MY LIFE WITH
CHAGALL

MY LIFE WITH CHAGALL

Seven Years of Plenty With the Master as Told by the Woman Who Shared Them

Virginia Haggard

DONALD I. FINE, INC.
New York

Library of Congress Catalogue Card Number: 86-80055
ISBN: 0-917657-73-X
Manufactured in the United States of America
10 9 8 7 6 5 4 3 2 1

This book is printed on acid free paper. The paper in this book
meets the guidelines for permanence and durability of the Committee on
Production Guidelines for Book Longevity of the Council on Library Resources.

FOR JEAN AND DAVID
WHO ARE ENDLESSLY INDULGENT,
UNDERSTANDING AND KIND.

CONTENTS

Preface   9

Chapter I   11
New York

Chapter II   50
High Falls

Chapter III   81
Orgeval

Chapter IV   89
St. Jean Cap Ferrat

Chapter V   101
*Les Collines—
Work and Friends*

Chapter VI   119
*Advice to Young Painters
Biblical Paintings
Ceramics and Sculpture
Israel*

Chapter VII   153
Denouement

Epilogue   189

PREFACE

Marc Chagall was born on the seventh day of the seventh month, 1887, of a humble Jewish family in a suburb of the small town of Vitebsk in Byelorussia, near the Lithuanian border. Art was far from the minds of the people he grew up with, and the birth of such an extraordinary talent in their midst was something of a miracle. His father worked in a herring warehouse, and his mother kept a modest little grocery shop to feed their six girls and two boys. Marc was the eldest child and they counted on him to contribute toward the livelihood of the family; but he was hypersensitive and emotional and, when upset, subject to fainting spells. He seemed unsuited to the sort of employment they had in mind. Instead, he began to show a remarkable talent for drawing. He was a beautiful, intelligent child and his mother could refuse him nothing. She paid a handsome tip to the master of the communal school for his admittance, for Jews, who comprised more than half the population of the town, did not have equal rights with gentiles. It was at this school that he learned Russian. At home he spoke Yiddish, and he learned to read the Holy Books in Hebrew at a Jewish school.

Later, yielding to his insistence, his mother got him into an art school run by an academic portrait painter in Vitebsk. From that moment he never looked back. He went to St. Petersburg, where he lived precariously (Jews had to have special permits to reside in the capital) and won a scholarship for a state art academy. Later, he went to the school of Léon Bakst, the famous designer of the Ballets Russes. Maxim Vinaver was democratic deputy to the First Duma, the elective assembly convened by the tzar after the failure of the first revolution in 1905. He had courageously spoken out for equal rights

9

for Jews, bought some of Marc's pictures and let him live and work in the offices of his political magazine, *Dawn*. Finally, Vinaver sent him to Paris for four years with an allowance. During those years he made the acquaintance of Blaise Cendrars and Guillaume Apollinaire and painted a series of astonishing works which he exhibited in Berlin, creating quite a stir in the avant-garde art world. He hurried back to Vitebsk, where his fiancée was beginning to weary of waiting, and arrived just before war was declared. He married Bella in 1915, and their daughter, Ida, was born in 1916. During the Revolution, Anatoly Lunarcharsky, an art lover and communist agitator he had met in Paris, became commissar for education and named Chagall commissar for art of his native town of Vitebsk. Chagall founded an art school and named as teachers a group of artists of the Suprematist school headed by Casimir Malevich, but they turned against him and tried to take over the school. Finally, the authorities began to condemn every form of avant-garde art. Lunarcharsky alone supported Chagall and facilitated his departure for Berlin, knowing that he had no intention of returning to Russia. Bella and Ida followed, and they were reunited in Paris in 1922, where they spent many happy and prolific years. Chagall's international fame grew steadily. At the outbreak of World War II, the Emergency Rescue Committee of the United States invited him to take refuge there. The Chagalls, together with Ida and her husband, went to New York in 1941. Bella died suddenly six weeks after the Liberation of Paris, in September, 1944, and Chagall was shattered with grief.

In the spring of 1945, there began for me seven enriching, eventful years as Chagall's companion.

I began collecting material for this memoir in 1950 when we settled in Vence, in the south of France.

Now, after all these years, I would like to pay tribute to a great artist and a lovable man, to contribute this modest study of his life and work as observed by me closely during those seven years.

—Virginia Haggard
  Brussels, Belgium

Chapter

I

New York

Marc had been feeling desperately lonely since the death of his beloved Bella the year before, in September, 1944. The New York summer was just beginning, and Marc's daughter, Ida, and her husband, Michel Gordey, who had been living with Marc since that fatal day and caring for him devotedly, were feeling the strain. The months since her mother's death had been wearing for Ida, and she was dreaming of a holiday, but there was no one to take over. The sharp-tempered, good-natured housekeeper had left after a tiff, and in any case, Marc had never learned a word of English, and communication with her had been difficult, even when he made her drawings to explain what he wanted. The drawings seemed to her as queer as his language, and though they gave her a good laugh, they seldom enlightened her.

Ida's most pressing problem was to find someone to mend her father's socks. They had been piling up over the months, for sewing was one of the few things Bella had not taught her daughter. She had been brought up as a cherished only child in the gay twenties, when her father was beginning to acquire celebrity and comfortable means. She was twenty-eight, a year younger than myself.

As for me, I was living in a shabby, furnished room with my

husband, John McNeil, a Scottish painter and theatrical designer, and our five-year-old daughter, Jean. For years, John had been suffering from serious depression. He had long since given up painting and was unable to earn a living. Our only means of livelihood was the little I managed to earn from cleaning and sewing. Jean accompanied me everywhere, for to leave her with John was out of the question. When my work was finished, I took her to play in Central Park, and it was there that we met a friend of Ida's, who sent me to 42 Riverside Drive to fetch a bundle of socks.

While I mended them, I thought of the time in Paris when I had first met Marc Chagall at a British embassy reception in 1933. It seemed an unlikely place to meet him, and he was playing an unusual part—that of a faun dressed in a dark suit and starched collar—but his gleaming smile was real. It made his slanting blue eyes slant even more, and I forgot the stiff collar and the stiff surroundings. I even forgot to be shy.

I was an eighteen-year-old art student, ill at ease in conventional society where my father, who was British consul general, was in his element. I felt more at home with my artist friends in Montparnasse than in my parents' polite circles, where I felt inhibited and clumsy. My father tried to initiate me to his infallible cocktail technique: "Prepare a few lively themes of topical interest, perhaps a good story or two, and if you catch sight of someone you know, excuse yourself and be off; always keep moving, that's the main thing." It was a technique I was never to master.

In his memoirs, written in retirement, my father speaks of me thus:

As a child, V. was much less accountable than her engaging sister, with an unaccommodating manner, tending to play by herself because she would accept nobody's leadership. Games involving teamwork were not for her. She had to put up with a lot of teasing, which she accepted with difficulty. In writing to her godmother, who doted on the queer child and believed in her, I note (unkindly) something "unholy" in her character. She was difficult to deal with along the ordinary lines, incomprehensible, I suppose, to nobody more than herself.

Her noticeable lack of judgment, which afterwards led her so astray, was perhaps due to the continuous search for her own convictions. It was the lamentably successful achievement of her husband, John, to kill her confidence in herself over ten years of a marriage which she

kept going by submissive devotion and determination. From that un-
speakable ordeal she has emerged, perhaps with enough resilience still
to fulfill her promise. She tells me she is glad it happened, because she
would never have learned any other way.

Reading those lines after my father's death, I reflected that if I
chose the hard way to search for my convictions, it was in order to
break with a life that was too privileged and secure, with people who
were too certain of their own superiority. No doubt my "unaccountable" and "unholy" traits were the most authentic side of my character, but they made life difficult and I found them hard to accept.

My father himself had some of these traits but he repudiated them;
the deep moral conditioning of his youth had soaked into his marrow
—the upper-class propriety, which he tried to pass on to me.

I went with Jean to deliver the bundle of socks, and when Ida saw
us standing in the doorway hand in hand she asked us to pose for
a drawing. This gave me time to study her. She was a handsome
woman with abundant curly hair of a reddish gold, like Titian's *Flora*,
turquoise blue eyes and a wide Chagall smile with the same perfect
teeth. She spoke in an elegant manner and walked with a dainty
mincing step. Some of her pictures stood around the walls; they were
delicate, vaporous paintings that tried modestly to shine with sincere
conviction.

Over her head a large painting by her father showed her naked in
a cloud of white drapery, floating over the town of Vitebsk. I thought
she was courageous to work under a picture by Chagall.

As she sketched us, I told her that I had made the acquaintance of
her father in Paris.

"Then I suppose you speak French?" She was absorbed in her
drawing, but also in her thoughts. After a while, she said, "Are you
by any chance in need of a job?" I replied that I was.

"Could you look after my father while I take a holiday?"

"Certainly, providing I can bring my daughter with me."

Ida gladly agreed and a weight seemed to fall from her shoulders.
She finished her drawing with increased application, then she led us
to the studio.

Chagall put down his brush and came forward. The smile I remembered was still there, a smile impossible to forget—dazzling, spontaneous, moving, but the eyes had lost some of their shine. They were misty, and the lights in them flickered like candle flames. His soft, fuzzy graying hair stood out in three tufts like a clown's wig. He shook my hand and Jean's when Ida introduced us, nodded approval when she told him I was coming to look after the house, and went back to his easel. His softly shod feet took short steps and his sturdy figure was supple and light. He was wearing sagging trousers and a many-colored striped tunic, open at the neck.

The next day I came to work as Chagall's housekeeper.

Everything was perfectly simple and straightforward from the start; I felt I knew this man already. I was immediately at ease with him, there was no strangeness between us. We were drawn to each other instinctively by our mutual solitude and shyness, but also by a fundamental joie de vivre that was temporarily smothered by our sorrow.

The day after Ida and Michel's departure on holiday Marc asked me to set him a small table in the studio because the big family table "made him feel like an orphan." When I brought him his meal, he said, "Well, aren't you going to keep me company? I can't eat all alone like a dog." So Jean and I sat down with him, and we were soon conversing in French. His Russian accent was warm and colorful, and his grammatical errors made me feel less self-conscious about my own.

I discovered that one of his favorite topics was Picasso. I told him I had been petrified by Picasso's penetrating stare when, as a student in Paris, I went to look at his paintings at the Galerie Pierre in the Rue de Seine. Picasso had sat there as I viewed the paintings, his hands dangling between his knees, focusing his black bull's eyes on me with such intensity that I fled. I said to Marc, "I wish I had not been so intimidated, I might have made his acquaintance." Marc grunted and said it wasn't a great loss. "But do you like his painting?" he asked.

"Yes, I do."

Marc smiled and shrugged his shoulders. "People of polite society adore him, also amateur philosophers and intellectual snobs. He enjoys showing all the most repulsive things in human beings—that's very fashionable. People with deep feelings are not moved by his paintings; he's not interested in human feelings, he only uses the visible, exterior aspects of human nature."

We discovered we had a common friend in the painter and engraver Bill Hayter, whose Atelier 17 had been founded in Paris in 1927 and moved to New York during the war years. Marc had recently been doing some engraving there. Bill favored a friendly workshop atmosphere where artists could communicate and share ideas, but Marc seemed not to have been impressed by this aspect of it. He wasn't interested in sharing his ideas with other artists.

I had been Bill's pupil at his atelier—it was in the Rue Campagne Première—at about the time I first met Marc. Max Ernst, Joan Miró and Alberto Giacometti came there sometimes to do their work; there was an atmosphere of intense concentration and Bill communicated his fervor to his pupils. His cheeks were etched with crisscross lines like his engravings, and it gave him a rugged charm.

"Bill is a first-rate craftsman," said Marc, "and for an artist, he's modest; so are Giacometti and Miró. As for Ernst . . ." Marc made a wry face.

"Ernst was friendly to me," I said. "He asked me to play a part in a film he was planning to make, but those eyes, those steel bullets, chilled me to the marrow!"

"I'm not surprised. I saw Max Ernst in Bill's studio only a few days ago. We don't get on well. He's much too clever. I'm just a simple person."

Giacometti came only once to the Rue Campagne Première while I was there, and I had watched him with fascination the entire afternoon. There had been deep gravity in his face; but suddenly he smiled and his eyes grew enormous. He spoke slowly and searched for the simplest and truest word to express what he wanted to say.

"Giacometti has a moving fragility," Marc observed. "I have more respect for a sculptor who leans toward fragility than for one who thrusts his way with violence, like Lipchitz."

I remembered that Miró had a ready smile for everyone. He shuffled around busily in string-sole shoes, dabbing and wiping his plates, wetting his paper and pulling off proofs in quick succession. Everything had to go fast with Miró, and when the print was good, he beamed with pleasure.

"Miró gets on well with everyone, even with me!" said Marc.

Teatime was always a welcome break, and Bill never lost that excellent English habit. He showed me a trick for warming the pot by putting it upside down over the open kettle. Each one came to fetch his cup, cigarettes were lighted and words were exchanged. I remember Giacometti saying that when he first arrived in Paris and went to work at La Grande Chaumière, he was met with crushing indifference from colleagues and teachers alike, simply because he was a foreigner.

"What did he expect?" said Marc. "Academies are not places of feeling. I got cold-shouldered too at La Grande Chaumière, not only as a *métèque,** but as a Jew."

"Then you can imagine how utterly insignificant *I* felt there!" I said. "Once a week, Gromaire came round to criticize our work. He had the face of an embittered mastiff, he was always so gloomy and severe."

"His paintings are gloomy and severe, as well," Marc grumbled, "it's that Prussian blue, a very dangerous color. It gets into everything. Maybe his dreams are full of Prussian blue."

Then I tried the Académie Ranson and Colarossi, and I finally opted for Scandinave. Dufresne came once in a blue moon to look at our work. I liked him; he was a good teacher. There was a rather more intimate atmosphere at Scandinave than in the other places. As well as being an art academy, it was a pension for young Scandinavian girls. Their parents may have imagined they were living in a respectable academy, but the Rue Jules Chaplin was a blind alley full of discreet brothels, and the students were on friendly terms with the prostitutes and their children. When our work was over, the easels were cleared for a ballet class, presided over by a splintery old man with a violin who screeched at the girls as he played and beat time with his foot. Occasionally, he swooped down on some offending leg with his bow. Once a year, Monsieur and Madame, who ran the academy, gave a masked ball which was quite an uproarious event. Students, artists, models and prostitutes mingled in exuberant dancing. Needless to say, my parents knew nothing of these goings-on.

Marc was amused by my stories of Montparnasse and began to look more cheerful; as soon as he finished eating, he went back to his

*a pejorative slang term for a foreigner

work. The pitiless New York summer had arrived, and the perspiration glistened on his face. I asked him why he didn't take off his soaking shirt. "Because I have a hairy chest," he said, smiling shyly. "But I like hairy chests," I told him, and after some insistence on my part, he complied.

I was an exceedingly shy person, and here I was talking freely to Marc Chagall as though I had known him for years. He spoke to me, also, with ease. Only later did I realize that with certain people he was overcome by shyness, and his famous play-acting was a cover-up. This, in time, became second nature, and the shyness was buried under a layer of amiable public behavior. But with me he never felt the need to bring out that public persona.

The immense studio had several windows looking out onto the Hudson River and the green hills of New Jersey. Boats and barges went up and down, and Jean watched them from the balcony where she had brought her collection of weird little people made from modeling clay, beads, buttons and miscellaneous trinkets I had saved up for her. She was always creating microcosms where a form of life went on that seemed totally real to her, a world of humor and whimsy, so unlike the one she had to live in.

When it was time for me to go home, Marc had a resigned expression at the thought of an evening of solitude. John, on the other hand, after a day to himself, was able to face us once more. Sometimes he was even in a gay and gentle mood. Those times he played with Jean, and his droll inventions and nonsensical humor delighted her; but often we were saddened by his negative attitude and his grim, determined pessimism.

When we went back to Riverside Drive in the morning, Marc was already hard at work. He had several paintings going at the same time, and when he got tired of one, he took out another. I seldom saw him without a brush or a pencil in his hand, and when he wasn't painting or drawing, he was scribbling notes in Russian on scraps of paper, or sketching rough ideas for future paintings. The studio was strewn with these, and there was a small leather chest full of them. He drew ideas from this treasure chest from time to time, sometimes for paintings, sometimes for poems. I gathered the scraps reverently whenever a draft blew them around, but I did very little cleaning, because it disturbed him.

Two paintings, especially, alternated on the easel at that time: *Nocturn* and *Around Her,* paintings full of tragic undertones. The first is a wind-swept, panic-stricken scene. The flying horse is a "nightmare," come to carry off the phantom bride across a stormy sky. This painting had a strong simplicity that bore no trifling with, and Marc sometimes looked at it for a long while without daring to touch it. In the second painting, he represents himself with his anguished head upside down, while Bella sits sadly beside an image of Vitebsk reflected in a crystal globe.

As he worked, his face was tense and painful. He seemed to be in a sort of rage, as if he were trying to put something back into the world that had disappeared with Bella.

As soon as lunch appeared he relaxed, and we resumed our conversations. We would discuss the other artists of the time, and he would often come back to the subject of Picasso. Sometimes his wit was caustic.

"Picasso changes his style more often than his socks," he commented as we looked through a book of reproductions. "Look! It's the same puzzle over and over again. He shuffles it around endlessly, and it always works. He tries to be ugly and grotesque, but it's of no use; he's always pretty."

I was in a vague, ambivalent state at the time. Living had become a grueling business, and the only way to get by was to let myself slide through existence. Now I began to absorb the elements that embodied Chagall's life as if they were food and drink. The delicious, all-pervading smell of linseed oil and turpentine brought back life-giving memories. I feasted on the sight of this man who worked from morning till night with such astonishing singleness of purpose. Slowly, I began to come alive again.

Here were paintings from the pre-World War I period that filled me with wonder and joy: *The Marriage Procession,* with bands of brilliant colors like flags blowing across the sky; *The Studio,* painted in bold brushstrokes like a Van Gogh; *The Cattle Dealer,* whose cart is drawn by a mare with a foal in her transparent belly.

Sometime later, this last picture had a fall. The family was sitting in the studio with friends, when a loud crash was heard in the dining room. Marc got up slowly. "It's all right, it's only *The Cattle Dealer.* I hung it up yesterday." There was a large gash in the painting, and

Ida remarked with a chuckle that if anyone else had hung it up, there would have been trouble.

Marc always dispatched his food hastily and without undue refinement. Eating was a time-consuming occupation, and work was waiting to be done; but he ate with such gusto that it was a pleasure to cook for him, and if it reminded him of his youth he became lyrical (*golupki,* blini, *schav* and borscht, which Ida later taught me how to make).

Whenever Marc was moved or excited it caused him to stammer, which I found rather charming. It seemed to betray a certain vulnerability. Marc told me his stammering dated from the time when, as a little boy, he was bitten by a mad dog. He still had a long scar on his arm as evidence of the incident. Entering the rabbi's house for his Saturday Bible lessons, he saw a big, ugly, reddish dog coming down the stairs. That was the last he remembered until he was picked up with a bleeding arm and leg. That very evening, his uncle rushed him to the Pasteur Institute in St. Petersburg, and he was put into a clean white bed for treatment. He felt like a hero for he had never had so much attention.

Marc often stammered when he mentioned Picasso. "I'm like a mosquito buzzing around Picasso," he said. "I sting him once, I sting him twice, and, bang, he squashes me."

And: "Picasso is always setting new fashions. The great fashion designers launch a green gown with purple gloves; Picasso launches a pair of eyes in a backside and everyone follows. Whatever he does, the result is a museum piece; it has that unquestionable aura."

Marc told me about Montparnasse before the World War I. "There were many trains going in different directions. All one had to do was to jump onto one of them and off one went. I never jumped onto any train. Now they have all slowed down or shunted them off onto sidetracks, but there's one train that still makes a lot of noise—Picasso's train. A lot of people jump onto it, but it doesn't go anywhere! As for Montparnasse, it smells of artistic corpses.

"Van Gogh," he said, "is like a peasant who enters a drawing room with mud on his boots, because he can't help it. Picasso also enters with muddy boots, but on purpose, to show he doesn't care."

Alexander Calder had presented Marc with an attractive mobile by

way of cheering him up in his solitude after Bella's death. Marc didn't
particularly appreciate Calder's generous gesture; he mistrusted
Calder's teasing humor and took his waggish ways too seriously. He
gave the mobile to Ida, who hung it in the studio where it moved
gracefully among the giant plants, against the glittering Hudson.
From time to time, I would give it a spin as I passed by. It didn't cheer
Marc, but it sometimes had its intended effect on me.

Some of the paintings were nearing completion, and Marc had
started sketching a new one. It was full of explosive movement, and
it promised to be different from the melancholy paintings he had
been working on for months. It was later called *The Flying Sleigh.* It was
daring in composition and high in color—a vibrant painting. It had
a strength that was lacking in some of those he was repainting at the
time, such as *Around Her* and *Burning Candles,* which were two halves
of a large work called *Circus People* that he had painted in 1933.

He never actually destroyed or abandoned any of his paintings;
instead, he would transform them. And this, I think, is fairly rare
among painters. He could not accept the failure of one of his children,
they all had to be turned out presentable. He hated to abandon
paintings; instead, he would put them away for a while. Sometimes
they matured, and sometimes, when he had forgotten their original
significance, they would suggest new paintings. Occasionally, he
turned them upside down and they became completely new pictures,
but he was careful to sign them before putting them aside, for fear
of forgetting which was the right side up.

This reluctance to destroy may have been in part motivated by a
sense of conservation, even of economy. "That's a good piece of
canvas," he used to say. But it also showed his love for rare materials
that had acquired a patina of age.

Whenever Marc worked over an old painting he would put the old
paint to new purposes, instead of obliterating it first with a coat of
white paint. The technical dangers inherent in the repainting of old
canvas were never a problem for him. The successive layers easily
adhered to each other because he worked them together with intuitive skill as he worked the new theme into the old one. He possessed
a flawless technique, an uncanny insight into chemical reactions.
With only a few exceptions (and these date from the very early

years), none of his paintings has ever shown signs of age, the colors have never lost their original hues, the paint has never cracked or flaked; and this in spite of difficult working conditions. During the very early years, he often worked on anything vaguely resembling canvas, such as bed sheets, shirts and tablecloths. The paint must often have been of inferior quality, except when he managed to swipe a few tubes of good paint from his master, Penne in Vitebsk. Yet, most of his canvases have remained supple and can be rolled without danger. This intuitive genius gave him such mastery over every kind of technique that he was able to try them all with equal success.

One day, as he was working, he called to me to sit down and keep him company. "Virginia," he said, I want to be talked to." He wanted to know what had brought me to my present state. Evidently my shabby clothes, my look of resignation, my thin figure and lank, despondent hair had roused his curiosity.

"It's a long story," I said evasively. I found it painful to talk about the last few years of my life. "Maybe I should begin right from the beginning, before I was born." I thought this might give me courage and even throw light on the events of recent years, events which I found it difficult to explain to myself, let alone to Marc.

"If you like."

"In those days, my father used to keep pet pigs in Venezuela," I began.

Marc looked puzzled. "Pet pigs in Venezuela? Whatever for?"

"He liked scratching their backs with a walking stick."

"But I thought he was a British consul."

"He was only a probationer at the time, he could afford a little eccentricity. He was a vegetarian, wrote poetry and traveled all over the country on a mule. He had flaming red hair and was in no danger of going unnoticed. Since his youth he so persistently tried to live up to what was expected of him as an official representative of his country that most of his eccentricity disappeared in the process."

"And your mother?"

"She is the thirteenth and youngest child of a Quebec farmer, and the odds were very much against her marrying a man like my father."

Marc smiled and attacked his painting with renewed vigor; he was feeling less lonely. "How did that happen?"

"Her elder sister married a Canadian diplomat and when they were sent to Guatemala, they took my mother along with them. That's where she met my father. Then they returned to England on leave with their two small children in a German boat, and landed in Le Havre the very day war was declared. But they managed to get safely to England. Then my father was appointed to Paris. That's where I was born."

Marc sat back and looked at his painting through narrowed eyes, pressing his lips together. He began to hum and squeezed some fresh paint onto his palette.

"So you're much Frencher than I am. You not only have French-Canadian blood, but you were born in Paris. I'm a naturalized *métèque*. When I first came to Paris in 1910, I was treated with condescension by some French artists. After the war, too, when I went back with Bella we were at the Rotonde (a popular café in Montparnasse) where we overheard Georges Braque saying "These *métèques* are all coming here to eat our food." My naturalization proceedings took years because I had come from Communist Russia.

"Finally, in 1937 Jean Paulhan (the poet) raised hell and I became a Frenchman. The French have always been chauvinistic. I feel no Frencher today than I ever did, less so I should say, since France has been ruled over by Hitler and Vichy, and all its Jews have been exiled or massacred. But Bella wanted to go back immediately after the Liberation. She was deeply attached to France. Perhaps she was somehow scared of America, as if she had a premonition of her death, and she begged me to have her body taken home if she should die here. When we left France, she had a terrible feeling she would never come back. Well, Paris was liberated on August 25, and on September 2, she was dead. Now what's the use of going back? I'm in no hurry. France will never be the same again for me, or anything, without Bella. And quite frankly, I'm afraid of rubbing shoulders with people who have sent Jews to gas chambers." Marc took a rag and wiped away something that dissatisfied him; he shook his head and frowned a little, then heaved a deep sigh.

"So you were born in 1915. That's the year we were married in Vitebsk. That painting called *The Birthday* was painted the same year. Do you know the one? Bella had brought me bouquets of flowers and colored shawls to deck my little studio, and I painted us flying up to the ceiling together. When I first went to Paris, I left her alone in Russia for four years. I was so innocent and trusting, I knew I could count on her fidelity. You can imagine what temptations assailed a beautiful young woman studying in Stanislavski's acting school in Moscow! When she wrote saying that a certain young man was paying her a great deal of attention, I boiled up immediately, suspecting my closest friend. I decided on the spot to go home. But I didn't go straight home, I stopped off in Berlin on the way and had an exhibition, which was a triumph, and I got back to Vitebsk just before war was declared. All my life I've got through scrapes by the skin of my teeth. I grabbed hold of my fiancée, and feeling strengthened by my new success, I announced to Bella's parents, (the Rosenfelds, very rich jewelers) that I was going to marry their daughter. The news didn't seem to delight them at all. I felt barely tolerated, and the marriage ceremony was an ordeal. I've painted it many times since then, but I've always turned it into a poetical, romantic ceremony. That's not the strict truth as far as I was concerned. But I was immensely happy with Bella, and we left immediately for the country."

I cast my imagination back to this distant period, enveloped in a legendary haze, and illustrated with such eloquence by the pictures. Marc began to concentrate with redoubled energy on a difficult part of the canvas; he liked to be talked to while he worked, he said it kept his mind off his worries and set his imagination free. But a moment later he began to sigh fretfully.

"If you only knew how hard it is to sit here all alone, battling with a canvas. I think of Bella all the time. I ought to have insisted she remain in that hospital." He turned toward me: "Of course you don't know what happened. We were having a holiday in the Adirondacks, and she suddenly got a bad sore throat. She kept calling to me to give her boiling hot tea. The next day she was so feverish that I took her to the hospital, and when she saw a lot of nuns in the corridor, she became upset. I must explain that in another place where we had been staying, in Beaver Lake, she had seen a sign saying that only white Christians were welcome, and she had been brooding on that. Strangely enough, just before falling ill, she finished writing her memoirs and said, 'Look, here are all my notebooks. I've put everything in order, that way you'll know where to find them.'

"Well, when she got to the hospital, they naturally asked for particulars—name, age—but when they asked 'religion' she wouldn't answer. She said 'I don't like it here, take me back to the hotel.' So I took her back, and the next day it was too late." Marc heaved a deep sigh. "But there was no penicillin. No penicillin," he repeated to himself, as if to try and quell his tortured sense of responsibility. Penicillin was reserved for military use in 1944, and when Ida finally obtained an exemption from Washington, Bella was past saving.

A few days later Marc settled down in front of a new painting of a pair of yellow lovers on a flying bed, ecstatically floating on a blue cloud, which afterward received the title of *The Naked Cloud.*

"Nu?" he said, "go on with your story."

I did so, telling him how we'd left Paris when I was four months old and sailed for La Paz. The journey took about four months, and after that ordeal we had to adapt ourselves to four thousand meters of altitude. I almost died of mountain sickness, after surviving dysentery on the boat. "I think it has given me surprising resistance," I said.

Marc looked at me dubiously, thinking I didn't look particularly resistant.

"Then when I was five I found myself in a Dorsetshire village, where my godmother tried to turn me into a Catholic. My father is an atheist, but he thought religion could do us no harm. He even submits to churchgoing himself occasionally, because its one of the recognized customs of an English gentleman. He sent us all to Protestant boarding schools in England."

"How strange to turn religion into a polite convention!" Marc said. "For *my* parents, religion was the axle around which their whole existence revolved." A fundamental difference, but not one that would become an issue between us—at least not for a while.

From time to time I left Marc to his work and his brooding. Jean needed my attention, too, and my work had to be done.

I cleaned Ida's part of the house to the best of my ability, scouring the kitchen and bathroom, soaking the hairbrushes in ammonia and disinfecting the dustbins as she had taught me to do. I wanted her to be pleased with me. She came back from time to time to see how things were getting along, and when she felt reassured by the peaceful atmosphere and relative cleanliness, she departed.

Domestic work is less irksome when the mistress is away. This experience taught me to spare my own domestic helper of my presence and to leave her as much freedom as possible. I even go to the point of cleaning up the worst of the dirt before she arrives, remembering the times when I felt disheartened.

But I was always anxious to return to Marc. I found him fascinating to be with and to talk to. "What other scrapes did you get through by the skin of your teeth?" I asked Marc.

"In St. Petersburg I had all kinds of adventures. I even went to prison."

"Well! I don't suppose many people know that Marc Chagall went to prison."

"Jews weren't allowed to live in the capital in those days, unless they had special permission. One day I forgot my permit, and they put me in a sort of cage with thieves and prostitutes, who were very kind to me. Then they put me in a cell with an old man and gave me a prison uniform. I spent my time drawing, dreaming and sleeping. It was perfect! It's all written in my book. I'll lend you a copy."

He got up at once, nimble and energetic, and went to fetch a copy of his autobiography, *Ma Vie*. It was full of splendid pen drawings, humorous, whimsical and sometimes weird. One of them caught my eye, opposite the chapter beginning with the word, "Idochka is born." It represents a naked bearded man lying in bed, with an infant lying beside him. Behind the bed, a woman with a jug of water attends to him. I laughed. "That reminds me of the Boccaccio story called "The Pregnant Man." Did you feel so actively involved with Ida's birth?"

"To tell you the truth, I'm ashamed. I was disappointed, I wanted a boy so much, and it was a girl. But I've made up for it since. She's more than a daughter to me—she's a real Chagall!"

Marc was working on the bold elemental shapes of the yellow lovers. The painting had a directness that some of the other recent ones lacked, and he wanted to leave it in a liquid state, respecting its freedom and strength. He screwed up his eyes to get a more general fuzzy impression of the composition, and a dimple appeared in each of his puckered cheekbones. He was not tense any more as he painted, but concentrated. His face had a fascinating mobility; it changed constantly from jocularity to wistfulness, from cheerfulness to solemnity.

I began to read *Ma Vie* and was even more fascinated by this extraordinary man. I sat up half the night, and John was intrigued. He was proud that I was working for Marc Chagall. A window had opened somewhere and fresh air was coming in. The book is a masterpiece of spontaneous poetry, halfway between painting and writing. It has a visionary quality like the best of Marc's paintings, and flows in a torrent of vivid colors, enchantingly carefree and exuberant, but also nostalgic and melancholy.

His description of his father runs thus:

Have you ever seen, in Florentine paintings, one of those people with never-trimmed beards, whose eyes are dark, but also pale as ashes, whose skin is burnt ochre and covered with fine wrinkles? That's my father. What's a man worth if he's worth nothing, if he's inestimable? It's difficult to find the right words for him. What a smile! Where did it come from? Everything in him seemed enigma and sadness. Inaccessible images. In his greasy workman's clothes with wide pockets, out of which he drew a dark red handkerchief, he came home, tall and thin, and the evening came in with him.

Of his relatives, he writes:

If my art played no part in the lives of my relations, they, on the other hand, greatly influenced my art. One of them found nothing better to do than wander around the streets of Lyozno in broad daylight clad only in a shirt, as if he were a painting by Masaccio or Piero della Francesca. The memory of this "sans culotte" fills me with joy, and I feel near to him.

A scene from Vitebsk:

I am bathing alone in the river, hardly ruffling the water. Around me the town is peaceful, the milky sky is a little bluer on the left and above is a celestial radiance. Suddenly on the opposite bank, over the roof of the synagogue, a cloud of smoke bursts forth. I can almost hear the cries of the burning scrolls and the altar. The windows are smashed. Quick out of the water! All naked, I run to fetch my clothes. How I love fires!

In his poem on Chagall, Blaise Cendrars writes:

> *He grabs a church and paints with a church,*
> *He grabs a cow and paints with a cow. . . .*

In his astonishing book, Chagall grabs words and paints with words, conjuring up dreams, visions and burning memories. His self-portrait in writing is as humorous and poetic as his painted ones, and the characters of this colorful fresco are as fantastic as those of his pictures. The book revealed to me many an absorbing aspect of Marc's extraordinary life which he hadn't told me about during our talks. During the prewar years in Paris, he worked like a madman; nothing else mattered. Vitebsk had become a dream town, and his friends and family were its dream inhabitants. Bella was a faraway goal, a fairy princess he had to work for and win. He wrote her many letters and thought of her constantly. His paintings were full of sensuality, like the people who bustled around him, his artist friends and their models. One of his friends offered to lend him his model (he was too shy to ask her himself) and after a posing session, she simply took him to bed with her. He was terribly innocent, he had never touched a woman. Bella had posed for him in the nude, but he had never touched her. Of course, no one in the town believed that. When his mother saw the sketch, she made him tear it up.

Before he fell in love with Bella he flirted with many girls, but he didn't love any of them. They were romantic creations of his own mind, and when the girls wanted to go a step further, he backed out. Bella had a friend, Théa, who was more intelligent than the other girls, more refined. She and Bella studied in Moscow and spent their holidays abroad, but the day he first met Bella in Théa's house, he knew it was all finished with Théa. There was something about Bella —a mysterious likeness to him. Not long before her death she wrote in Yiddish about that first meeting.

"Her text is pure poetry," Marc said, "like my paintings. She really *felt* me, she was part of my crazy inventions, they never seemed strange to her. She was a brilliant student, one of the three best in Russia the year she left school, and of course she was beautiful; intensely so, with her deep dark eyes, a trifle sad. Look!"

Marc went to the massive fireplace with a high stone mantelpiece and took down his favorite photo of her as a young girl: pale oval face with enormous eyes, dark hair tied behind her head—the image of soulful intensity. Then he brought out an album and showed me photos of his family. One picture shows his father, Zachar, and his mother, Feiga Ita, sitting bolt upright, their hands resting on a small round table. His tiny grandmother, with wig and kerchief, sits on the other side of Zachar; his two married sisters stand next to their stiff-collared husbands; Marc is superb in a white waistcoat and tie.

"Were your parents very reserved and chaste? Is that why you were so innocent in your twenties?"

"Yes, no doubt. I remember the others boys laughing at me for my ignorance, and it upset me. I was shy, I stuttered, I was scared of growing up. Even in my twenties I preferred dreaming about love and painting it in my pictures. But girls were drawn to me. I was good looking, and I started flirting. I loved flirting. But I wept a lot too, I was melancholic."

"Yes, I was impressed by the frequency of the word 'weep' in your book. In one passage, even the houses weep!"

Marc laughed. "Perhaps you wouldn't understand that. For English people, to weep is to lose face; they're reluctant to show their feelings."

"I don't feel very English in that respect. Once, when my father kissed me good-bye before leaving for Rio de Janeiro for a year, I saw a tear in his eye and it moved me. I didn't know he was capable of weeping."

"Thank God my parents wept and laughed without restraint," he said.

Marc confessed that he had never been much drawn to the English. Bella got on better with them; she had been friendly with the ambassador's wife in Paris, which explains how I'd had occasion to meet Marc at the embassy.

At about the time that Marc was sometimes frequenting these circles, I left them forever. I had fallen in love with my Scottish painter, who had communist ideas; his dream was to go to Russia. We went to Russian films—Eisenstein, Dovjenko and Pudovkin. We were thrilled by the new world the communists were building.

Marc said that he was, too, until he had spent a few years in communist Russia, in the first years of the Revolution. It was a fantastic period. Everything became suddenly possible; Jews were given full status, no more passports, no more pogroms. Anatoly Lunacharsky came back from exile with Lenin and became commissar for education, and named Marc commissar for art in Vitebsk. Marc founded a school there; he wanted to create new artists and liberate the old ones. He brought in avant-garde teachers, Casimir Malevich and his Suprematist disciples, but they were jealous, and they finally threw Marc out. Then the Tcheka broke into the Rosenfeld's house and took away everything they could lay their hands on, gold, jewelry and money, and he, their son-in-law, a commissar, could do nothing. He was having trouble himself. The Proletkult was beginning to disapprove of his pictures. Soon they clamped down on the Suprematists as well, and all the rest of the avant-garde. Only Lunacharsky defended him obstinately—he was a freethinker and a romantic. He gave Marc permission to go to Berlin and see what had happened to all the pictures he'd left behind there.

"He knew I wouldn't come back; he knew my art wouldn't survive communism. But I've never been anticommunist; that would be siding with my bitterest enemies. And now that we've crushed the Fascists, I even feel a solidarity with the communists. But my first great disillusionment began with the Nazi-Soviet pact. Bella and Idochka said I didn't understand, it was pure strategy, but it shocked me profoundly."

I told Marc that John had said the same, and after that I no longer believed in communism.

Talking to Marc was beginning to thaw me out, but I was still not altogether conscious of the slow, relentless destruction of my personality that John had wrought during the ten years of our life together. I lived from minute to minute, without thought of past or future, numbed to the reality of our difficult life together. John held me in his power. I feared and pitied him, but I didn't love him. Jean and he had a deep attachment, and for her sake we got along on a platonic basis. Since her birth, our physical relationship had come to an end.

Jean and I clung to each other through thick and thin. She was the only person who loved me and I was the only stable element in her life. We read books and painted pictures, walked and talked together, visited the elephants in the zoo and the stuffed shrews in the Mu-

seum of Natural History. She loved to survey the bustling world from
the safety of my shoulder.

When I arrived one morning Marc was working as usual, but now
he had an expectant look. He beamed at me as I came in. "The nights
are so lonely in this big empty apartment," he commented.

The yellow lovers were nearing completion and he put the picture
away, to forget it for a while. In a week or two, he would look at it
with a fresh, new vision, but first he wanted my opinion. I said it had
been exciting to watch it grow like a living thing with a throbbing
soul of its own.

"Do you like it?"

"It's beautiful!" I began to discover a trait in his character that
played an important part in his life. He often needed to be reassured,
not because he didn't know perfectly well which were his best paintings, but because he wanted other people to like them. He often
asked the opinion of inexperienced people, who were more spontaneous in their likes and dislikes than specialists. He was afraid of
antagonism and incomprehension.

Bella had been his own private specialist, his ultimate judge for
every single picture, his oracle. "Now I try to see my pictures through
her eyes. Ida would be only too pleased to play the part her mother
used to play. She has taste and intelligence and she knows me well.
Perhaps in time . . ."

Marc told me, "My whole life is made of work; the other things
are secondary. Of course, love and death and birth are great shocks,
but the work goes on just the same. After Bella's death I didn't work
for months. It was the first time in my life I ever stopped. If the work
didn't go on, it would kill me, it would consume me from inside.
Holidays are made for work. A day without work is never a real day
for me. I have to feel I've taken a step forward, solved a problem or
made some discovery. Why this constant drive? It's an eternal quest
for something I shall perhaps never find. How merciful that an artist
is never contented, otherwise, what would keep him going on and
on?"

In the course of our many conversations Jean was beginning to pick
up a few words of French, but Marc remained impervious to English.
"It's a language I'll never learn, but everyone seems to speak Yiddish
in New York, or French, or even Russian," he said.

When on the rare occasions that he had to buy something, he usually went to a Jewish shop. He loved shopping, especially discussing the wares with the shopkeeper, and bargaining for a good price.

He possessed a collection of colorful shirts and jackets, most of which Bella and he had purchased from what he called the "pederast" shop, on Lexington Avenue, where they spoke French. Bella had excellent taste, he said, and was daring. He didn't dare enough. The summer shirts were checkered mauve and pink, or green and yellow, and the velvet jackets were plum-colored or ultramarine. A striped coat of many colors had been bought in Mexico, where they had gone to launch the ballet "Aleko," with Marc's designs. "If Bella hadn't bought me all these things, I'd just wear anything. Clothes are of no importance to me. As you see, I like to work stripped to the waist; it saves my shirts and makes less work for you." But in spite of what he said, he had no lack of interest in clothes. When he met friends he combined shirts, ties and jackets with originality, and knew that he would attract attention and maybe receive a compliment.

One day Marc drew me toward him and sat me on his knee. There was a gentle familiarity between us, as if we had been a part of each other's lives for a long time. We had begun to love each other almost imperceptibly.

We didn't fall in love, we grew in love like two plants that grow in the same soil. I felt secure in this love, and slowly I began to yield to it. For years I had been starving, shriveling in apathy. Now I felt very young, as if I were discovering love for the first time. Marc, too, was like a shy young lover.

We began to steal kisses in the bedroom, while Jean was running around the apartment. Then I found a play school a few blocks away, where I left her each day. I can't remember how she reacted to this unprecedented event. It was the first time in her life that she had ever been separated from me. I was much too elated to take this into account. I was falling in love.

One blissful afternoon was spent downtown on the Lower East Side, where we browsed around the little shops and stalls. Marc bought me a moonstone ring as a token of his love.

Marc confessed to me that only a few weeks earlier he had asked a friend of Ida's, a young woman, if she would be willing to come and live with him, just to keep him company. He had told her: "I can't offer you love, only companionship." But she declined the offer, confessing that she had a secret lover. "What a good thing she refused! We wouldn't have got on at all well together, but you see to what lengths I was prepared to go for company. It's difficult to live with one's daughter and son-in-law."

I reflected that so desperate was he for company, I might well have missed my chance if the young woman had been otherwise inclined.

Marc had started a new painting, which later received the title, *The Soul of the Town.* In it he showed himself as a two-faced artist, painting a picture of a crucifixion. Bella had become a disembodied heavenly bride, a flying soul with a twirling veil, and below was a light-haired, earthly woman holding a cock tenderly in her arms.

His choice of themes was largely subconscious, growing out of an overwhelming urge to express something mysterious inside him. He drew spontaneously from a rich store of themes and put them to new uses in an infinite variety of combinations. Sometimes, however, his choice of themes was more consciously affected by actual events and states of mind, such as the tragic paintings inspired by the war and the Holocaust, and the melancholic series he had painted since Bella's death.

In this painting, *Soul of the Town,* I believe he made a subconscious allusion to the fact that he felt "two-faced" in his devotion to Bella and his attraction to me. Often the titles were invented by Ida and Marc's dealer, Pierre Matisse (the son of Henri Matisse), when a new series of paintings was completed and ready to be exhibited. Marc always approved of the titles, as he had approved of Bella's and, before her time, the titles suggested by his great friend, Blaise Cendrars: *The Holy Carter, To Russia, Asses and Others, A Russian Village from the Moon, Half Past Three.* Titles were not of great importance to him and only served to identify, but he was fond of those with a poetic quality. "My work is finished," he'd say. "Other people can do the rest, I know my pictures too well. They're part of me, but I don't know what they're *about.*"

One morning, Marc announced that Idochka was coming home that evening. The next day was Marc's fifty-eighth birthday, the seventh of July. I hurriedly got things straightened up and was rather

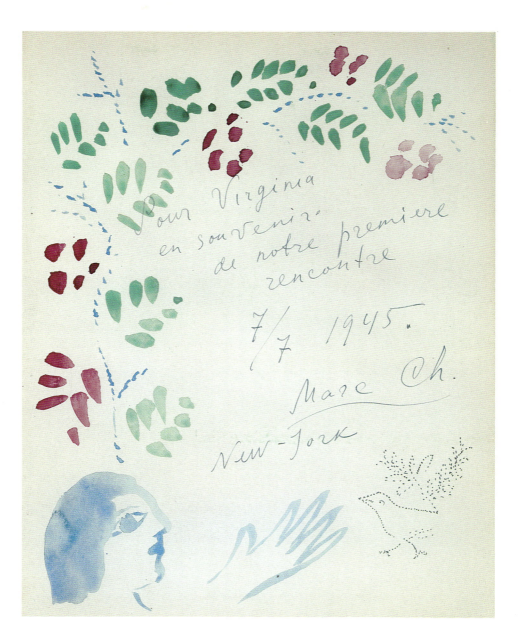

Pour Virginia
en souvenir
de notre première
rencontre

7/7 1945.

Marc Ch.

New-York

fig. 1

fig. 2

fig. 3

fig. 4

fig. 5

fig. 6

fig. 7

fig. 8

List of Color Illustrations

Fig. 1 Watercolor and inscription: "For Virginia, a remembrance of our first meeting." New York, July 7, 1945

Fig. 2 Watercolor in *Ma Vie* by Marc Chagall (Stock, Paris, 1931) 1947

Fig. 3 Watercolor, 1947

Fig. 4 Watercolor, 1947

Fig. 5 Watercolor and inscription: "For dear Virginia from Marc." High Falls, New York, 1947

Fig. 6 Watercolor and pen drawing. Portrait of Jean McNeil, 1949, inscribed to Jean.

Fig. 7 Watercolor and inscription in *The Complete Works of Plato* (Pleiade, Paris, 1951), 1952

Fig. 8 Watercolor and inscription in *The Complete Works of Plato* (Pleiade, Paris, 1951), 1951–52

nervous at the thought of her return. Would she sense the intimacy of our relationship?

But Ida was relaxed and charming as usual. The next day there was a small party and she called me from the kitchen to drink a glass of vodka to her father's health. One of the guests was Lionello Venturi, an elderly, bearded gentleman with an aristocratic air, who had brought along the first copies of his new book on Chagall. The deluxe edition contained an original etching, the one Marc had been working on at Bill Hayter's studio. The next day Marc secretly gave me a copy. A few months later he added a watercolor and the following inscription: *"En souvenir de notre première rencontre, 7/7/45."*

Marc always had a superstitious preference for the number 7, having been born on the seventh day of the seventh month, 1887, and although he'd said, "It *could* be that my father lied about my age and gave me two extra years so that I and my younger brother, David, would be exempt from military service," he preferred to stick to the official date of 1887, because of the magic number, and the mystery remained. I never managed to clarify the matter; his answers became more and more vague whenever I questioned him about it. He simply didn't know. What he did know, however, was that he had been frightened of adolescence; he wanted to go on being an innocent child. Perhaps he was launched into adolescence a little too early because of these two extra years. But later, he enjoyed the thought of having two suspended years to play with.

Marc was pleased when he discovered that I was also born in the seventh month, and when the day came, he presented me with an inscribed copy of *Ma Vie,* containing a watercolor of an artist at the easel, half-man, half-faun, a revealing version of the self-portrait.

I took home the Venturi book before it was inscribed and showed it to John, but I left *Ma Vie,* with its telltale painting, hidden away on Marc's shelf. John was impressed by the beauty of some of Marc's pictures, but the next day he said something unkind about Jews. Was he beginning to feel a bit jealous?

Ida certainly sensed the change in her father and the easy friendliness between us, though we were careful to show as little familiarity as possible, and I continued to address Marc as Monsieur Chagall. But his eyes could hide nothing from Ida, nor could mine. She had a way of looking at me, kindly, but with a certain insistence, until I felt uncomfortable.

I seldom saw her husband, Michel Gordey, who was a journalist with the Voice of America and rushed in and out of the house all the time in tremendous haste.

Sometimes a cheerful crowd of young friends blew in, some in G.I. uniforms, and the lunch table was often the scene of lively conversations in French, English and Russian. The months following the end of the war in New York were charged with tremendous vitality. The G.I. Bill was creating a vast movement of learning, a thirst for culture, and the European exiles had brought and received a powerful stimulus.

Fernand Léger and Piet Mondrian were quickly assimilated to New York; it was their element, and it made their art flourish. The sculptors, Ossip Zadkine, Amédé Ozenfant and Jacques Lipchitz also developed in very positive directions under the strong impact of New York.

Pierre Matisse organized an exhibition of illustrious exiles in 1942 in his New York gallery. A photograph shows them all together: Max Ernst, Kurt Seligman, Ozenfant, André Masson, Piet Mondrian, André Breton, Léger, Zadkine, Yves Tanguy, Lipchitz, Pierre Tchelitchew, Eugene Berman, Roberto Matta—and Chagall.

In the photograph, Marc appears severe and rather ill at ease. He avoided his famous colleagues in New York as much as he did in Paris. His contacts with other painters were always difficult. Against his fear of being misunderstood was the inevitable conviction of his own superiority. In short, he had an inferiority-superiority complex.

As for painters of Jewish origin, he was even more distrustful of them, and when the less successful ones showed him friendliness and admiration, he imagined they sought to be associated with him so as to take advantage of his prestige. He was particularly anxious not to be considered a Jewish artist, but a universal one.

At the luncheon parties on Riverside Drive, Marc was usually gay and talkative. I occasionally caught snatches of conversation when I was passing dishes. Sometimes he was teased about his various aversions, and once when someone mentioned Moise Kisling and Mané Katz, two other exiled Jewish artists, he made a comical grimace of disgust, and everyone laughed.

Marc had a more friendly relationship with poets and writers.

Among the exiles were Jacques and Raîssa Maritain, excellent friends
of the Chagalls for years. Jacques was a Catholic philosopher, and
Raîssa was a Russian Jewess converted to Catholicism by Jacques.
They, in turn, converted Pierre Reverdy, Jean Cocteau, Max Jacob
and Georges Rouault, but their fervent proselytizing had never been
aimed at the Chagalls, who were all too obviously not interested.

Another couple, Claire and Ivan Goll, both poets, had been friends
of Bella and Marc since the twenties. Marc illustrated their *Poèmes
d'amour.* Yet while in New York they were still living their chaotic,
romantic lives; still faithful to their communist principles, especially
Ivan, who often gave vent to solemn sermons of political faith. Communists, Marc thought, were even worse than devout Christians in
their desire to convert everyone.

Marc also became friendly with André Breton after the publication
in New York of a text in which Breton stated that the Dada and
surrealist movements had underrated the importance of Chagall.

Marc was very proud of this homage, since Breton's prestige was
enormous. But it amused him to be considered a forerunner of the
surrealists, with whom he felt he had little in common.

One day Marc told me that he had been commissioned by the New
York City Ballet to design the sets and costumes for Stravinsky's
Firebird, with Ballanchine's choreography. Ida decided to rent a large
house in Sag Harbor on Long Island so that he could combine work
with pleasure. A real holiday was something unknown to him;
his sojourns in country places always turned into opportunities for
work.

Ida asked me to accompany them with Jean, and the prospect filled
me with pleasure. Ida packed heavy suitcases with household linen
and groceries, and Marc, in a short-sleeved shirt with green and
mauve checks, a straw hat perched on his fuzzy hair, picked them up
without effort and carried them onto the train. I admired his brawny
arms and youthful energy.

The house had vast rooms with threadbare carpets; an oak staircase
at the head of which dusty stuffed sea gulls and cormorants perched;
and a wide balcony that linked all the bedrooms together. Often,
when everyone had settled down for the night, I would slip out of
my room and into Marc's. One night, Jean woke up and, finding me
gone, screamed in fear. I ran back to my room just as Ida was coming

out of her's, and we bumped into each other with embarrassment. I wish we could have laughed instead!

Ida was kind to me, but our relationship was bound to be delicate. I admired her strong personality, her excellent intellect and her sense of humor, but she made me feel ill at ease. Sometimes she scrutinized me until I was completely out of countenance and blushed hotly. She was seductive and charming, but I didn't know what she was really thinking. I was awkward, naive and inhibited; she was emotional. Marc avoided speaking about me, and Ida was discreet.

Marc and Ida spoke together in Russian, and I could tell by the winsome tone of her voice when she wanted to please him (the charming way she had of calling him "Papochka") and her indignation when he was hard and unyielding. There were sometimes passionate quarrels, followed by kisses of reconciliation. Marc shouted, Ida protested tearfully, but there was no sulking; everything blew over quickly. As she was deeply attached to her father, Ida needed frequent demonstrations of affection, and these were not always forthcoming, especially when they were most needed. It was not easy being a famous man's daughter. As a child she was adulated, spoiled perhaps, but not always loved the way she needed to be loved.

For days, Marc listened to the *Firebird* music in a huge bedroom, with three windows looking out over Long Island Sound. At once he began to float in Stravinsky's music, thoroughly tuned in to its powerful archaic rhythms. He started sketching feverishly, jotting down ideas, sometimes in color, sometimes in pencil. They were barely more than abstract shapes or colors, but they contained the living seeds out of which would grow birds, trees and monsters. He let them soak in pools of color until something started moving. First, a bird woman emerged with outstretched wings of awesome beauty, sweeping into a sky of ultramarine; then a mysterious forest emerged where trees grew upside down and the bird was a twirl of gold caught in its branches. In the third scene the bird became a cloud-palace with a ladder leading up to it. Finally there was a celestial wedding scene in reds and yellows where the canopy, the cakes and the candles exploded joyously to the last majestic chords of Stravinsky's music. Everything was flying in Marc's *Firebird;* the dancers would have to be celestial.

Everything that happened at Sag Harbor was full of shattering contradictions: the promised bliss with Marc—the growing suspicions of John (when Jean and I paid him fortnightly visits in Manhattan); Marc's astonishing eyes that had regained their former brilliance, his sun-browned, radiant face; Ida's watchful eye, her unrestrained enjoyment of picnic parties on the beach with amusing friends, her full-blown beauty; Jean's fascinated discovery of the sea and her bewildered fear each time I was out of sight; and, dominating everything, the *Firebird* designs that grew in intensity with our love. Michel came occasionally, and was kind to me. One day, I put too much salt in the soup, and he called to the kitchen teasingly, "They say that when you put too much salt in the food, it means you're in love!"

One hot summer evening, Jean and I were returning from New York by train, when suddenly a tin can came hurtling through the window, striking me violently and showering us both with a dark purplish powder—some kind of chemical used by farmers, it turned out. No one came forward to comfort us. I have often witnessed this indifference in America, the fear of other people's misfortune.

Ida was upset when she saw us. She ran a bath and sponged us soothingly, and I was touched by her tenderness. *"Comme vous êtes belle!"* she said spontaneously. *"Vous aussi!"* I replied. Ida was wearing her Titian hair in pigtails, and it made her more girlish.

A Soviet Russian friend of hers, Nyla, came to stay in Sag Harbor, and the two young women, both handsomely endowed, roused the truck drivers on the country roads. Nyla flirted with Marc and enticed him to the bottom of the garden one hot evening, but he was always reserved and shy, especially with enterprising young women.

On each of my visits to New York, John became increasingly alarmed by my silent reserve, and he began to question me fiercely. Finally, I broke down and confessed that I was in love with Marc. His rage was violent. He stormed up and down the room for half the night and finally left the house, threatening to put an end to his life. I was terrified and trembled with fear for hours, but in the early morning he came back. He was calmer. He said that I must go back to Sag Harbor to fetch my things and break with Marc. I was so shattered and frozen with terror that I put up no resistance.

I boarded the train like a sleepwalker. To leave Marc was only possible in that state. My mind was empty. I had been carried away by my love; now I was suddenly confronted with the problem of Jean's happiness as well as John's, of John's possible suicide. I must go back to him, I thought. There was no other way—at least for the present. I had often reacted with blind acceptance to circumstances that seemed momentarily inevitable, biding my time until the storm blew over, and this patient attitude in the face of disaster had got me unscathed through many a scrape. I knew suffering was part of the game, and that when the storm abated, there were sometimes new and beautiful things strewn on the shore.

Marc was numb and expressionless when I told him I had to leave him. He said nothing. He only lowered his head as he sat at his easel, brush still in hand, submitting to the blow in stony silence. He was motionless as I kissed him and fled. Then he returned resolutely to his work. Marc had a Jewish fatalism (born of thousands of years of persecution) which is also a trust in fate, a mystical belief that events are written into our lives. His destiny was to be a great artist and everything else that happened to him was subsidiary. He had only one direction, and his remarkable instinct for self-preservation had got him safely through many adversities.

Renoir talked of his capacity for letting himself be carried along like a cork on a stream which preserved him from the biggest shocks. This resembles the Taoist philosophy of *"wu-wei"* ("going with it") and suggests a serenity that Marc did not possess. Marc was perpetually anxious, yet he had an instinctive trust in destiny. It was as if he believed in a jealous God who observes us constantly and will punish us if we are too content.

Later I sometimes noticed that the better things were, the more Marc complained. He never dared to admit that he was happy, it would be inviting misfortune. And sometimes he even went to the extent of marring his happiness by fussing and complaining, perhaps from a guilty fear of being too fortunate. Paradoxically, he was never really happy unless he was worrying about something. I often saw him literally wring his hands in anguish over some seemingly trivial thing, the outward sign of a deep anxiety. He was prepared to suffer for the sake of his work, but he had a terror of anything that threatened to disrupt it—noisy children, bills to pay, other people's problems, all the usual day-to-day interruptions, even a rainstorm; every unexpected thing had a jarring affect on him and distracted him from his work. Once he told me, "Sometimes there are waves of sadness blowing through me, like wind in a field of wheat—you know the way it scurries through the wheat in a dozen places at a time. It's beautiful to see, but it's always sad." When it rained he was miserable, as if ink were falling from the sky. Once when I played him a Mozart record to cheer him up, he listened for a while and said: "Ah, Mozart! There's a happy man for you!"

"Mozart had his share of sorrows too," I reminded him.

"Yes, but nothing ever killed his joy."

Back in the drab furnished room in New York, I broke down and sobbed for hours. I felt crushed, as if a boulder had rolled over my body. John tried to cheer me up. He took Jean and me for a walk in Central Park and bought us ice cream. Jean was aware that something serious was happening, and she tried bravely to comfort me. John was half-reassured by my return, but he began to realize the extent of my despair and couldn't face it. His own was heavy enough to bear. He knew that our unhappiness would continue as before, the numbness that crushed us, day after day. After the third day, he broke down as well.

Finally, he sent me back to Marc, making me promise never to leave him completely. Again, I was letting myself be carried along by this stream, resolving, with my usual confidence, to tackle each problem as it arose.

Marc was glad to see me, though a little dazed, and Ida was extremely edgy. She left us alone in Sag Harbor until our holiday drew to a close.

Our return to New York produced a difficult situation. Marc was anxious to keep our liaison absolutely secret. Only the most intimate friends knew about it, the others considered me simply as the housekeeper. Ida had very mixed feelings about me. She had witnessed a dramatic separation in Sag Harbor, a repetition of which was not impossible. There was a tense atmosphere in the Riverside Drive apartment, and it was out of the question for me to live there, so in the evenings Jean and I returned to the furnished room, where there was even more tension.

I felt more and more each day that John was a stranger; he was so far removed from everything I wanted out of life, that I had nothing whatever to share with him. My fear of him was fading and turning to animosity.

Fortunately Marc and Ida got to work immediately on the sets and costumes of *Firebird* and I was employed in helping to sew the costumes. There I met a theater friend of my brother's, Elizabeth Montgomery, a member of the Motley group of theater designers. Before the war my brother, Stephen Haggard, had been a well-known actor in London. From acting he had turned to writing plays, and one of these, with Peggy Ashcroft and himself in the leading parts, was playing when war was declared. He had been sent to the Middle East in the intelligence service and was killed there in 1943. Elizabeth and I spoke with deep nostalgia of those prewar years when Stephen and the Motleys had made the sparks fly in the London theatrical world.

Balanchine blew in and out of the costume studio, as were the New York City Ballet's principal dancers, Maria Tallchief and Francisco Moncion, who came with the corps de ballet to try on their costumes. It was good to be back in the theater world again. I had worked in a scene-painting studio in London when I first left my parents' house, and it was there that I had met John McNeil.

Marc supervised the execution of the back drops at the Metropolitan Opera House for two arduous weeks, wielding the long-handled brushes expertly and adding brilliant finishing touches that made the whole thing come alive.

Ida was following in the footsteps of her mother, who had supervised the costumes of the ballet *Aleko* in 1942. After Ida had dressed the dancers, Marc came to inspect them; sometimes he took a brushful of aniline color and dabbed it directly onto their costumes, breaking up a line here and there, flicking a few dots or heightening a tone.

When I saw the ballet a few days after the triumphant opening, the moment of greatest intensity was, strangely enough, the prelude, before the dancers appeared—the first spine-shivering bars of music in the darkened theater, the slow parting of the curtains and the dazzling apparition of Marc's celestial bird. Never had music and painting been so miraculously one. As soon as the dancers appeared, the spell was broken. But the magic returned when the monsters tumbled onto the stage, and the music exploded in a whirl of greens and purples.

When the Yiddish novelist, Joseph Opatoshu, saw the ballet, he exclaimed, "Marc, you must be in love!" Marc chuckled and kept his secret, but a month or two later, we took Oppen, as he was called, and his wife Adele into our confidence.

Opatoshu wrote poetical, spicy tales of the Old Country, which appeared weekly in a Yiddish paper. He had a fascinating ugliness— a protruding lower lip, flat nose and enormous ears. He was playful, even flirtatious, and Adele was romantic and sentimental. We became fast friends, and their friendship was one of the most positive elements in my life at the time.

Marc had the impression that Ida and Michel were on the point of separating. A friend of Michel's, a young French journalist, was often with her, and Michel was seldom there. But Marc preferred to ignore this possibility as long as nothing was official. Both Ida and Michel planned to return to France in the near future.

Michel and I had little contact, but later in France I began to appreciate this intelligent man who, apart from broadcasting on the Voice of America, had worked all through the war at the Office of War Information under Pierre Lazareff. In France he joined Lazareff's newly founded newspaper, *France Soir.* He was of Russian-Jewish origin, his real name being Rappaport. Gordey was a non de plume, taken from the village of Gordes in the south of France, where the family had spent their last months before emigrating to America during the war.

At that time Marc and Bella seemed incomprehensively reluctant to leave France. They imagined that no harm could come to them in that southern, nonoccupied territory. They had bought a handsome seventeenth century schoolhouse in the spectacular, half-ruined village that their friend, the painter André Lhote, had discovered, and all Marc's pictures were taken there. The sale of the house was completed on the very day the Germans invaded Holland and Belgium, and they seemed unconscious of the danger that threatened them. When the American Emergency Rescue Committee arrived in Gordes with an invitation for the Chagalls, they hesitated to accept. Finally, Michel and Ida persuaded them, and they left Marseilles on the seventh of May (the day Marc had chosen because of the lucky seven), embarked from Lisbon in extremis and sailed for New York. Michel and Ida stayed behind to save the pictures, which the Spanish authorities had seized on the orders of the Gestapo. Finally, thanks to their skill and devotion, and after running into many dangers (Michel was arrested, but liberated by the Vichy ambassador in Madrid), they saved Marc's entire collection of some 500 paintings, plus hundreds of drawings and gouaches. They left with several crates on a grueling forty-three day journey to New York.

Ida and Michel had both been under twenty when they married in 1934, although they were not anxious for marriage. Marc told me that he and Bella had persuaded them to marry after discovering that they were lovers. Marc shrugged his shoulders as if to say, "What else could we do?" He regretted nothing, even now that the marriage was breaking up. Ida and Michel remained staunch and loyal friends, often companions in adversity, but they never raised a family. An atmosphere of melancholy hovers over the picture called *The Bride's Chair*, painted the day after their marriage—a bouquet lies there abandoned, the bride has gone.

When Ida packed up and went to stay with friends, somewhere in New York, Michel stayed on in their half of the big Riverside Drive apartment, and Marc considered that I could now move in with Jean, at least temporarily.

I was tremendously relieved not to have to return to purgatory every evening. As for Marc, he was at last reassured. Every night he had imagined that John would again threaten suicide and hold me prisoner.

The ballet work was finished, and Marc went back to his easel at last. Several paintings were awaiting completion, and he was glad to be able to tackle them again. The embarrassment and tension with Ida was forgotten for the moment, and in the still of the evening, once Jean had been put to bed, we could talk freely.

"*Nu?*" he said on one such evening. "You never told me how you came to America."

"I'd rather not, it's a painful story." But he insisted. I explained how my father had been appointed consul general in New York just before the war, and when war broke out I asked him to send affidavits so that John and I could come as well. He did so, and my parents very generously put us up in their apartment on Sutton Place South. It was the first time they had ever met John, although we had been married for four years. He and my father took an immediate disliking to each other, which grew into bitter hatred.

Shortly after our arrival, I discovered I was pregnant. John had decided that he wanted no children and I had acquiesced, but this was an accident. He refused to believe it. All through my pregnancy he reviled me without mercy. No doubt I unconsciously desired a child, but I hadn't really thought about it. John had killed all my conscious desires. In the first month of our life together he had managed to quash my hopes of becoming a painter.

Living with my parents became a nightmare for everyone. John relapsed deeper and deeper into depression and refused every promising chance to make a living from his drawings. So we went to live in a tiny sordid furnished room under the el on Fifty-third Street with our baby daughter.

Now John vented all his bitterness and exasperation on me. I was to blame for all his troubles: I had brought him to America, I had given birth to Jean. She was the only person he loved, but he wasn't grateful for her. He made me feel unworthy of her, and responsible for all her little woes. I was cut off from my family and friends, I felt guilty toward him and Jean.

I stuck to him because he had no one else, I believed in him because no one else believed in him. I knew he was a highly intelligent, talented person.

I didn't see my father again for many years. He went back to England when America joined the war and became chief of the Department of Anglo-American Relations at the Foreign Office. When the war was over my mother joined him. Even the appalling tragedy of my brother's death couldn't reconcile my father and me.

Marc remained silent for a long while, shaking his head gravely. "I never quarreled with my parents. For me, parents are sacred. Nothing in the world could have turned me against mine. How could you let John do that?"

I explained how I was torn between conflicting loyalties. John had had a disastrous childhood, he was embittered against the ruling classes; I felt I had to defend him. I could never talk to my father, he would listen to nothing. He said what he wanted to say, then he went off and slammed the door. My mother was more tolerant. I could talk to her, but she was scared of my father, too. When I visited her with Jean I went in by the servants' entrance so as to avoid the two liveried porters who always bowed obsequiously. I also avoided my father that way.

Marc looked at me with a smile and a frown, half amused, half disapproving. His first reaction was to defend my father. "You must write to him immediately and make peace."

His mistrust for John grew into hostility and disdain. When Jean was upset and consequently difficult, he blamed John for his bad example, seeing in her a reflection of her father.

Marc treated Michel with a slightly suspicious coolness and Michel, offended, complained that Jean disturbed him. The last weeks had been a strain on her and she didn't quite know where she stood, so she was particularly demanding and tearful. Marc was extremely nervous and exasperated. I felt torn and aching, still prey to guilt and feelings of unworthiness, instilled by John. My love for Marc was very gradually drawing me out of these feelings, but in my unconscious mind Jean represented my unworthiness; she was a constant reminder of it. I began to have a helpless feeling of being incapable of giving her all the love and attention I gave her before, plus the extra dose she needed since she had been separated from her father.

As Marc became more and more tense his work made no progress. I was deeply concerned about this.

The Opatoshus volunteered advice: They had friends who ran a small boarding school in Plainfield, New Jersey, and they suggested I send Jean there for a few months. Marc urged me to consider this and we all went to visit the school. The atmosphere seemed friendly and one teacher, especially, took to Jean and gave her warmth and affection. I tried to quiet my conscience and decided that I must sacrifice Jean for the sake of peace with Marc until things settled down, and I persuaded myself that things would turn out all right in the end. But I didn't keep my eyes open to Jean's suffering, to the profound transformation that was taking place inside her. Perhaps my own weakened state prevented me from doing so. She hardly complained, she numbed herself to the suffering, but the strong symbiosis that had linked us together for five years was broken.

Whenever I went to see her at the school or brought her home, she was politely reserved; friendly, but somehow absent. She became a quiet, secretive little girl, overanxious to please and be accepted, and when the strain proved too great, she often broke down. I hoped that John would visit her, but he feared the emotional impact of seeing her again.

It was at this time that another little person who would be named David chose to begin his life on earth. No doubt he already looked very much like a broad bean beginning to sprout, having got well on his way before I noticed his presence; with marvelous disregard for our muddled lives he took root uninvited—in spite of precautions— as Jean had done six years earlier. Since then, they both continue to be wonderfully unpredictable. They are now in the prime of life. They have always avoided adhering to established forms of thought and behavior, and have usually succeeded in steering clear of everything that cramped their lifestyle. They are surprisingly tolerant toward me, in spite of my failings as a mother and their difficult beginnings, and both have brought me immense joy and confidence.

Marc was terribly upset by this inescapable evidence of our new love. The traditional one-year period of celibacy after the death of a wife (which Jewish custom prescribes) had not yet elapsed. This was a grave matter for Marc, although he was not a practicing Jew. He felt guilty toward Bella and scared of Ida's reaction; he feared the opinion of friends who venerated Bella's memory, even though he maintained that he felt at peace with his own conscience.

I went to the country to be alone. The village of Walkill in New York State was unpaved in those days and the roads were muddy. It rained incessantly for two weeks. Bleak houses were lined up along a wide straight road as they are in most American villages, no doubt because they were doomed to become cities in the future.

I spent two miserable weeks of reflection, profoundly upset by Marc's reluctance to accept this child.

I had written my parents a joyful letter about my new happiness with Marc. My father's answer was cool and skeptical with regard to Marc, and overly triumphant with regard to John. He wrote:

"You must not think you are obliged to live with this man of thirty years your senior, simply because you need a home."

I was hurt that he should set so little store by my love for Marc. I answered that it was thanks to Marc that I had found the courage to leave John at last. My frayed nerves couldn't take his sermonizing, and I wrote a hard letter which I later regretted. I wrote words that I would never have said to his face. This rash practice is a common one in the Haggard family. With characteristic impulsiveness, we send our letters immediately, for fear of changing our minds.

I had forgotten my parent's own wrought up state, the difficult conditions of their life in blitzed England, and the terrible pain of losing Stephen in the war and shortly after his three-year-old son, who had come to New York with his mother and elder brother to stay with my parents.

I immediately wrote back asking my father's forgiveness. After this stormy exchange we became true friends, and our friendship continued to gain strength until the end of his life.

Finally, I emerged from despair and went back to Marc.

I already loved this child of ours, and my stronger attitude began to influence Marc. I said that *I* wanted the baby, whatever happened.

But I needed guidance from someone completely outside our problems and had no one to turn to. I had heard of an Englishwoman named Quest Brown, who had a remarkable gift of clairvoyance. She was an experienced intuitive psychologist who used palmistry as a method for stimulating her natural faculties.

I asked Marc to accompany me, and far from scorning such irrational practices, he approved of my idea of seeking guidance in this unusual fashion.

She studied our hands in silence, glancing rapidly at our faces from time to time. She had a birdlike face with a beak nose and fuzzy red hair. She began to make surprisingly pertinent remarks about our lives; then, quite suddenly, she announced that we would have a son and be very happy together.

I told her about my life with John. I still had a haunting fear that some harm might come to him and I would feel responsible, but she assured me that he would never commit suicide. She said I must cut myself free of him once and for all. Marc nodded with vehement approval.

She explained that I was doing John more harm than good by consenting to be his victim, that my pity was weakening him. As for myself, I had been very near to destruction, and Jean would also be in danger if she remained too close to him.

When we left the bird lady, we were both in a considerably happier mood. Then and there we decided to name our son David, after Marc's younger brother, who had died in a Crimean sanatorium. The thought of having a son had suddenly filled him with joy, but he said nothing to Ida for the time being.

Marc begged me to leave Jean at school; he said our peace and happiness depended very much on this for the time being. Her presence had begun to weigh on him considerably; now he honestly confessed that her presence might prove a threat to our relationship. Ida observed his nervous state and agreed with him, and I complied.

The final break with John was painful, but not stormy. He accused me of breaking my promise never to abandon him completely, but he agreed to give me a legal paper declaring that my expected child was not his. He was taking it much better than I expected.

The next day he wrote to me:

> Don't be upset please, you're married now to a very fine painter. You have what you dreamed of. Please be reassured and reassure Marc. I have written to your father and to mine, and I'm telling everyone how right it is for you to be Marc's wife.
>
> I have said bitter things and gross things to you but I am not like that any more.

He also wrote to Marc:

> "Dear Marc Chagall, I am glad that Virginia has gone to you. I know that you are both happy and that you are a kind man. I know that it is unfair of me to ask any woman to be a part of my home. Sometimes I was bitter towards you. You will forgive me, I was very ill. Best wishes. I love you both."

I was profoundly touched by these letters and heartily relieved that my decision to break with John (thanks to the bird lady) had such positive effects. John decided to go back to England as soon as possible. Marc found the affectionate tone of John's letters embarrassing and mistrusted their sincerity. I knew they were perfectly sincere, but I also knew his violent contradictions and changes of mood.

Marc told Ida my husband was leaving, and seeing his immense relief she, too, was reassured.

On the eve of John's departure, I took Jean back to our old apartment to say good-bye to him. This was the moment I most dreaded. But on the door I found a note which read, "Forgive me, I can't face it." Jean's plush penguin and two teddy bears were sitting on the chairs. John had expressed a wish to take one of the bears with him.

Suddenly Jean realized the whole extent of her sorrow. She knew she would never see her father again in this home of hers, and she let out a heart-rending wail. She sobbed disconsolately all the way back to Riverside Drive. Many years later I spoke to her of this incident, but she remembered nothing, it had been thrust so deeply into her subconscious.

Chapter

II

High Falls

In *Ma Vie* Marc wrote that he couldn't understand why people crowd together in the same places when there are thousands of miles of beautiful country everywhere. "My wife likes culture," he wrote, "but I would be content to live in some quiet place, where I would do nothing but paint pictures that would astonish the world."

He developed this theme dreamily, but seldom put it into effect. Since those Russian days when he and Bella had opted for "culture," he had undoubtedly hankered after quiet places, which only holiday periods could offer. The war sent him to the quiet village of Gordes where, in spite of the dangerous situation, he threw himself into his work with zeal, and had a last illusion of calm before the storm of uprooting.

Now Marc at last saw a possibility of settling in the country. Michel had left and Ida would also be returning to France shortly, and he had no intention of staying in the Riverside Drive apartment. Also, my pregnancy would soon be visible, and he wanted to hide me away for the time being. Ida, who of course knew nothing of this particular reason, approved of the plan, providing that it was temporary; she expected Marc to return to France within the following year.

The atmosphere was now more peaceful in Riverside Drive; Ida came back and forth, taking care of business matters and watching the evolution of Marc's work. There was a much easier relationship between us, with even a few laughs here and there, encouraged by their intimate friends, who were now familiar with our relationship.

One day Marc said: "Virginichka [he had Russianized my name], go and see if you can find a house in some quiet country place." Without hesitating I went to Walkill, where I had landed in a haphazard fashion a few weeks earlier. I had seen some countryside on the way that reminded me of Dorset. The thought of returning to the country after all these years of city life filled me with joy. There was one real estate agent in Walkill and he only had one house to offer, for rent or for sale. It was in High Falls, in the Catskill Mountains, and the very next day Marc and I went to see it.

It was a simple wooden house with screened porches, near a superb catalpa tree. It had been fondly built by a contented carpenter who had enjoyed it to the end of his days. A grassy valley lay before it; behind, the ground rose to a jagged ridge of rocks, crowning a wooded ravine. Next to the house was a small wooden cottage that immediately enchanted Marc—it reminded him of an isba.

"That's my studio!" he said, and at once decided to buy the house. It wasn't expensive; besides he loved buying houses. He would return to France sooner or later, but meanwhile he wanted to have an illusion of settling down. He was accustomed to tearing up his roots.

On our way home, he explained that he intended to knock out the inner walls of the little house and put in big studio windows. We were as excited as children and hugged each other delightedly. Marc immediately went to tell Ida the good news.

She was somewhat taken aback when he announced that he was going to buy a house. Cautiously, she went to look at it. She found it rather primitive, but didn't altogether disapprove. She gave me a lot of good advice about improving it, and there was not a trace of tension between us. She saw that her father was in high spirits and she was happy for that.

Our muddled life was gradually beginning to sort itself out. The next step, and perhaps the most difficult one for Marc, was to break the news of my pregnancy to Ida. But the time had not yet come.

There were a few essential pieces of furniture in the house, as well as pots and pans, so we lost no time moving in. Marc wanted to start working immediately on the illustrations for the *One Thousand and One Nights,* commissioned by Kurt and Helen Wolff of Pantheon Books.

Before I even had time to unpack, he was already at work, and the musty house came to life at once. I read him the stories while he made rapid sketches and spread them all over the living room floor to dry. We had to pick our way through them carefully. From these he produced a series of luminous gouaches.

He seemed remarkably unconcerned by the inevitable blots and smudges, and he plodded away with inspired concentration, making them all serve his purpose. Sometimes he poured a glass of water over the gouache, then drained it off. A few minutes later he called for more water, but before I had time to bring it, he said, "Never mind, I spat."

He explained that there were no rules for technique; anything was permissible as long as the motives were genuine.

I was impressed by the way he plunged headlong into creation, regardless of pitfalls, carried away by an idea that kept flashing in his mind, eliminating all obstacles that threatened to extinguish it. "Art is a deluge," he said, "but a controlled deluge."

Altogether he made thirteen gouaches for this project. From these, color lithographs were executed in Albert Carman's studio on City Island in New York: a mermaid reclining beside a stormy sea where shipwrecked sailors struggle; a flying horse carries lovers away into a deep blue sky; a naked couple is awakened from sleep by a dazzling sun bird. "Then, said the king in himself, 'By Allah, I will not slay her until I have heard the next of her tale.' So they slept the rest of that night in mutual embrace till day finally broke."

Marc and I were happy to be alone together; it was a mercifully peaceful period. I began to retrieve my lost equilibrium and I was feeling healthier than I had felt in years.

Marc was a delightful companion. In spite of our completely different origins and the thirty years that separated us, there was perfect harmony between us. I never felt the least intimidated or inadequate with this man. It was a blissful change, both from John's constant criticism and the exacting ambitions of my father. I had developed an obsessional fear of my unworthiness and inferiority, and Marc began to free me from it. I was never troubled by feelings of inequality between us, whatever obvious inequalities existed between a great painter and an immature young woman who had been through a traumatic experience. At last I had freedom of speech and was no longer tongue-tied.

As for our difference in age, it simply never occurred to us. Marc was astonishingly youthful and energetic, and we felt like the pair of exuberant young lovers he was painting in the *One Thousand and One Nights.*

Occasionally we traveled to New York and spent a night at Riverside Drive. Ida had returned. Marc was still apprehensive about his friends' reaction to his new companion, but they did all they could to reassure him and I was readily accepted by them all. Ida's sense of humor lightened the atmosphere, putting everyone at ease, and we spent delightful evenings at their houses.

One evening our host was an immensely rich art collector and lawyer, Louis Stern, a fanatical perfectionist who spent his life adding new and ever more lavish items to his palatial home. No woman shared this flawless opulence with him; perhaps women tend to feel cramped by too much perfection. I felt certain Marc and Ida saved the man from boredom and melancholy.

Another friend was Max Lerner, the journalist, who was always talkative, spontaneous and witty. Marc and he spoke Yiddish together and laughed a good deal. When Marc was in need of advice on weighty matters he often asked Max, in whom he believed implicitly.

Marc's French doctor, Camille Dreyfus, had an affectionate, protective attitude toward him. He treated Marc like a younger brother, and teased him for being wrought-up, excitable and squeamish. When Camille had to draw blood for a checkup and Marc let out a pitiable "Ai! Ai! Ai!" he chuckled delightedly. He had the gray face of a mouse, a small bristly mustache and dark circles under his eyes. Camille had an excellent effect on Marc's health and humor, and always managed to dispel his obsessions by drawing from his store of subtley absurd Jewish stories. He was kind to me, and occasionally gave me a sidelong smile and a wink, as much as to say: "You're okay."

One day in the dining room at Riverside Drive a violent quarrel broke out between Marc and Ida. Russian is a particularly expressive language for quarreling and the scene was quite theatrical. As I came out of the kitchen I saw Marc suddenly lift a chair and brandish it over Ida's head. Quietly, I seized it from behind and the torrents of abuse subsided.

Marc explained to me afterward that Ida had asked him repeatedly to honor his obligation to give her a certain sum of money, or its equivalent in pictures, as her legal share in her mother's legacy. He protested, "I'm not dead yet, but my daughter wants to deprive me of my paintings!" He refused to accept her legal and moral right to inherit from her mother, and this gave rise to several quarrels.

I tried to have a moderating effect on him in this matter. Louis Stern and another lawyer friend of Marc's, Bernard Reis, who, like Stern, was a Chagall collector, supported Ida discreetly in this matter and finally managed to persuade Marc. But it was not until 1948, in France, that the ridiculous litigation was settled and Ida inherited an important collection of pictures.

Marc's tempers were legendary. In *Ma Vie* he has recollections of one of his roommates in St. Petersburg, a sculptor who pounded his clay and attacked it like a wild beast. Finally Marc, exasperated by the sculptor's fury, flung a lamp at his head. Another story has it that Katia Granoff, the Parisian dealer, caught a flying statuette on her (fortunately) well-padded bosom during some disagreement concerning a contract.

Back in High Falls, we decided to buy a secondhand Oldsmobile, and I asked our farmer neighbor, Victor Purcell, to give me driving lessons.

The Chagall family had never owned a car, nor had the Haggards, and we were proud and excited on our first drive to New York.

Marc enjoyed strolling through the Jewish quarter of lower Manhattan, where the merchants set their stalls in the street. No one knew him but everyone was his friend because they all spoke Yiddish. He could behave exactly as he pleased. He was no longer a celebrity; he could bargain for a good price with the best of them. He bought me a silver star of David on a chain and put it around my neck delightedly.

"Don't leave the car too near," he said, "they'll put up the prices." He bought Yiddish newspapers and read them as he walked along, munching strudel and discarding the pages one by one as he read them, until the pavement was strewn with floating sheets. We bought Jewish bread and gefilte fish.

"You must learn how to make that," he said. "Adele will teach you. All I know is that when the sauce is good, the fish is ready. My mother always gave me the sauce to taste; I was the only one she trusted."

The Opatoshus came to see us in High Falls. They were affectionate and humorous; they called me "goy" and "shicksele" when they were in a teasing mood, and declared they were godparents to our unborn David. They invited us to celebrate Passover in their house, and Oppen donned a white satin skullcap with gold embroidery and recited the Haggadah (the story of Israel's bondage and flight from Egypt), giving me an occasional wink. We ate gefilte fish, soup and dumplings. A chair was set and a glass of wine was poured out for the Prophet Elijah.

Marc felt at peace in High Falls; never, since then, did I see this anxious man so free from anxiety. Life had been simplified, and Marc had no need to worry over money matters. His dealer, Pierre Matisse, gave him a monthly allowance and came every few months to take away his share of the paintings. Every year, he held an exhibition of Chagall's latest work in his handsome gallery on Fifty-seventh Street in Manhattan. Marc's intrinsic insecurity, which had a tendency to increase proportionately with wealth and fame, seemed dormant for the time being.

He told me that Bella had once asked him (at a time when he no longer had any financial worries) how much money he needed to feel totally secure and he replied, "I shall *never* have enough money. I shall *never* feel secure."

It is interesting to note that in periods of his life when his material insecurity was acute—the years of poverty in Russia, the first Paris period and his return to Russia during the revolution—he did most of his finest work. Yet he sought fame and riches, perhaps to avenge himself for past humiliations; it was his answer to some of the older and more famous artists in Paris who once showed contempt for this humble Jew from Vitebsk. He had certainly been humiliated by the superior attitude of Bella's family, the Rosenfelds, and though they lost their riches in the revolution, he seemed to have been unconsciously trying to get square with them ever since. When his brother-in-law, an unsuccessful doctor, left communist Russia for a mediocre life in Paris, Marc could not help treating him in a patronizing manner. He had done the same to Marc during his own years of plenty.

Marc's family were Hasidim and his attitude toward religion was relaxed, almost cheerful. The credo of the Hasidim was, "Serve God in joy." They placed emphasis on feeling rather than on intellectual merit and for them, as for Spinoza, joy was a virtue, and sadness a sin. They also preferred storytelling to theological discussions. Marc gave up religious practices when he left his family, but he never forgot them; ultimately they left a deep impression on him. Because neither he nor Bella were practicing Jews, Ida subsequently had not been brought up to observe the faith.

In High Falls, he became friendly with a group of devout Jews who took him to the synagogue one year to celebrate Yom Kippur. I believe it was the first time he had done so for many years, and during the seven years we lived together, he never repeated the experience. Perhaps so soon after the tragic Holocaust years, Marc felt a need to manifest his profound identity and solidarity with the Jewish people.

But strict kosher practices seemed to him ridiculously sectarian, and when his niece, Bella Rosenfeld (who adhered to them), came to stay with us later in France, I had to try and defend her as best I could from his intolerant exasperation.

As this was his attitude toward religious practices, I was surprised when a short time after settling in High Falls, he began, first delicately and then with slightly more insistence, to suggest that I might adopt the Jewish religion. He said he had discussed the matter with the Opatoshus, and they thought it was a good idea.

I explained that I had no religion at all and desired none, but I was careful not to show too much opposition, lest Marc should take it as an unfriendly gesture toward Jews. He was touchy on this point, although he was himself often hard in his criticism of Jews, even calling them "dirty Jews" on occasion. Once he said, ironically, "Sometimes I feel positively anti-Semitic." But he considered them a superior people—God's chosen—and his criticism was all the more severe. His disapproval was chiefly directed toward "assimilated" Jews, because they had "lost touch with the Bible." He once wrote,

"Were I not a Jew, with all the significance I put into that word, I would not be an artist at all."

It was plain that he felt conscious-stricken about his "Goy" companion, but I thought his misgivings would wear off.

Marc knew that I was attracted to Jews, and I playfully reminded him that I had received a sprinkling of Jewish blood from my Russian great-grandmother. Our family coat-of-arms, strangely enough, carried a six-pointed star, which amused us. I told him my great-uncle, Rider Haggard, had written a weird adventure story called *King Solomon's Mines,* which he'd found equally intriguing.

But perhaps this difference of background between us was more important to Marc than I had imagined. In later years he had a tendency to blame it for the other differences that would come between us, thus needlessly aggravating those differences.

I let the matter of my conversion slide, as I usually did when faced with delicate problems. One day Ida got wind of our discussions and came to my rescue. She declared that it was an absurd idea, and nothing more was ever said about it. I was relieved, and Marc seemed satisfied.

Still, he wanted David to be brought up as a Jew, and insisted that he be circumcised. I realized then that it was for David's sake that he had wanted me to be officially "Jewish," for Jews consider that the mother's origin determines that of the child.

He often spoke to me of Bella; he believed that her spirit lived on somewhere and was watching over us. He said I must try and be worthy of her; needless to say, I felt that that was impossible—Bella was a sort of saint. From her girlhood photograph, she contemplated us with great dark eyes like an El Greco Madonna. Still, Marc had once said, "It was Bella who sent you to look after me. Rembrandt had his Henrickje Stoffels to console him after Saskia's death; I have you."

Among the many qualities Marc admired in Bella (and which Ida inherited) were a meticulously practical mind and a refined taste and sense of propriety—she had a flair for doing just the right thing at the right time. Marc had hoped to discover these same qualities in me to compensate for his own lack of them, but he soon realized that I didn't possess them either.

Before his marriage Marc had been madly excessive and daring, marvelously careless of his masterpieces and totally confident in his judgment of them. His relationships to people were tempestuous and impulsive. Bella had somewhat of a refining effect on him, perhaps to the detriment of the more savage side of his nature that produced such unaccountable creations.

Bella's childhood and girlhood memoirs, written in Yiddish, had been finished just before her death, translated into English by Norbert Guterman and published in 1946 by Schocken Books in New York, with drawings by Marc, under the title *Burning Lights.* The following year a second volume, *Die Ershte Bagegenisch,* describing her first meeting with Marc, was published in Yiddish by the Jewish People's Fraternal Order, a communist organization, also accompanied by a series of beautiful drawings by Marc.* The publication of these moving and poetical texts in which Bella, after so many years of complete devotion to Marc, had rediscovered her secret self and her talent to express it, was, for Marc, both redemption and consolation. Perhaps he had an obscure sense of guilt toward her for the difficult life she had led. He must have realized that this work showed the real, the complete Bella, who had given up her personal life for him; and Bella, the writer, seemed to have let herself die once her own personal work was finished, as if she were weary of the fight. Bella's personal creativity had been diverted in the direction of Marc's work, in which she participated as his supreme critic. In *Ma Vie* he'd written: "May our deceased parents bless *our* painting."

Bella's role of muse, which brought Marc such powerful inspiration, became a dominating one. She was a brilliant intellectual, an ultrarefined woman. Marc was not aware of her domination, so completely did their personalities melt into each other. In many paintings representing himself and Bella, the artist melts into the loved one, sharing her breasts and body. The most interesting example of this is a picture called *The Black Glove,* begun in France before the war and finished in High Falls in 1948. It represents a particularly beautiful double portrait of Marc and Bella with their heads joined together,

*Both books were translated by Ida into French and published by Gallimard in 1973 under the title of *Lumières Allumées.*

his arm encircling their single body with its breasts, and his hand working at the easel.

I busied myself with the house, which was still far from comfortable. Not a soul in the village would do any work for me. I was a stranger, a foreigner; I lived with a much older man and I was pregnant. The cisterns had to be cleaned out, so I went into the water with rubber boots and brushes.

Every week I went to see Jean in New Jersey, and brought her presents which didn't interest her very much. They were a poor substitute for the warm home she had left. As always, Jean was quiet and uncomplaining. The teacher who was fond of her tried to give her the maternal affection she so badly needed, but nothing could take the place of mine. We walked around the fields (Plainfield was a country place in those days) and I explained to her that very soon she would come to a beautiful new house in the country with a brand-new baby brother.

I stopped going to Riverside Drive and Ida began to ask questions, innocently. Perhaps she had already guessed I was pregnant, having noticed my buxom appearance, or perhaps she had caught a trace of embarrassment in Marc's eye. Suddenly the truth was out. It was a difficult moment, but Ida didn't overdramatize the situation. Marc felt guilty and uneasy. When he came home I resolved to write Ida a letter. She replied kindly and reassuringly:

> You must on no account be sad about any possible misunderstanding or discord between us, because there isn't any. You mustn't blame yourself for anything. Papa felt guilty and embarrassed; that was normal, inevitable. It could only have been avoided if there had been complete frankness between us; but that's difficult with one's daughter. I hope everything is smoothed over now.

I was very touched by this letter and, needless to say, no longer apprehensive.

Riverside Drive was full of bustling activity. Ida was busy collaborating with James Johnson Sweeney on preparations for a big retrospective exhibition of Chagall at the Museum of Modern Art. She was also preparing for her departure to France, and a lot of things had to be settled between Marc and herself. He went to New

York more frequently, and came home exhausted from these trips.

His relationship to Ida was partly based on mutual possession. Marc knew how to turn on his humility and vulnerability when he needed her protection, and Ida made use of her irresistible "chantage sentimental." Occasionally he felt an urge to disobey her as a child would do, to show his independence. Wonderfully disarming Marc, so childlike, yet so artful!

In the early spring, Sweeney opened his splendid exhibition, with Marc and Ida in attendance. He also published an important catalogue with the picture *I and the Village,* from the museum's own collection, on the cover.

A few days later I went alone to see the exhibition, and came back to Marc in high spirits; I had been bowled over by *The Pregnant Woman, The Soldier Drinks, Homage to Apollinaire* and *The Burning House,* which had come over from Europe with many other astonishing early works. Marc confessed that he had been amazed when he saw these paintings again. "I knew they were fine paintings, but they are even better than I thought." His joy was that of a father retrieving his lost children. The splendid *Praying Jew (Rabbi of Vitebsk),* from the Chicago Art Institute was there as well, and he loved it particularly. Marc told me that for years in Russia, he had kept the *Rabbi* under his bed to protect it from the vicissitudes of his precarious life. He prized it as his masterpiece and said it was the nearest he had ever come to the sublimity of Rembrandt. He loved it so much that in France, when he had been obliged to sell it for want of money, he first made a copy of it. Finally he sold the copy as well and made a third, which he also sold. The first of these versions (1914) is in the collection of J. Im Obersteg in Geneva; the second (1923) is in Chicago and the third (1928) is in the Museo d'Arte Moderna in Venice. Each time he sold the picture he was bereft, but he needed money badly. He called these copies "variants," although they were almost exact replicas (except for their slightly different dimensions; also, the first version was painted on cardboard, while the others were on canvas). These copies were freely and beautifully done and as good as the originals, he assured me, but he kept quiet about them, because there was some trouble with the collectors when they discovered that their pictures were not unique. Marc told me he had made variants of one or two other pictures he had been obliged to sell. In the case of *The Praying*

Jew, his favorite work, this meticulous copying was certainly not distasteful to him; perhaps he enjoyed going through this act of creation a second and a third time, trying to probe its mystery.

In November of the same year, the retrospective exhibition moved to the Chicago Art Institute and Marc flew there for the opening. It was the first time he had ever flown, and he sent me a telegram on arrival so that I shouldn't be worried. He said the exhibition was magnificent, and I visualized the rooms I knew so well, for I had studied at the Art Institute in 1930, when my father was stationed in Chicago for three years, between Rio and Paris.

After the New York opening Ida left for France, determined to sow fruitful seeds on the scarred soil and obtain a big retrospective exhibition for her father at the newly reopened Musée d'Art Moderne in Paris. It would be the first one organized by Jean Cassou, the curator, since the outbreak of war.

Ida settled in Montmartre and returned to her own painting for a while, but it was difficult for her to close herself in and concentrate in the exciting atmosphere of postwar Paris. This was a period of intense activity in the art world. The survivors were licking their wounds and searching for their old friends. Each one had a hair-raising story to tell. Ida herself, though impatiently awaiting the return of the exiled hero, was living one of the most interesting periods of her life. Most of her friends had been in the Resistance movement and some held posts in the new government. Everyone was asking when Marc was coming back.

To that end, Ida wrote excited letters, urging Marc to come at once. Dealers were vying with each other for exclusive rights. Marc's three great engraved works, Gogol's *Dead Souls, Fables* by La Fontaine, and the Bible (comprising 300 plates in total) were to be bought back from the heirs of Ambroise Vollard so that the famous editor, Té-riade, could at last take them down from the dusty shelves, where they had been lying ever since they were finished.

Vollard, one of the first great speculators in the modern art world, was never in a hurry to bring into the light of day the treasures he had commissioned years before. Marc was dismayed by his apparent indifference. Every time he brought him a new plate Vollard would simply say, "Put it down over there with the others," not even troubling to look at it. Because of the collector's hoarding and speculation, some other painters, such as Georges Rouault, André Derain and Maurice de Vlaminck, suffered virtual extinction for many years, as far as the public was concerned. Their works had been bought on contract for very modest sums by Vollard, who then tied them up in packages and put them away in vaults. He had a cynical disregard for the feelings of artists, and he treated their works as merchandise and hid them from the public eye; he had a thirst to possess and was in no hurry to sell. Gauguin once complained bitterly that when he would send Vollard a picture from time to time he received "just enough to pay for a crust of bread and some medicine." He was miserably poor during the last years of his life, and he blamed Vollard for the fact that he failed to make a name in the art world because his paintings were never shown.

It must have been disappointing also to Marc, after the completion of these three gigantic works, to see them disappear into oblivion, but he nevertheless felt he owed Vollard a debt of gratitude for having commissioned the work.

When Marc first went to Paris in 1910 he immediately visited the big picture galleries, Durand Ruel and Bernheim, to see Gauguin, Van Gogh, Renoir and Matisse, and to Vollard's "shop" (badly lit, dusty and piled with newspapers) to see the Cézannes. But when he saw Vollard sitting in the middle of the shop in his overcoat, he didn't dare go in. Vollard always put on a disagreeable expression to keep people away.

Now it was time at last for Marc to follow Ida to Paris. He was apprehensive about seeing old friends again—he was coming home without Bella. Her place had been taken by someone else and a child was on its way. How would they greet him? With condolences or congratulations? The entire situation made him feel guilty. Finally he decided to leave in May, so as to be absent at the time of David's birth in June.

Of course I was disappointed, but I knew that he couldn't be expected to behave like any other normal father. He was obviously scared of birth, as he was of any physical suffering. When a member of the family fell sick, he unconsciously vented his ill-humor on the victim.

Birth had frightening associations for him, as one can see from the dramatic pictures he made on the subject in his youth. In one well-known painting, *Birth* (1911), he imagined the scene from the description his mother gave him, putting into it all the love, awe and respect he felt for his mother. His own birth, as described in *Ma Vie*, was a traumatic event:

> "The town was in flames, the poor Jewish quarter. They carried the bed, with the mother and the newborn baby, to a safe place at the other side of the town. But first of all, I was stillborn; I didn't want to live. Imagine a white bubble that doesn't want to live, as though it were stuffed with paintings by Chagall. They pricked it with needles and plunged it into a bucket of water and finally it let out a feeble whimper."

His mother and father were almost sacred figures to him. Marc had a positive influence on my relationship with my own parents, persuading me to be understanding and grateful, which I had often failed to be. For himself, the sacred role of father had to be divided between his painted children and his human ones, and when there was a sacrifice to be made, it was the latter who had to make it. In *Ma Vie*, he writes that he couldn't stand the shrill cries of a baby and when Ida screamed with hunger (milk was scarce during those years of famine), he caught her up roughly and flung her down on the bed. He was shocked at his own brutality. He also confesses with shame that when Ida was born, he didn't come to see the child and her mother until four days later because he was so disappointed that she wasn't a boy.

But now, when his son David was born, it was two long months before he came home. I missed him enormously, but I was full of joy and confidence. I also realized that Marc's anxious presence might have done more harm than good. I understood well Jung's description of the artist's life: "It cannot be otherwise than full of conflict, for two forces are at war within him; on the one hand, the common longing for happiness, satisfaction and security in life, and on the other, a ruthless passion for creation, which may go as far as to override every personal desire."

But this dichotomy didn't prevent Marc from becoming a demonstratively affectionate father. He thought his son was some kind of unique phenomenon, and he was filled with wonder at each stage in the child's development. He often seized David in his arms and smothered him with voracious kisses. Children didn't interest him a lot as such, but he considered his own children superior beings, and David's endless good humor was a tonic for Marc. However, when his children developed their own distinct personalities, there were inevitable clashes with their overproud, exacting father. Ida had experienced these run-ins and David would encounter them later.

In my eighth month of pregnancy Marc left for Paris accompanied by Louis Stern and a large quantity of crates containing food and scarce commodities for friends. Conditions were still very difficult in France, but in England, they were worse. My father wrote:

> We may have to pull in our belts a bit more, but there are still one or two more holes. Many thanks for the food parcels. We haven't been invaded since 1066; now we are talking of the next war and we know we shall be in the vanguard. It's a stimulating sight to see us pull ourselves together for the approaching struggle. Between the two last wars, I was a Utopian. I ought to have been put away as a dangerous lunatic.

It was at this time that I could, at last, bring Jean to her new home in High Falls. I was immensely happy to have her back, and she began to open up and enjoy herself. With Marc absent, I could at last devote myself to her exclusively, and our loving link began to grow again.

Tante Phine, my dear Canadian aunt who had brought about the first meeting of my father and mother in Guatemala, came to live with us until Marc's return, and the neighbors, hitherto politely guarded toward our strange ménage, gradually became warmer and more helpful. Our neighbor Victor, a self-satisfied, puritanical but kindly farmer, agreed to knock down the dividing walls in the little cottage to make a studio for Marc, and his son Donald dug up the soil for a vegetable garden. We acquired a black cat (who immediately became Jean's confidant and inseparable companion), then a flock of chickens. Tante Phine, full of good sense and experience, taught me how to pluck and boil an old fowl, then roast it until it tasted like turkey. We had many good talks together, and her tolerant, broad-minded attitude was helping to bridge the divergencies between my parents and myself, over my new life with a much older man and the expected birth of an illegitimate child.

Marc's letters brought me immense joy. They were spontaneous and lively, like everything he did, and full of love, which he expressed simply and with delicate sincerity. He was not a man for passionate declarations or promises of eternal fidelity.

> You don't know yet how much I love you. You know very well I don't say such things lightly, but you feel, you know you're my life.
>
> France has changed a lot. I don't recognize it. I know I must live in France, but I don't want to cut myself off from America. France is a picture already painted. America still has to be painted. Maybe that's why I feel freer there. But when I work in America, it's like shouting in a forest. There's no echo . . .
>
> I lunch and I dine. I see endless people. Impossible to be alone and *work*. . . .
>
> In the art world, the same names are still on everyone's tongue: Picasso and Matisse, Picasso and Braque, Picasso and Picasso. André Lhote turns himself inside out to please Picasso. I went to see him at Le Rancy and got all my pictures back. That was a great joy for me!"*
>
> Paulhan and Aragon are "Intellectual Odalisques"—Eluard and Char are *real* poets . . . Eluard is an excellent friend.

Like Marc, Paul Eluard had recently lost his beloved companion, Nusch, and this double tragedy gave them a strong bond, along with the fact that they both represented the struggle for true democracy against anti-Semitism and repression. Eluard was foremost among French writers to form strong attachments with painters, and he was a great admirer of Marc's work. They immediately planned to make a book together—*Le dur Désir de durer (The Lasting wish to Last)*—a book of poems with twenty-five drawings by Marc. In the meantime, Marc's letters continued to come:

> I avoid Montparnasse as much as I can . . .
>
> You can't imagine how much I long to work in my little house. Don't take too much trouble. All I need is *walls*, windows and big tables . . .
>
> I know our house is a paradise . . .

*Lhote was one of the first Cubists, also a great teacher who founded an art academy. He took care of Marc's pictures and other possessions during the war, saving them from destruction or confiscation.

I wrote to him almost every day, my letters written as though I were talking to him. I imagined him walking with me in the long grass, watching the sunset. I was preparing his big tables, whitewashing the walls of his studio, looking through piles of unfinished sketches. I wrote him my love and gratitude, for he had saved me from disaster. I was happier than I had ever been. I felt full of energy and fit as a fiddle, in spite of my pregnancy.

To await the birth of David, I went to New York. Jean stayed in High Falls with Tante Phine, and wrote me that she was playing all day long on the porch with her imaginary brother. Quest Brown had become a valuable friend and adviser, and her company was reassuring; the Opatoshus were kind and attentive. David arrived on the Jewish Sabbath on June 22, in the sign of Cancer like Marc and myself. We exchanged jubilant telegrams. Oppen presided over the circumcision ceremony prescribed by Jewish doctrine. I brought David home to his excited sister, and his first photos were taken by Tante Phine, first in Jean's arms and then in mine.

Marc wrote:

> I got your letters and David's first photos. You can't imagine my emotion! He looks all right, but I'm worried. Does he eat enough? Was Jean like that, with a big head and a skinny body? . . .
>
> I'm so happy for us both. Thank you for the child. I hope he'll be strong and healthy. We shall love him with all our might.

I sent him a drawing I made of David, and he replied:

> It's the first time you showed me one of your drawings. David looks wonderful. Oppen says he's a real little Chagall.

In July, he wrote:

> The retrospective is at last definitely fixed. The *Affaire* Vollard is a tremendous business.* All these *"affaires,"* Vollard, Pierre Matisse, Carré, Maeght, the exhibition, give me a pain in the belly. What I would love most of all is to come home and *work*. I don't like the atmosphere here, especially alone . . .
>
> I'm sending you these articles so that you can judge the vanity of all these empty words. There's too much writing being done; it's an intellectual inflation . . .

*There was a legal battle going on between the heirs.

I'm just the same as ever. I love solitude with you and a simple life.
All I want to do is work. I have plenty of faults, like a child. You can
criticize me if you like.

In spite of all his preoccupations, Marc managed to make a series
of astonishing sketches in gouache and pastel, inspired by his return
to Paris. From these he made the oil paintings of the "Paris Series"
in 1953 and 1954. The central figure of several of these is a mother
and child. The *Pont Neuf* shows a mother lying in the foreground with
her baby. Hovering over her on each side are the artist with his
palette and easel and the bride in her wedding gown. Three others,
the *Madonna of Notre Dame,* the *Banks of the Seine* and *Quai de Tournelle*
were also inspired by the birth of David.

Meanwhile, in High Falls, Marc's studio was ready, the garden was
full of flowers and the sweet corn was ripening.

David became the object of Jean's passionate love, not without
occasional torture, which he took with surprising good humor. The
children and I were settled in, and Tante Phine went back to her
home in Springvale, Maine.

In August, Marc returned at last. We flew into each other's arms
on the dock. He looked marvelous in a new summer suit. "Thank
heaven *that's* over!" he said. "Now quick, drive me home!"

He was terribly excited to make the acquaintance of his son and
to see his new studio.

David was by this time quite presentable. He had blue eyes
like all of us—Marc, Ida, Marc's father, myself, Jean and practically
all the Haggard family. His hair was very fair. "So was mine when
I was a child," said Marc, "and his eyes are full of wonder like
mine."

Marc was in high spirits. He had brought with him a number of
unfinished paintings, which he unrolled on the long trestle tables in
his studio. At last he took out the palette and paints that had been
put away for so many months. I made him bouquets from the garden
and he painted them with explosive joy. They were the starting point
for many a picture: the splendid blue delphiniums set off the flaming
hair of *The Redhead;* the phlox, peonies, arum lilies and roses all served
to awaken his fantasy and were the basis for many a painting: *Green
Dream, Arum Lilies, Bouquet with Flying Lovers* and others. Two other

important paintings made at the time were *Self-Portrait with Wall Clock* and *Flayed Ox.*

He would worked tirelessly through the heat of the day and into the evening, and when the crickets went to sleep and the fireflies lit up, we often took walks in the cool valley. We were blissfully happy to be together again. Our bedroom was in the cottage, over Marc's studio, and it smelled of linseed oil and turpentine, a smell I never tired of. First thing in the morning, we would go down to the studio to look at the work Marc had done the evening before. He often asked my opinion, and though I watched him with intense curiosity, I didn't feel it was right to talk about a painting until it was finished. He wanted to finish a lot of them before his return to Paris in October, for the opening of his exhibition.

He worked in shorts, stripped to the waist, and when he was tired, he read his Yiddish paper on the cool veranda, rocking himself in the rocking chair.

When he heard the toot-toot of Mr. Goldwasser's traveling store, he would go down to the road to buy pencils, paper and colored crayons and have a chat in Yiddish with Mr. Goldwasser.

There was plenty of magic to be found in the New York State countryside, but there were also a number of threatening elements: Jean couldn't wander off into the fields for fear of poison ivy; the windows were screened against the hordes of mosquitoes, and the Japanese beetles ate all our sweet corn in a few hours, much to the amusement of our neighbors Victor and Donald, who teased me for my ambition to grow vegetables without pesticides.

My parents were happy to hear of the birth of a new grandson, and my father immediately inscribed him on the family tree. He bore the legal name of McNeil, his mother being lawfully married, so for the time being, my father could keep up appearances. He was extremely worried about the whole situation. Of course, Marc and I had been incautious; we had not gone into the matter of David's legal status before his birth, in spite of the fact that two of Marc's best friends were lawyers. Marc had been so anxious to keep David's birth a secret that he had not even dared to consult his friends until it was too late. John had signed a statement before he left for England to the effect that he was not the expected child's father, but when we finally consulted a lawyer, a few months after David's birth, we discovered to our dismay that the paper was valueless. According to American laws at that time, a legal father could deny his paternity only during the two months *following* the child's birth, failing which he remains irrevocably the child's legal father. The only solution to the problem was to divorce John and marry Marc; thus, as Madame Chagall, I would be in a position to give my name to David. The adoption of David by Marc was ruled out, since the French adoption laws at that time prohibited the adoption of a child by a man who already had one. But Marc and I were not particularly worried; we believed that the matter would be settled in good time.

In October, 1946, Marc returned to Paris for the opening of his exhibition. It had been delayed due to transport strikes, as well as the fact that some collectors had refused to send their pictures because of threats of a postwar revolution in France. But George Salles, the director of the National Museums of France, solved one problem after another.

Marc wrote:

> A retrospective exhibition gives me the painful feeling that people consider my work finished. I want to cry out, like a man condemned to death: "Let me live a little longer. I shall try and do better." I feel I've hardly begun, like a pianist who is still trying to settle down comfortably on his stool . . .
>
> Everyone asks me, "Well, are you back for good this time?" But I'm counting the days until my return to High Falls . . .
>
> The exhibition is a great success. It's really good!
>
> It's difficult to live without working. I have no peace and quiet, interruptions all the times, visits; I can't even write. I've started this letter three times.
>
> Sometimes I see some people from the British embassy who invite me to concerts of chamber music. I like the English people better because of you. I search for similarities.

From the *Mauretania,* on his way over, he wrote:

> I share a cabin with Martin-Chauffier. I sleep with my shirt and trousers on. I'm a bit crazy. You know how shy I am!

I'm a bit too well known on this boat. People ask me: "Aren't you Marc Chagall?" and I answer, "no," or "I don't think so," or I point to someone else and say "maybe that's him." The English stewards are all gracious and courteous like people from a Gainsborough picture.

When he got home, Marc proudly handed me a present of a dress and a blouse he had chosen for me, quite on his own. Ida sent me a luxurious crocodile bag and a handsome velvet cloak, tailored especially for me. She had a flair for gift-giving and real generosity, and I was deeply touched by her gesture of affection.

She had confided in her father that she and Tériade (the famous editor of Greek origin, who later bought the Vollard engravings) were on very close terms, and Marc was proud of his daughter. The period of adjustment to her father's new life had been much less problematic than he feared, and all had gone smoothly and happily between them during his visits to Paris.

It was a joy to have my vibrant companion back for good. He threw himself into his work with renewed intensity, and insisted on no interruptions.

The children were sometimes disturbing, especially as Jean was very possessive of David and often incurred his noisy reactions. Her jealousy, alas, was to be expected. Once more, she had to make a sacrifice for the sake of peace, and we sent her to a little boarding school in a village nearby for a few weeks. I can remember nothing whatever about the school; no doubt I buried the memory deep in some corner of my subconscious, such was my remorse.

Thinking back on this episode, I am angry with myself for giving way to Marc once more, and sacrificing Jean. As always, the threat of Marc's displeasure counted more for me than Jean's suffering.

When winter came to High Falls, the snow was a yard high and Donald carved a neat passage down to the road, cutting the snow into square blocks and dragging them away on his shovel. Sometimes, to relieve the monotony, he scooped up slices and tossed them over his shoulder like pancakes. When all was clear, the children coasted down on their sleds.

Marc was elated; he felt that he was truly in his element. The coal stove in his studio burned red hot, reminding him of his home in

Vitebsk. He never felt the cold, especially when he was hard at work. When I went in to ask him if he was warm enough, he would answer, "I'll have a look," and went to read the thermometer.

He was working on another new painting, *Resurrection on the River,* a strange and fascinating composition where all the elements are arranged around the frame and a crucifixion flies horizontally across the sky, like a terrifying bomber.

One of the most powerful paintings of that period was *Lovers at the Bridge* in which Marc and Bella are framed within a picture, Marc sitting at his easel and Bella consoling and caressing. Marc's right hand has left the frame and is painting another picture showing a fair-haired woman with long legs, resembling me. The composition is divided sharply into two equal parts, perhaps unconsciously symbolizing the break in his life after Bella's death.

"I must have walls to paint on!" he often sighed. For years he had been longing to paint large-scale murals. Every time he saw a vast empty wall, he would stare at it pensively. Once, in a New York cafeteria, he watched enthralled while a man painted a large mural decoration at tremendous speed. Suddenly a tree sprung up, with long branches. Marc grabbed my arm excitedly. "Virginichka, look! That's the way I must do it!" and while I looked, he grabbed my coffee and drank it up. He had the irresistible charm of a child.

Now that he had a moderately large wall, he rolled out the enormous *Revolution* that he had brought with him from Riverside Drive. He had painted it in 1937 from a series of studies and a small painting of great quality, but this large picture lacked their strength and cohesion. He was puzzled by his failure to enlarge the successful, smaller painting. Somehow the composition became confused and woolly on a larger scale. Though it had already been exhibited by Zervos in Paris, and later by Pierre Matisse in New York, it continued to disappoint him. He was determined to pull it together, but after weeks of effort, he was more and more dissatisfied.

Quest Brown came to stay with us in High Falls, and he asked her what she thought of the painting. Whenever he felt at a loss he liked to ask the opinion of people who were relatively unacquainted with his work. She had been to see his exhibition in New York and had written to me:

I would like to know more about Chagall's unconscious mind that compels him to paint with an inspirational force such as I have never before encountered. It is a challenge to try to analyze the direction of Chagall's genius.

Quest had received her name as a little girl because of her insatiable curiosity. As an adult, her natural curiosity had evolved into a mixture of intuitive flair and penetrating logic. Our friendship continued from our first meeting, and she had been an important positive element in my life during a painful period, when I had been torn between my new life with Marc and my old one of self-negation and suffering that had brought me to the brink of destruction.

She said that the painting "disturved" her (there were a number of words she pronounced in her own fashion, giving them a peculiar character). She said she felt that Marc had no real conviction in that chaotic mass of unrelated elements, that he seemed to have thrown into it all the paraphernalia he could invent in an effort to awaken some meaning.

Marc decided to cut the painting into three pieces and suddenly felt liberated. Perhaps that is why the title *Liberation* came to his mind. He gave it to one of the paintings and called the others *Resistance* and *Resurrection*.

It is interesting that of the four paintings of mural dimensions that he undertook in France after his return from Russia in 1922, *To My Wife, The Fallen Angel, Circus People* and the big *Revolution,* all were repainted later and the last two were cut up. He seemed never to have retrieved the powerful construction of the early murals he had done for the Jewish Theater in Moscow in 1920.

The Fallen Angel is now in the Museum of Basel. It had hung for years over the staircase when we had our house in Vence, in the South of France. I had leisure to examine it daily, and never got over a feeling of slight discomfort at the tortured construction of this painting into which Marc, perhaps aware of its lack of real strength, flung his frustrated rage. But he finally managed to pull it together with cunning refinement.

His obsessional desire to do mural paintings may have sprung from his first superbly successful undertaking and his less fruitful subsequent attempts. When he had set his will on some accomplishment, he never gave up until he succeeded. He believed that the first mural was powerful because it had been painted for a special wall in a special theater.

This conviction was to grow over the years, but it was not until 1956 that he had an opportunity to tackle really monumental works. Then he began to work in collaboration with craftsmen of exceptional talent, on stained glass with Charles Marcq, on mosaics with Lino Melano, on ceramic panels with Ramié. These craftsmen infused him with new blood and moved him to new heights. The monumental works he created in these media are among his finest work. The same cannot be said of some of the gigantic mural paintings, which he still had a tendency to encumber with needless detail, driving on in pursuit of some elusive perfection to which he seemed to have lost the clue.

Marc was often troubled by the thought that as an exiled artist, he lacked the contact with his native soil that seemed to him so vital to his art. The richness of the Russian Jewish culture into which he had been born had nurtured visions that made him produce some of the most strangely wonderful works ever made. He often pondered whether that powerful heritage would continue to nourish him indefinitely.

When he first went to France in 1910, the stimulating uprooting made these inner visions explode with even greater intensity. The first Paris period was a voyage of discovery; the earth of his country was still clinging to his shoes.

His return to Russia reawakened that powerful source of inspiration, and his voluntary exile to France in 1922 proved a difficult period of uprooting and adaptation. He was back in Paris, but this time it was not with the illuminated eyes of a discoverer, free, unknown and possessing nothing. He now had a reputation, and it had to be defended.

Returning to La Ruche to claim the paintings he had left there, he found that they had all disappeared.

He had taken forty important paintings and 160 gouaches to Berlin in 1914 before leaving Russia, and they had been shown by Walden in his famous gallery Der Sturm, where they aroused tremendous enthusiasm. Eight years later, after the end of World War I and the revolution, Marc traveled through Berlin on his way to Paris. There he learned that Walden had sold everything, but the titanic inflation had reduced the proceeds to a ridiculous sum. Marc refused it and threatened to bring suit against Walden. Finally, in 1926, he received three large paintings in compensation—*To Russia, Asses and Others, I and the Village,* and *The Poet*—as well as ten gouaches, but he was cruelly deprived of most of the works of that prolific prewar period.

There were two other occasions on which he lost a large number of his paintings. When he was living in St. Petersburg in the house of Vinaver he made a copy of a painting by Levitan. Badly in need of money, he sold it to a framer for a good price. A few days later, he saw the painting for sale as an authentic Levitan, and the framer smilingly asked for more copies. This time Marc modestly offered his own paintings and drawings and left a large quantity of them on deposit, but a few days later when he came to inquire if anything was sold, the framer pretended not to recognize him. "Who are you? I've never seen you before," he'd said. With no proof of his ownership, Marc was helpless. When he returned to La Ruche after an absence of more than eight years, the paintings he had left in his little studio had vanished, not surprisingly, since he had "locked" the door with nothing more than a piece of wire, intending to return shortly with his bride. Some of the paintings were found in a rabbit hutch, where the concierge had used them as roofing. Others turned up in various collections with a certificate of authenticity signed by Cendrars. Marc suspected his friend of treachery and never forgave him, in spite of the fact that after eight years of war and revolution, and without a sign of life from Marc, everyone presumed he was dead.

These additional breaks with the past were a blow to Marc.

He settled down with his family in Paris and the paintings became more refined, with bursts of the old fire from time to time. The engravings commissioned by Vollard were a strong new stimulus. *Dead Souls,* witty, cynical and sublime, plunged him back into Russia; the *Fables* of La Fontaine, first planned as color engravings, demanded a completely new technique, capable of transcribing into black-and-white the richness of the gouache texture. The result was truly fabulous. The Bible crowned the series with its grand and moving sincerity; its primitive, childlike truth; its absence of cleverness and scholarly pretensions. These works sent him on journeys to Poland

and Palestine with Bella. Deeper roots came to light; new discoveries of old sources were made. Bella began to reclaim some of the luminous memories of her childhood.

The anxious years of Hitler's rise to power and the beginning of the Holocaust provoked powerful works, such as *The Martyr* (1940). Another war and a new uprooting, though full of pain, had a stimulating effect on Marc's work. In New York Marc's friendship with other Russian Jews charged him with new dynamics. They were all exiles together and they shared the same feelings of nostalgia. Perhaps he still felt something of a foreigner in France, where he had sometimes been treated with contempt and envy by less fortunate colleagues.

All of this might explain why he was now delaying his return to France. He had been away from his native land for so long, that going farther still had somehow sent him back to his secret sources.

Speaking of these sources, Marc once said, "Bartok carries the earth away in his claws like an eagle and rises to vertiginous heights. Bartok, Seurat and Van Gogh remained faithful to their native soil. There's plenty of earth in their art."

In *Ma Vie,* he wrote: "Don't call me fantastic; on the contrary, I am realistic. I love the earth."

But perhaps Marc felt more at ease in America because he felt more of a Jew. High Falls, with its simple people and its animals, was about as near to Marc's home in the suburbs of Vitebsk as any other place he had known since then.

Animals played an important part in his childhood; he observed them in a symbolical way. In *Ma Vie* he wrote lovingly of the cows and bulls slaughtered by his grandfather, the butcher of Lyozno, and his feeling of guilt even as he ate their meat with relish.

He often painted the horses of Vitebsk that pulled small carts, the goats and donkeys, and the poultry kept by his parents. In High Falls, he could watch the cows from his studio window, and the noise of our cocks and chickens created a familiar atmosphere. But he had no sentimental attachment to animals; for him they had a universal character. Dogs are noticeably absent from his paintings. He disliked them and had a fear of them, ever since he was bitten as a child.

One particular incident that took place when Ida was a child had left a deep mark on him. He was walking with her in a field when suddenly she fell. He saw that a small pointed stick had pierced her cheek, and he drew it out immediately. The blood came profusely, and Ida's eye was damaged. The night before this accident he had dreamed that Ida was bitten by a dog. Once when he was walking with Jean, a vicious dog rushed out and snarled at them. He gathered the frightened child in his arms and reassured her. Later she heard about his own phobia of dogs, and every time a dog appeared she ran to protect him.

Jean went to the village school in Mohonk, on a hill, and walked a mile there and back each day. When motorists offered her a lift, she declined politely. Driving bored her, she said. Jean lived in a fairy-tale world, and the country scenes she observed served as a backdrop for the stories she made up for herself along the way. In the winter she peopled the road to school with snowmen and snowwomen, who greeted her like friendly milestones. She protected herself as best she could by withdrawing into her secret world, where animals played an important part. "The cat," she said one time, "takes all my sorrows on his poor little heart." David was the prince of her fairy-tale world, and the only person to receive her confidences. She began writing poems:

> *I saw many things when I was small*
> *Oh many things I saw*
> *I saw the playroom carpet*
> *I saw the playroom door*
> *I saw my mother get undressed*
> *I saw the cook make cakes*
> *I sometimes saw the other things*
> *But those were my mistakes.*

Marc was proud of her poems and encouraged her to copy them into a special notebook he gave her, which she illustrated. Later in France, he showed her notebook to the poet Octavio Paz, who copied out some of the poems for his private collection.

Jean considered Marc benevolently as a spoiled and very special grown-up child, who had a right to every kind of privilege. She had long ago realized that she had no choice but to accept him as a formidable rival for my favors. Now David was also getting a lot of my attention, but I tried as much as I could to divide it equally between them. There were now kindly feelings between Marc and Jean, especially when she applied herself to be obedient and predictable. She called him Papa and in her pictures of happy families he played the role of father. Her own father was put out of her mind for the time being.

On the occasion of David's second birthday, Ida wrote us a warm letter:

David, Virginia, Papa,
    I think it must soon be David's birthday.
With all my heart I wish him the best things in the world. May his blue eyes see good things and bright things around him as they grow bigger. May you be happy because of him, more and more happy.
                                                                Your Ida

And on that occasion Michel wrote as well:

Dear Marc Zacharovitch and Virginia,
    Congratulations for David's birthday and all my good wishes for today and tomorrow for him and for you. Paris is waiting for you and so are we. Kisses for the little *"imeninnik."*
                                                                Your Michel

Marc was delighted with these letters and felt totally reassured about taking me back with him to France, but he was not quite ready to go.

Ida's letters to her father became more and more insistent. We had been in High Falls for two years and it was time Marc returned to France. All the other war exiles of the art world had already returned: Léger, Zadkine, Ozenfant, Breton, Tanguy, Seligman and Ernst. The dealers were waiting impatiently to promote Chagall's rise to the summit of fame. He was liable to lose his standing, Ida said, if he didn't return. The three great Vollard books, now taken over by Tériade, had to be completed and signed.

All of these arguments seemed logical enough, but Marc was not a logical man. Ida's letters could be forgotten for a while, whereas her presence would certainly have defeated him. Sometimes we felt like Ida's unruly children and the spirit of revolt possessed us. Did Marc instinctively feel that this wonderful "honeymoon" would be broken by our return? Never again would we be so close to each other or so free from worry. In France, the battle for fame would swallow up our intimate family life as well as the quiet working days. He would have to worry about his standing, his market price, his reputation.

Everything was going smoothly in High Falls, and Marc wanted desperately to finish a series of paintings he was working on. The children were growing well, and I had found a wonderful Irish girl who adored them. The Opatoshus paid us regular visits, much to our delight, and had no difficulty persuading Marc that he should listen to his own heart. The four of us conversed in a mixture of Yiddish, English and French, drank wine, laughed a great deal and ate the Jewish delicacies Adele brought along until far into the night.

Marc was always the life of the party. Whether with these or other friends, he entertained us all with his colorful stories and clowning.

In the spring of 1948, most of the pictures exhibited at the Musée national d'Art moderne in Paris were transported to London for a show at the Tate Gallery, and Ida was present at the opening. This was something Ida loved to do and did very well. She was pleasant to everyone, dressed elegantly and was interesting to converse with.

My parents also went to the opening and my father later wrote:

> I enjoyed the Chagall exhibition immensely, especially the Bible engravings and the *Firebird* designs. There were several big luminous rooms, a riot of color. But I came away feeling desperately uncomfortable and rushed for relief to the other rooms, even to the Blakes which, though weird, are at least "of my time." Nevertheless, I am determined to be broad-minded and anxious to be convinced. You say there is "nothing to understand" so what am I to see in it all? Why headless men and trains upside down? There must be some *reason.* Tell me that and you'll send me away, if not quite happy, at least satisfied.

Marc and I laughed and thought it would be impossible to content this rational mind that wanted explanations for everything and couldn't consider painting purely as painting. That same year, Faber and Faber in London published an album in the "Faber Gallery" series on Chagall with a particularly good introduction by Michael Ayrton. Under each color reproduction was a text by Marc, and I did the translations of the quotations from *Ma Vie.*

While Ida was taking care of Marc's celebrity, he was able to discard it for a while like a cumbersome piece of clothing, stripping himself bare and coming face to face with his work. Never again would he be as far removed from the agitated life as he was in High Falls, except for short holiday periods.

Ida was more and more concerned about her father's putting off his return to France. She wrote to me, hoping I would have some influence on him:

> People are waiting for him. Their expectation is something to be treasured, not despised. He owes to Paris at least a semblance of a return. It's like a gift; it must be given at the right time. Paris is Paris, beautiful, decaying, full of sweetness and bitterness. The artistic, literary and political battles are often fruitless, but they are indispensable.

Ida was making new friends, new admirers of Chagall, new admirers of herself; now full-blown and liberated, she was surf-riding on the waves of postwar reawakening.

Of course, Marc knew that he would soon need the incomparable, seething, fertile world of Paris, but at present he needed seclusion more than anything else, and he nourished a hope of keeping both. As the time of our departure grew near he said that Victor would look after the house, and we would come back every year. In any case, Pierre Matisse must not have the impression that we were leaving America for good.

In that spring of 1948, when the apple and cherry trees were in full blossom in High Falls, a Belgian photographer, Charles Leirens, came to stay with us. He was a man of about Marc's age, tall and loose-limbed, quick and restless, with big ravenous eyes.

He had made a remarkable series of portraits of Marc at Riverside Drive before my arrival, and I had admired their originality. His photography showed an extreme sensitivity toward the model, who often became his friend after the sitting, so closely did Leirens work with his subjects. His was a warm, human approach, and his subjects felt more like collaborators than models. Marc and he had friends in common, such as Kurt and Helen Wolff, who had commissioned the *One Thousand and One Nights* lithographs.

The Wolffs had invited us to dine in Leirens' company, and he brought along a portfolio of splendid portraits of André Gide, Paul Valéry, Colette, Malraux, Mauriac, Bartok, Maillol, Chagall and Kurt Wolff, among others; we were all impressed by the almost draughtsmanlike quality they possessed. Each photograph was a work of art; it had texture and substance and a wonderful scale of rich tones.

Leirens was also a musicologist, and had been the first director of the Palais des Beaux Arts in Brussels, where concerts and exhibitions were held. He had organized the first retrospective exhibition of the Belgian painter James Ensor, which created a sensation, and also important exhibitions of Bourdelle, Carpeaux, Cézanne, Permeke and African art. Then he founded La Maison d'Art, where he organized concerts of chamber music, exhibitions and lectures, and took up photography. On the eve of the war, he went to New York at the invitation of the New School for Social Research, where he taught musicology and photography.

Leirens had a great sense of humor and, as Marc and the Wolffs had the same gift, the evening was very enjoyable. Kurt showed Marc a small Chagall drawing of Adam and Eve he had bought and was fond of. Marc took one look at it and exclaimed: "That's a fake! I'll tear it up."

"No, no. I like it; I want to keep it," Kurt said and took it away from him quickly. Marc shrugged his shoulders and turned down the corners of his mouth with such a comical expression that we all burst out laughing.

Leirens wanted to do a new series of photos of Marc in High Falls, so it was decided that he would come and spend a couple of nights with us. Many of these photos are included in this book.

We all enjoyed posing for this man of intelligence and charm, brimming with wit and enthusiasm. But I never imagined he would come back into our lives with such far-reaching consequences.

Chapter

Orgeval

Finally, the inevitable upheaval took place, and we locked up the house, leaving some unfinished works and other belongings as a token of our intended return. But we were never to see High Falls again. A page had been turned, and there was no going back. Two years later, Ida came over to America, packed our dusty belongings and sold the house. She often had such thankless tasks to perform for her father. Her practical efficiency and lucid view of immediate realities always kept her afloat.

Victor Purcell wrote us that the F.B.I. had been searching the house for incriminating documents. McCarthy was beginning his reign of repression. Marc had been honorary president of the Jewish Writers' and Artists' Committee, a left-wing organization, and when he went back to France, he was honorary president of the Committee for the Suppression of Anti-Semitism and the Promotion of Peace. To be anti-Fascist at that period aroused suspicion.

We sailed to France in August, 1948, on the *De Grasse,* a small but excellent passenger liner, together with Jean Wahl, the French poet and philosopher, and his family. We liked this warm and exceptionally intelligent man. He wrapped his small frail body in a long overcoat, with only his nose and feet protruding, and several times a day he strode around the decks at top speed. The children ran wild, and Jean was invaluable in keeping David from falling overboard.

I was happy at the prospect of living in France again. I considered it my own country, at least as much as England. I also looked forward to seeing my parents.

Ida came to fetch us at Le Havre and drove us to Orgeval, Seine-et-Oise, near Paris. She had found us a fantastic chaletlike house with gables and a rotting wooden turret. It was like a fairy-tale ginger-bread house, surrounded by enchanted woods. The moon shone brightly when we arrived, and David exclaimed, "Look, there's my moon. It followed me over from America!"

Marc chose two large light bedrooms for his studio and unrolled the unfinished canvases he had brought over from High Falls. Most of the recent paintings had been finished and left behind with Pierre Matisse, but there were some too fragile and elusive that needed perhaps to be forgotten for a while and taken up again in another time and place. Marc looked at these now with a fresh eye, but he also looked around him for inspiration. There was a crumbling eleventh-century church in the tiny village of Orgeval, and its pointed steeple and lichen-covered walls aroused his curiosity. There were orchards and avenues of graceful elms and a black shimmering pond in the woods, full of mysterious shadows.

Marc's pictures had been returned from the London exhibition, and Ida had hung several of them in the vast, beautifully empty living room with three French windows opening onto a terrace. Rarely had they been hung to more advantage. All the old pictures that had hung in Riverside Drive were there, the big *Marriage Procession, The Cattle Dealer* (now perfectly restored), *The Studio,* the *Little Drawing Room,* and one of the oldest and most important of his paintings, *The Dead Man.* This had been painted before Marc's first visit to Paris and had created quite a stir at the famous "Donkey's Tail" avant-garde exhibition in Moscow in 1912. There were also more recent paintings such as *The Red Horse* and the *White Cock,* painted in America.

We had an excitable Italian housekeeper who covered her pregnant daughter's eyes when ever she entered the living room to prevent her from seeing one of the latest pictures, *The Fiancée with a Double Face,* lest she give birth to a monster.

The Germans had taken possession of the house during the Occupation. We learned that they had imprisoned, perhaps executed Resistance fighters in the stables where we parked our car. It cast an imperceptible shadow over the place that I was never able to shake off.

We had many visitors in Orgeval, and there were as many animated meals around the big oval table. Among the visitors I especially remember were Tériade and Zervos, the two most famous avant-garde art editors in Paris at the time. Zervos had created the superb art magazine *Minotaure,* where Picasso was an uncontested king. Marc was more especially drawn to Tériade, whose art magazine was *Verve.* A group of art critics and historians were frequent visitors, especially Jacques Lassaigne and Charles Estienne. Louis Carré and Aimé Maeght were two of the most dynamic, up-and-coming gallery directors. Jean Cassou, writer and art historian, had organized Marc's first big retrospective exhibition at the Musée national d'Art moderne. Paul Eluard, Claire Goll and Pierre Reverdy were Marc's favorite poet friends. Jean Paulhan also came once or twice; he had been a friend of Marc's and Bella's for many years. He had an intimidating air about him, with a mouth that turned down at the corners and staring brown eyes like an owl. Three other writer friends, Lionello Venturi and Jacques and Raîssa Maritain had also returned from New York, and their conversations were always vigorous and lively. I caught on as best I could, but most of it was over my head.

Marc was one of the rare artists the Maritains didn't try to convert to Catholicism. He was never completely natural with them, as if he felt he had to be on his good behavior. Raîssa was writing a book on Marc entitled *L'Orage Enchanté,* and they often had spirited telephone conversations in Russian. One day, Marc was dressing when I called him to the phone.

"Hurry up, it's Raîssa."

"Tell her to hold on, I can't speak to Raîssa in underpants."

Charles Estienne was a poet as well as an art critic and historian. He had a soft, teasing voice that was forever scurrying like a busy mouse in pursuit of wisps of poetic humor. He felt at home in the world of Chagall. In his writings on art, he was always breaking away from the jargon of art critics, from the pedantry of some and the florid eloquence of others. He not only criticized and appraised, but also stimulated artists in their work.

Ida came for weekends, followed by a troupe of brilliant and amusing friends. Her special friend, Géa Augsbourg (a high-geared, spontaneous Swiss artist with a rare gift for humor, all qualities the Swiss are not supposed to possess); Jacques Lassaigne, the art historian and his writer wife Assia, in whose apartment Marc had stayed on his two trips to Paris; Michel Gordey and his new wife Marina; Claude Bourdet, the editor of the newspaper *Combat,* soon to found the weekly magazine *Observateur,* and his wife Ida, tennis champion of France. Claude Bourdet had played an important part in the Resistance movement and miraculously survived internment in Buchenwald, where he remained until the Liberation. He had founded the clandestine newspaper, *Combat,* with Albert Camus during the occupation and directed it after the war, defending anticolonialism and neutrality. He later led the movement of opposition to the Algerian war and often got into trouble. Today he is still in the front line, fighting for disarmament and nonalignment, the only guarantees of peace in the world, as he sees it.

All these witty and highly intelligent people kept the conversation bouncing back and forth. Marc said it reminded him of a tennis tournament. He was impressed, but sometimes exhausted.

We had some unforgettable meals in Paris bistros where Ida's presence was a promise of good fun. She always encouraged everyone to go for the tastiest delicacies on the menu, and Papa had to pay without complaining. Sometimes the laughter became so riotous that people turned around with amusement. Marc, like Ida, had the gift of a ready laughter, and their voices could be heard above all the others. The standing joke was Marc's well-known jealousy of Picasso and Matisse, and he was relentlessly teased about this. He rose to the occasion infallibly and provoked riotous laughter, but strictly speaking, it was no joking matter for him. Picasso and Matisse (in that order) were undisputed kings, and Marc felt he would never attain their tremendous prestige.

Ida and I were now on very pleasant terms; there was no strain in our relationship. She and Géa Augsbourg had fallen in love, and their happiness was evident. I liked Géa very much and even Marc found him congenial, but Marc was always cautious where Ida's passions were concerned, and waited to see if it was a serious affair. Géa was not a future husband for Ida, he thought; he was too carefree and unconstrained. Besides, he wasn't Jewish.

Like Marc, Ida often caught David in her arms and covered him with kisses, regardless of his squeals. He was a slippery little devil and when people were overeager to hold him, he wriggled away, laughing. If he received exaggerated praise or attention, he began playing the fool from a sort of bashful modesty. Sometimes he spoke to me earnestly, looking straight into my eyes and nodding gravely, to convince me of the importance of what he was saying. I listened intently, holding back my emotion; I recalled how grown-ups used to laugh at me as a child, when I said things of importance.

In the meantime, my parents were eagerly awaiting my first visit to England with the children. A new friendship was beginning to form between us, linking up with my childhood affection to bridge a breach of misunderstanding. Their numerous grandchildren had taken to calling them Godfrey and Georgiana, and I immediately adopted the practice, having failed to find a suitable substitute for the childish Mummy and Daddy and the too severe Mother and Father. The use of first names helped me to facilitate the change from a parent-child relationship into a very special sort of friendship.

Arrangements were made for our trip to England, and our arrival in Broomfield, Essex, was a happy event, followed by Georgiana's visit to Orgeval. Marc enjoyed her warm conviviality and was delighted to see the family circle expanding. I always hoped he would accompany me to England one day, but he seemed to have no curiosity whatever for England. (He went there for the first time with his wife Vava in 1959, when he received an honorary degree from Glasgow University.)

Jean had been corresponding with her father ever since their separation. She never did this spontaneously but had to be reminded, and she never expressed sorrow at being unable to see him; no doubt her feelings for him had been smothered under a protective layer of forgetfulness. John sent her letters and little parcels now and then. He was back in Scotland, living with some painter friends and seemed to have returned to the bohemian company of his art school days in Glasgow.

Godfrey pressed me to commence divorce proceedings and put me onto a lawyer friend of his in London, but there still didn't seem to be any urgency for settling the matter.

In September, we went with Ida and Géa Augsbourg to Venice, where Marc's graphic work had received the Biennale award. It was the first time I had ever been to Italy and it was Marc's first visit to Venice. We were graciously greeted by Umbro Apollonio, the director of the Biennale and an eminent art historian. At the same time we made the acquaintance of the painter, Giorgio Morandi, a shy, gentle person with whom Marc was perfectly in tune. His relationships with painters were not always that smooth.

Marc was elated and untiringly curious about everything. Speechless with emotion before the Giottos in Padva, he could only shake his head slowly in wonder. But Tintoretto gave him the biggest shock of all. He was bowled over by the flying figures and the savage strength of the gigantic "Paradise" painting in the Council Hall of the Doges' Palace in Venice. Hundreds of people float up to heaven on dark clouds, their billowing robes sweeping them into the sky. It was a rare experience to accompany Marc on his first visit to the Scuola San Rocco. He said, "Titian gives you the tips of his fingers delicately, but Tintoretto presses your hand tight and hurts you."

We wandered in the dark passages of the Jewish ghetto under festoons of laundry, and Marc poked his nose into doorways and glanced into windows, trying to discover the atmosphere of the people who lived there. We visited the luxurious shops in the arcades around the Piazza San Marco, and Marc bought me a white silk embroidered blouse. We were perfectly happy. This was a sort of honeymoon trip for Ida and Géa, as well as for us. They were happy, too, and we felt all the freer. High Falls seemed very far away; we didn't miss it any more.

As a couple, we were like adolescents compared to Ida and Géa. We were more romantic than sensuous, and our pleasures were simple. Marc's sensuousness went into his paintings; mine, because of my unhappy marriage, was still developing.

Having breakfast in the sun on the Grand Canal was a glorious combination of sights, sounds, smells and tastes. Going to the Fenice Theater one evening in Peggy Guggenheim's private gondola (Peggy, in a tight lamé sheath, had to be lifted in by the gondolier) to hear

Don Giovanni; visiting San Marco and the Academia; walking for hours without a trace of fatigue, carried away, almost in a trance—such was our week in Venice.

Marc concluded, *"On aime la France, mais on est amoureux de l'Italie."* One loves France, but one falls in love with Italy. I agreed.

Chapter

IV

St. Jean Cap Ferrat

Tériade, who had a house in St. Jean Cap Ferrat in the south of France, suggested that Marc spend a few months there to work on the illustrations he had commissioned for Boccaccio's *Decameron* and to consider settling there himself.

In the early spring of 1949, we went with the children to St. Jean and settled in a *pension de famille,* a modest yellow stucco building. There were cool tiled floors and big tables spread with white cloths and crowded with heavy jars of mimosa and anemones. When the sun became hot and the green shutters were half closed, the light that filtered through them made everything glow like a Bonnard painting.

We had a tiny corner bedroom with two windows looking out onto each side of the peninsula of Cap Ferrat, and Marc excitedly brought out his gouaches and his large sheets of pure chiffon paper. It was fun to have him working right in our bedroom, spreading his paintings out on the white cotton bedspread. He gave me a delightful smile from time to time. "Virginichka, this is terrific!"

An explosion of new ideas was suddenly released at the sight of the Mediterranean. He had always been directly stimulated by every new place where he stayed (except New York) and his store of "Chagall" material was jolted and injected with new substance, producing a series of variations around a theme. Here, it was the sea, the beach, the boats and flowers of St. Jean that tumbled out in exuberant succession. He had never worked his gouaches so richly. He invented a mixture of media, obtaining depth and luster by adding touches of oily pastel, and playing with the antagonistic elements of oil and water to produce unexpected textures.

The *Fishes at St. Jean, The Blue Landscape, The Green Landscape* and *St. Jean Cap Ferrat* are paintings that announce a new style, where the components are bold and large and there are no unnecessary embellishments. Marc presented me with a big blue *St. Jean Cap Ferrat* gouache, full of liquid brilliance, and said that the blue profile in it was an evocation of me.

Tériade was hospitable in the grand manner. Meals at his house were always served in handsome china on delicate tablecloths; he took care of every detail himself. Madame Lang and her daughter, Marguerite, were his collaborators. They were the mother and sister of his beloved Angèle, who died some years earlier. They carried out his every wish and produced champagne lunches under the orange trees.

Marc and Tériade had just enough difference of character to make them mutually stimulating. Tériade was a brilliant intellectual, cultivated, sensuous, refined and secretive. Marc was demonstrative and humorous, full of fantasy and wit, sentimental, dramatic and melancholic. Their friendship was fruitful. Tériade had a true understanding of the artist's nature; his own ideas served to kindle a spark, always keeping with the artist's secret desires.

As Marc and I started searching for houses, I realized that his taste in homes had become somewhat grander. He had often talked of retiring into the country with cows and chickens, but this dream, like the famous "monk's cell," was a sort of fantasy. Here in France he was somebody of importance, he said, and he couldn't live as he did in High Falls. "Chagall can't live in a house that has cow dung on the driveway," he explained. Cows were extremely rare in St. Jean, and they were kept in dark and cruel sheds where the children went with cans to get milk, so there was no way for this problem to present itself.

Finally, Marc fell for a tall, dignified house with cement paths winding in and out of rock gardens, high old-fashioned windows and enormous bedrooms. The latter attracted him particularly; he planned to make his studio in three of them, and with our usual impulsiveness, we then-and-there decided to buy the house. We were like excited youngsters, and, as there were other would-be purchasers that day, Marc immediately signed a three months' option. But when Ida hurried over to take a look, she scolded us quite justifiably. The house was all stairs and there was very little sun. Sadly Marc agreed, but as the house was completely furnished, we moved in for the three months' option.

I wrote Godfrey:

> We are both inclined to let ourselves get carried away. Now I find myself obliged to act as a brake, which is funny, considering my character! Life on Cap Ferrat is languorous. If it rains, by some odd chance, everyone stays at home; even the children miss school. The flowers never wither; it's like the Garden of Eden. I long to see some untidy grass, or some trees that have grown up where they weren't supposed to.

One day a couple of Englishwomen knocked at the door. They introduced themselves as theater people from London, Elisabeth Sprigge and Velona Harris. They had recently founded a repertory theater in London called Watergate, and they wanted Marc to paint murals for their auditorium. Marc asked them how much they could pay, and they confessed cheerfully that they hadn't got the first penny. We all laughed and changed the subject, but meanwhile, we became friends. Marc was attracted by the idea—it was the first time anyone had made such a suggestion since Granowsky had commissioned the murals for the Jewish Theater in Moscow so many decades before.

They then suggested that Marc create two paintings and lend them to the theater for a year. Marc accepted, and the plan was carried out in 1950. The paintings were called *The Blue Circus* and *The Dance.* I took them to London with me and I remember the puzzled look on the customs officer's face when he asked me to unroll them. "You call that art?" he said.

Marc had sent me to be present at the inauguration of the two impressive paintings, and it felt good to dip once more into London's theater life, giving me the same taste of excitement I had felt in the days of Stephen's glory.

While in London Marc had also wanted me to investigate a case of fake Chagalls. They proved to be so ludicrously bad, however, that they were hardly a threat to Marc. It was later, in 1968, that a much better imposter, David Stein, a Frenchman, was able to make a considerable fortune by turning out "Chagalls." He went to prison. When he had served his sentence he continued creating "Chagalls" and "Picassos" and many other paintings, but he now signed them David Stein.

At St. Jean I read Boccaccio's *Decameron* to Marc while he sketched ideas with brush and pen. These monochrome wash drawings were commissioned by Tériade to accompany the famous fifteenth-century Franco-Flemish miniatures that already illustrated the *Decameron.* Marc's work was full of strength and truculent humor, like some of his earlier Russian drawings, and contrasted wonderfully with the delicate miniatures.

Picasso drove down to Cap d'Antibes with his liveried chauffeur for a visit and we strolled along the shore with him. At that time we had a modest Peugeot 201, the kind that looked to me as if it were squinting, because its front lights were so close together. In those days it was one of the few available cars. There was a long waiting list, unless (as in our case) the car was paid for in America and carried a tourist number plate. Also, gasoline was severely rationed.

Marc asked Picasso, "How do you manage to get petrol for that big car?"

Picasso waved his hand toward the sea with a smile. "There are oceans of petrol for those who can pay for it."

On another occasion we had met Picasso, with Françoise Gilot and their children, coming out of the Musée Grimaldi in Antibes, where we had been looking at the handsome, playful paintings Picasso had made on huge white panels. Marc liked them; they had none of the aggressiveness of the previous period. They filled the impressive castle with light and gaiety. Marc told him so as we passed him in the hall and Picasso seemed pleased. But the meeting was brief. It was some time before the famous lunch in Tériade's garden, described by

Françoise Gilot in her book, *Life With Picasso,* during which the two great painters provoked each other with subtle cynicism.

As a prelude to this meeting, Marc had sent Picasso a friendly letter (at Ida's suggestion) from High Falls, enclosing a photo of himself with David, and saying how much he hoped to see him on his return to France. Picasso was touched and pinned up the photo in his studio. Ida followed up this overture by organizing the lunch at Tériade's house.

The lunch was a festive event even though, as Françoise also remembers, Picasso was in a devilish humor. Before the meal he obliged Tériade to take down a Bonnard painting because "it made him sick." According to Françoise, Picasso was always upset by the sight of skinny women, and she and I were skinny at the time, as was Jean, who was growing tall for her age. I was going through a vegetarian stage (but not, as she said, from theosophical convictions, for I never adopted ideas even vaguely religious). Such fads were utterly unthinkable for Picasso. He was even more intolerant than Marc, but Marc could be even more scathingly cynical. They enjoyed tormenting each other, and this meeting was a perfect occasion for amusing their audience. Picasso insinuated that Marc had been much too comfortably off in America to return to France after the Liberation. As for Marc's own country, Russia, he didn't suppose Marc would go there, as there was not much business to be done. Marc retaliated that Picasso, the great communist painter, should go first to show the way, though unfortunately his paintings were not at all appreciated there. Picasso made a sour face. The repartee continued throughout the luncheon; they were both prodigious performers.

Picasso had a great respect for Marc's painting, (much more than Marc had for his) but he couldn't help provoking him with flourish and brio, irritating Marc to such an extent that he became like a maddened bull. After this discordant meeting, there were no others.

We returned to Orgeval for the summer months and found Ida in poor health. Eventually, she had to have a serious stomach operation. I realized later that she needed some "mothering" at this period, but I was not at all effective as a mother, nor was Marc much of a father. We always considered Ida herself as a sort of mother—she was protective, efficient, practical and businesslike, all of which we were not.

But thankfully Géa was both companion and father to her and his good humor and kindness helped her through this difficult time. She was soon back to her jokes in her hospital bed: "Papa, you're a happy man," she said, "you can fart, I can't." Once released from the hospital, she spent her convalescence in Oregeval.

It was there that Marc painted one of the great works of the later period, *The Red Sun.* It has the exuberance and powerful structure of the earlier works, and something like a passionate joy that is irresistible. There is no unnecessary detail, no hesitation, the original impulse is intact; it is an explosion that sets off a series of explosions in those who view it. Later, this painting was chosen to be transformed into a Gobelins tapestry and Marc painted a "maquette," but the project was never carried out.

The summer months in Orgeval were very pleasant. Jean went to the village school in a checkered pinafore; she was learning French quickly and adapting to her surroundings with surprising ease. She watched over David constantly—perhaps a little too constantly for his liking, but they were very fond of each other. Several American friends came to visit us during this time: Max Lerner, James Johnson Sweeney of the Museum of Modern Art, Pierre Matisse and his wife Tina.

Marc was growing more and more handsome. The tufts of hair on each side of his prominent cheekbones had become almost white, lending a softness to his face. The contours of his upper lip were without clear definition, constantly changing, but his lower lip was hard and slightly protruding, like a ledge cut out of rock. It showed strength and determination, but also revealed the more difficult side of his character, the untrusting, uncharitable side. His smile had the astonishing power to light up his features from inside, producing the dazzling effect of a new moon that spread suddenly across his face. David once said of his father, "He can hypnotize people, he can't help turning on that magnetism—he's a real magician!"

Few painters have been more fascinated by their own faces than Rembrandt and Marc Chagall, and few have painted so many self-portraits. It is interesting to follow the endless transformations that Marc's image underwent through all these variations. Two of the best known of these self-portraits are *Laughing Self Portrait,* inspired by

Rembrandt, and *Self-Portrait with a Grimace.* From these two drawings he later made etchings.

In the earliest painted studies, made while he was still an art student, the face is swarthy and virile. But the description he gives in *Ma Vie* where he admires his reflection in the mirror of his parent's sitting room is of a "mixture of paschal wine, ivory-colored flour and rose petals." When he started flirting with girls he confesses: "I didn't hesitate to outline my eyes and add a little red to my lips" and when I asked him about this he laughed: "Somehow painting my face was not so very different from painting a picture of my face in the mirror." There is no doubt he was narcissistic.

In later years, his self-admiration depended very much on the admiration of others. At times he would speak of himself in the third person. I recall him asking a journalist, "What are they saying about Chagall? Do they love Chagall?"

In *Self-Portrait with Seven Fingers* he schematized the elements of his person into a strangely beautiful design. Another striking self-portrait is *Double Portrait with a Wine Glass,* in which he appears joyfully straddling Bella's shoulders (a significant allusion to her total support of him) with Ida as a small child flying over his head. It is one of his most powerful paintings and now belongs to the Musée d'Art Moderne in Paris.

To the end he continued to incorporate his features into hundreds of paintings, but these were no longer self-portraits; they were more along the lines of romantic self-fantasies.

At the end of summer in 1949 I took Jean to England. Godfrey and Georgiana kept her for a year, sent her to school and cherished her. They were like young parents with an only child, caring for her more attentively than they had cared for their own children. Notwithstanding, Jean still suffered intense homesickness.

Marc's understandable desire to have David to ourselves and to free him from Jean's possessive love and jealousy (the frequent skirmishes were becoming more disturbing) was satisfied for the time being. The two other men in Jean's life had to be considered as well: Godfrey and John, but their mutual love for her only aggravated their bitter hostility to each other. John's aggressiveness had flared up again over Godfrey's jealous protection of Jean and the mention of divorce.

John was at last earning his living as a painter of railway carriages
in London. He worked solidly for a number of years with a view to
earning a pension so that he might retire early and return at last to
his painting. He visited Jean occasionally in Broomfield, until relations with Godfrey became too strained.

Marc and Godfrey continually urged me to commence divorce
proceedings. I had every intention of doing so, but as long as Jean was
in England, I was afraid this action might increase John's bitterness
toward all of us, and make Jean suffer. I was constantly torn between
the desire to please Marc, content Godfrey, appease John and spare
Jean.

Godfrey's main concern was that Marc and I should get married,
and until we did so he was not overly anxious to meet Marc. He
wrote me:

> You are complicating things for everyone by not going ahead with
> the divorce *now*. You cannot invite Jean to share your household unless
> it is put on some more regular footing. Otherwise she will be fair game
> for every man in the place, and willing game, because she will think
> it is all right.
> I do think we are doing something to start her off right in life. She's
> an impressive young woman with remarkable potential. When she
> gets stronger she ought to be pitted against keen competition, and
> you'll see the sparks fly!

In Godfrey's mind my ten-year-old daughter was already a brilliant young woman, in danger of leading a dissolute life! Quest
Brown wrote me:

> I understand the difficult situation brought on by Jean's trying to
> impose her will on David. This was inevitable. Jean is a dear little girl,
> highly talented; she has good bone marrow and there is something
> very English about her. It is better that David should not be exposed
> to Jean's unconscious hostility for a while. She loves him dearly but
> obviously he is a real threat to her security. Now she will be the sole
> center of attention. Inevitably there will be moments of anguish over
> Jean, and with your tender heart it could not be otherwise. But, my
> dear child, this is the best thing for all concerned and never for one
> moment feel that you have failed Jean. You have done a wonderful job
> when one considers the tremendous difficulties you had to cope with
> in all directions.

Drawing and inscription, December, 1945.

Sketches made in a letter from Chagall to the author, 1946.

Drawing made of the author and their son, David. High Falls, New York, 1946.

Notebook drawing, 1948.

Drawing and inscription (Bonne Année), 1948.

Drawing and inscription ("For Virginia—my love") made in a copy of Chagall ou
L'Orage Enchanté, *1952.*

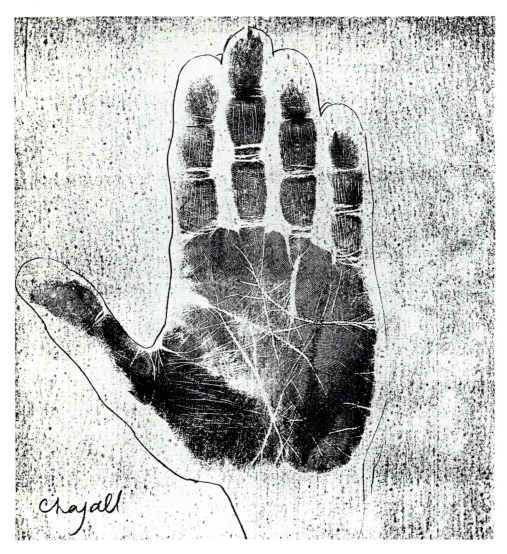

Inked imprint of Chagall's hand, made by Quest Brown.

Drawing made by Chagall, 1949, before the author and David left on a trip to England.

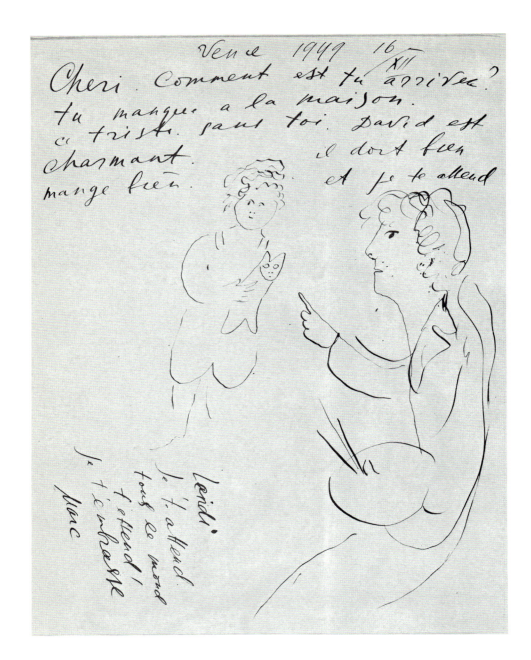

Sketch in a letter from Chagall, 1949, which reads, "Darling, How was your arrival? We miss you at home. It's sad without you. David is charming. He sleeps well and eats well and I'm waiting for you." And at the bottom: "Monday. I'm waiting for you. Everybody's waiting for you. I kiss you. Marc"

Drawing, 1949.

1950 vence.

Pour Virginia en souvenir de notre cinquième anniversaire — Marc.

Drawing and inscription made in an old English Bible found in the flea market in Nice, 1950, on the occasion of Marc and Virginia's fifth anniversary.

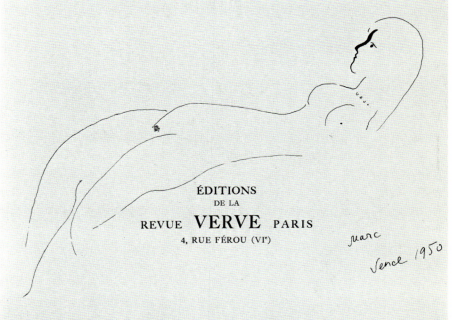

Pour Virginia

VERVE

REVUE ARTISTIQUE ET LITTÉRAIRE
DIRECTEUR : TÉRIADE

VOL. VI, N° 24

ÉDITIONS
DE LA
REVUE **VERVE** PARIS
4, RUE FÉROU (VI°)

Marc
Vence 1950

Drawing made in Verve, *Tériade's art magazine, 1950.*

Drawing of Chagall made by the author, 1950.

But the deep trauma caused by Jean's first feeling of rejection (her six months away in boarding school) continued their ravages. Recently she wrote me:

> I still have the greatest trouble forgiving and forgetting what for me was the opposite of your seven years of plenty with Marc. I hope this doesn't sound too hard on you, but I feel that Marc ruled your emotions to the extent that your maternal instinct was diverted, otherwise how can one account for the discrepancy between your nurturing and devotion to him and your displacement of me?

Of course she was right. Marc ruled my emotions very subtly. He was certainly my new child, and I sacrificed Jean from a fear of jeopardizing this new life that was so full of promise. Now I was sacrificing her again, and her separation from me and her adored David was causing her new pain. She came to Orgeval with Georgiana for the Christmas holidays—a joyful reunion but all too short to console her.

October of 1950 saw us back on the Cote d'Azur with David. The three of us lived very harmoniously together. David was angelic and constantly entertaining. As he no longer had Jean to play with, he spent all of his time with us. We all three adored traveling, and we also enjoyed looking for houses. David is still the same today, always on the move and always in search of the perfect, the ultimate house.

Godfrey wrote, "I don't see you settling or wanting to settle anywhere." Of course he was perfectly right, or more exactly, Marc and I were constantly "settling down" somewhere. If there is anything whatever in astrological signs (an amusing and harmless hypothesis) this might be due to our Cancer tendency to "carry our houses with us everywhere." We Cancers love houses, but we are not scared of tearing up our roots. However, Marc was approaching the age when it became advisable to settle down, if only to gather all the paintings together under one roof.

His life had been full of uprootings, but he had always followed his star faithfully, through all kinds of vicissitudes. When, between the two wars, there were no longer any threats to the artist, the furious urge became more tempered, but the rise of Fascism and the war years brought back a haunting uncertainty. Again he became a wandering Jew, following his star with a blind faith, and his paintings were filled with revelations and more vital statements. Chagall the man longed to settle down, but Chagall the artist always unconsciously sought uprooting and renewal. Now the man's infallible instinct for self-preservation won the day.

One day we drove to the village of St. Jeannet, in the mountains beyond Vence, to see Georges Ribemont-Dessaignes, the great surrealist poet. He smiled graciously from behind his large horn-rimmed glasses and held out a long bony hand in greeting. He was one of the most sincerely tolerant people I have ever met, and I have rarely felt so readily accepted as I was by him. But it didn't prevent him from being ferociously attached to his own opinions. He was anxious to persuade us to settle in that rocky village where each little square had a trickling fountain and a few trees for shade, and donkeys loaded with grass from the valley climbed up the winding paths. Despite this charm, we found it somewhat isolated.

Instead, Vence seemed the ideal place, and we found a large furnished house, appropriately named Le Studio. The tall French windows, the balconies with stone balustrades, the fruits of Vence in ceramic bowls and the tea roses from the garden inspired a whole series of monochrome wash drawings. Marc also made a number of sketches in gouache, ink or pastel of the children and myself seated at the round table. His oil paints had been left behind in Orgeval, and he was reduced to these simple media and stimulated by new impressions.

Marc felt free in this new temporary abode; it was not charged with the accumulations of the past. His canvases were forgotten, as was his self-imposed obligation to finish them. I believe this obsessive conscientiousness sometimes produced negative results. Some of the reworked canvases lacked a primal impetus. Technically, they were flawless and the reworking was unnoticeable, in terms of paint. But the freshness of texture was misleading. These paintings often had as much success with dealers and collectors as the more vital and spontaneous ones, a success that confirmed Marc in his obsessive desire to finish everything. It never occurred to him that the judgment of people who made very important gains from his paintings was in any way distorted.

In addition, Marc's fame was such that critics rarely gave vent to totally spontaneous opinions. Chagall became more and more sacred and untouchable as the market value of his works increased. When, on rare occasions, a critic was outspoken in his criticism, Marc was understandably upset, for his ear had become accustomed to a chorus of approval. An article that was not all praise plunged him into gloom; it saddened him to be thus "misunderstood." I don't know whether he was assailed by doubt when an honest man spoke his mind, but I know that the opinions of art critics affected him more than he cared to admit.

I don't believe he was disturbed by criticism during the first great period of his life, in Russia and in Paris, it only increased the tremendous conviction he had of being absolutely true to himself. The result is a series of staggering masterpieces, so full of mystery and beauty that one doesn't seek to fathom their secret, one is simply filled with wonder.

Some unconscious doubt must have crept in during the second half of his life, for he was obviously shaken by adverse opinions.

Chapter

V

Les Collines—
Work and Friends

It was time to look for a permanent house where Marc could at last assemble his large collection of paintings from every period of his life —all the unfinished canvases and the hundreds of drawings, water-colors and gouaches. Our next move was to Les Collines.

Claude Bourdet's mother—Catherine Pozzi, separated from her husband, the playwright Edouard Bourdet—had lived in Vence for many years, and since her death the Bourdet family had taken over her house for the holidays. During Claude's activities in the Resistance, his hideout had been a room in a separate building, with a door opening onto the fields behind. A bell from the house warned him of danger, and allowed him to escape to safety.

It was in this house that Paul Valéry came to stay in secret with Catherine Pozzi, and the house was full of his watercolors and portraits of Catherine.

Claude and Ida Bourdet rarely came to Les Collines, but their three children, who came with their grandmother, considered it paradise on earth. The house was falling into serious disrepair and when we first

saw it it had an air of melancholy about it. The iron railings around
the leaking terrace roof had left long rusty trails down the yellow
walls, and the shattered glass porch and cracked cement steps contributed to its dismal appearance.

The two Idas were very keen for Marc to buy the house, but apart
from the sad state of the building, he was somewhat put off by the
fact that Matisse had lived farther down the road. The chapel he
decorated had just been inaugurated, and there was talk of naming
the road "Avenue Henri Matisse."

Renoir's house in Le Cannet was also for sale and we went to see
it. The glass studio in the garden had collapsed, but the garden was
beautiful and the house was simple and full of charm. I loved it, but
Marc knew he would never be himself in Renoir's house. He wanted
to live in virgin soil, far from the aura of other great painters.

Finally he was won over by Les Collines, because there was a
separate two-story building with an outside staircase that was an
ideal studio—in fact it had already been one. A man who made fake
Matisses had rented it from the Bourdets, and when his fraud was
discovered he fled, never to be seen again. The artichokes he planted
were still flourishing and we picked some for our supper.

A long driveway lined with cypresses climbed up to the house,
swerving around a clump of eucalyptus trees to a terrace shaded by
vines and roses. From his big studio window Marc could see the
Mediterranean over the crests of date palms and orange trees, and the
ancient walled town of Vence, which later inspired many paintings.
Behind the house, two rocky crags—the Baou Blanc and the Baou
Noir—rose like a pair of venerable Sphinxes to a height of eight
hundred meters.

It took me several months to have the dilapidated house transformed into a cheerful white one, with green shutters and a roof of
curved tiles.

In the spring of 1950 we moved all our belongings from Orgeval
and took possession of Les Collines.

I wrote Godfrey:

The moving has drained away every ounce of my energy, but to lie in
bed and listen to the croaking frogs and the nightingales is a reward
that soothes away all fatigue. The sun comes in and warms the newly

polished floors, and a delicious smell comes up from the garden with the cheerful sound of pickaxes and workmen's voices. I shall almost miss the workmen when at last they will have finished digging our drains. David will miss them especially. They make him brown-paper hats and bring him sand and pails of water, and he squats on the edge of the trench and translates stories for them from his English book.

Marc says he is sure this is much better than paradise. Today he said: "These are the best years of my life."

I began putting the studio in order. It was the first time since the war that all Marc's belongings were under the same roof. Ida sent the handsome old furniture that André Lhote had been keeping safe. She was pleased to see the rooms arranged with some of the familiar things that reminded her of her mother. Claude Bourdet's hideout behind the house became Ida's bedroom.

Over the mantel piece in the living room was the splendid *Lovers of the Eiffel Tower* and in the dining room we hung *The Cattle Dealer*.

There were two small sculptures, Renoir's standing bronze nude and a terra cotta figure by Laurens. These were the only works by other artists that Marc possessed. He could have exchanged paintings for the work of the best artists, but he preferred to keep his own. Other artists disturbed him. This is understandable, since an artist's own vision seems to him the only absolute reality.

At last Marc set to work really seriously. First he made the two large paintings for the Watergate Theater, *The Blue Circus* and *The Dance*. I helped him square them off from smaller sketches, as I had done for *The Red Sun*. It was a mechanical process that he didn't relish. When he enlarged a sketch he often gave it a free interpretation, but for these particular paintings he especially wanted to preserve the quality of the sketches.

When Marc started a painting he sketched in the broad lines with charcoal, and when he was satisfied, he continued accentuating the basic drawing with a brush dipped in turpentine and some neutral gray color. The turpentine mixed with the charcoal, and the drawing was often very beautiful. Then he laid out the main colors. Sometimes he picked up a piece of colored paper or cloth and held it against the canvas to judge the effect. There were many color samples lying around. Sometimes he would carry off unexpected objects and, if ever I lost something, I would look for it in his pile of treasures.

Once he took some brightly colored socks from the children's room, much to their amusement.

Though his small hands moved with incredible speed, the painting grew very slowly. The texture and color modulation was infinitely varied and subtle. He never worked in pure, flat tones like Matisse. He worked on very small portions, slowly, patiently, his hands quivering and fluttering like birds.

I have seen him work on the same canvas for weeks and months, at intervals. He always had several paintings going on at the same time and these sometimes became a series; there was often something common to them all. Sometimes he would put aside a painting for years and resume it when all the problems he had encountered when first painting it had worn off, and he could look at it with an entirely fresh perception.

He had an intrinsic understanding for the life of matter, for its vibrations and transformations. He respected its autonomous behavior and never abused it. Like a Taoist craftman, he sought the mystery that lived in his material, and worked in harmony with it. The result is that his works can stand a comparison with nature. His famous test consisted of setting a picture in the grass or against a tree, to see if it held its own. It illustrated his idea that a good painting is made of authentic, living substances and explained his pet theory of the indispensable "chemical" quality of a painting. What he meant was that there is a mysterious element, without which a painting cannot rise above the realm of pure matter into the realm of pure creation, without which it cannot become a *new living thing.* That element is like a piece of living tissue.

What for him was the result of an intuitive gift is difficult to define, but art critics, who adore definitions, often asked him to explain this particular flair, and as famous painters are supposed to theorize about their paintings in interviews, Marc repeatedly detailed this theory of his.

I don't agree with this craze for interviews; it is my belief that artists who lend themselves too freely to them do themselves harm.

Nothing irritated Marc more than the attempted explanation of his thematic material. The mere mention of the word "symbolism" in connection with his work made him sigh with weary vexation. In fact, when he talked repeatedly about "chimie," or chemistry, he was deliberately leading people away from considerations about the meaning of his themes and what they owed to his subconscious.

Marc knew that there was some mysterious force working within him, filling his paintings with dream forms, but he didn't feel a need to elucidate their origins, and it disturbed him when others tried to do so. He knew very well that they were charged with significance, but to his conscious mind they were purely arbitrary forms, elements that he used in the construction of his paintings, sometimes drawn from visible sources, sometimes from memories. He used them for their shapes, their colors and their mysterious qualities. The bride sometimes provides a strictly vertical line, shooting into the sky like a comet, with her long veil trailing behind her. Sometimes her head grows out of the twirling veil, like a genie out of a wisp of smoke. Christ on the cross provides a sharp division of the pictorial space. The ladder and the easel are architectural elements. Two lovers' heads, two circles, sometimes melted together, sometimes metamorphosed into sun and moon, are often the basic elements of a picture.

The authentic artist's vision of the world is constantly colored by the visions that he projects on things around him. One can practically say that Chagall actually saw fishes climbing ladders and trees growing upside down, as long as his reason didn't interfere. They seemed as real to him as all the tangible things that make up our lives.

Marc never spoke to me of his dreams. Perhaps he never consciously remembered them, because the borderline between sleeping dreams and waking ones was too fine for him to be aware of the difference. He used to tell me that he was a dreamer who never woke up. But in *Ma Vie* he offers three very vivid descriptions of dreams, one of them so vivid that he afterward made a painting of it, *The Vision:* "The ceiling opens and a winged creature descends in an explosion of light and noise, filling the room with movement and clouds, the rustling of feathers. I think it must be an angel. I open my eyes, it's too bright, too blinding."

A critic once asked him whether his fantasies were directly inspired by reality and Marc, in a playful mood, replied, "Of course. When I see a face I make a picture of a horse, and when I see a horse, I paint a picture of a cow."

"And when you see a cock?"

"When I see a cock, first of all I want to eat it, and when I've eaten it, I make a picture of a pair of lovers in the sky."

Marc later said, "Painters have always been mad. Why do they expect us to talk sense?"

Jean, at the age of seven, made a definition of Marc's painting. She said, "Picasso paints crazy things and puts them in their right places, Chagall paints things as they are and puts them all upside down."

There is a complete antithesis between the two artists, yet they both dominated an entire century of modern painting.

No other painter has shown us the chaos of our era as did Picasso. Chagall gives us a glimpse of the mysterious equilibrium that has always existed beyond chaos, that he believes might one day triumph over it.

Picasso was a Titan who sought to shock and shake the world. At first he was a true and loyal instrument of the tremendous fire that burned within him, but he became bewitched by his own magic. The volcano Picasso erupted lava which had destructive effects, as well as immensely positive ones.

During the first part of his life Chagall lived in a fever of creation, hardly eating or sleeping, hardly stopping to consider or to judge, indifferent to approval or recognition. The works of that period strike one dumbfounded. They have an inner radiance which is inexplicable, a mysterious life of their own. An artist builds a world in which life begins all over again. If we believe in it implicitly, we are so carried away by it that no other world seems as real. These paintings, these new live beings, are sent out into the real world still warm from the fire of creation, and they begin a separate life of change and evolution. They are carried away on the ebbing and flowing tides, and their relationship to other creations and other times fluctuates incessantly. They undergo dynamic transformations in the minds of men and follow mysterious patterns of history. Their life is long, but they are in danger of destruction, like any other living being. They even have moods and reactions. Perhaps they suffer when they are put away in vaults. Perhaps their souls only come alive when they have been loved and understood. Perhaps they are harmed in some way by hostility.

Someone asked the English painter Francis Bacon why the people in his pictures scream, and he answered that they scream when one looks at them, but who knows whether they still scream when one looks away.

Some of Chagall's paintings go out of their way to please; they sell for enormous sums of money and hang in their valuable frames for years, but nothing further comes out of them. Others, especially the earlier works, are transcendent, they shine with an inner light and have the faculty of transporting us.

But our views are distorted by fashion and hypnotic fascination, also by the money value of a work of art. The critics, whose work it is to observe the fluctuations of an artist's life, to criticize, guide and stimulate, are often in league with the dealers. They work to promote, not to criticize. Critics like Charles Estienne are rare today. The dealers have made a hugely successful business out of the artist's absolute necessity to express his new world vision, but if he becomes too affected by his success on the art market, he may never rise to anything timeless.

An established painter is no longer free; he cannot begin working on a new canvas without an involuntary reflection on the market value of the finished painting, unless he has the courage to reject the whole system and refuse to sell his pictures to dealers.

Marc said to Carlton Lake: "If I were free, I would not paint pictures to sell, I would not exhibit in galleries where people can pay large sums of money to own one of my paintings, either to decorate their apartments or because it is a good investment. I would spend the rest of my life painting my Bible." Carlton Lake ought to have asked him to explain why he didn't consider himself free to do so immediately.

Some of the last really free painters were Van Gogh, who was not concerned about success; Toulouse-Lautrec who had no need to sell; Cézanne, who chose to work in isolation; and Gauguin, who fled from civilization. The young Chagall was of their world.

He said to the art critic and historian André Parinaud:* "I have often dreamed of the great day when I shall be able to isolate myself completely, like a monk in his cell. Work is all I need, and some quiet corner with a hatch through which my food can be given me."

Chagall by André Parinaud, Club d'Art Bordas, Paris 1966.

But fame is a ruthless despot, and the dealers and critics are its agents.

Chagall's last lair was not a monk's cell but a gilded prison where the dealers and critics were admitted in turn; gone the simplicity, gone the direct contact with an unspoiled way of life, gone the innocent and spontaneous experiences. He could have hung on to these if he had really wanted to.

Among the dangers that beset an artist is that of the intervention of other people's judgment in the course of creation. Marc was too easily impressed when people of authority, armed with irresistibly convincing arguments, criticized a work in progress. I sometimes saw paintings go awry because of their intervention. The fragile and elusive mystery of Marc's paintings was not to be caught like a butterfly in a net but should have been observed silently, from a respectful distance, lest it take fright and fly away. I believe the basic spiritual structure of a painting can be destroyed by structural changes that come from without.

Marc told me that Bella was the first person in his life to play the role of permanent critic. No painting was finished until Bella declared it so. She was the supreme judge; she stuck to her opinion, even if it was different from his, and he usually came around to hers in the end.

On one of Ida's visits to Vence, she criticized a whole series of works that were in the course of creation. Marc obediently walked around with her, "correcting" some of the paintings with a brush dipped in neutral gray and turpentine. When she had gone, I expressed surprise at his docility.

I recall another time during one of Pierre Matisse's visits to High Falls to fetch a new series of paintings. He strapped a wet painting, face up, on the roof of his car, in spite of Marc's feeble protest that it wasn't quite finished.

Chagall's greatest pictures are, without doubt, those in which the original conviction remains powerful and complete. No critic, even if he were endowed with visionary powers, could come anywhere near the artist's original experience. An artist who willingly lends himself to interference consents to a form of sacrilege.

There are many intrusions into a famous artist's life, and the dangers that beset him are great. His work becomes public property even before it leaves his hand. His family and friends, his dealer, everyone feels entitled to an opinion before the work is finished. Even the artist himself becomes equivalent to public property—a symbol of success. The camera has penetrated into the sanctuary of the artist's studio and millions of television spectators can watch a work in the course of creation.

The artist is asked to become a performer, which is not his natural state. Clouzot's film on Picasso, *Le Mystère Picasso,* is a demonstration of Picasso's virtuosity, but the painting he did especially for the film ended up in confusion. Matisse, with his tranquil sense of measure, was filmed producing a typically accomplished work, but it lacked the usual enchantment.

In one film, made in the 1970s, Marc was interviewed while he worked:

> *"People say you draw badly."*
> *"Of course, I draw badly. I* like *drawing badly."*
> *"You hesitate a lot, your line is feathery, as if you were searching for something."*
> *"Yes, of course I hesitate, it's necessary. I'm searching constantly."*

The questions obviously irritated him, but he continued working, regardless of this niggling, provocative interference. Photographers are notoriously aggressive too; they don't all work in Charles Leirens' respectful manner. I have an unpleasant recollection of Marc's sitting for the excellent American photographer Philippe Halsman. He had a brusque, authoritative manner and invaded the living room without consideration, throwing cables around and rolling up rugs, moving sculptures without permission and ordering his model around in a rather patronizing manner. The children and I posed for him as well, and the result was particularly static and unnatural—we all had pained expressions. Halsman showed us a portfolio of "indiscreet" portraits that were never shown to the models, because he had lighted them in a diabolical fashion to stress every defect. They were the equivalent to caricatures. There was one of the duke and duchess of Windsor making grotesque grimaces. I wondered if he had done this to Marc when my back was turned.

Marc was an excellent performer and he knew how to be winsome and charming. He got so good at playing the part of Chagall, (the "Chagall" people expected him to be) that it was impossible to say whether he was acting or not. But he had a secret shyness as well as a simulated one, and he was never totally at ease, except with his family and his closest friends. On the other hand, everyone felt at ease with him.

His company was so enjoyable that many visitors came to share it. The jade green, wrought-iron table with the slab of polished stone set into it was constantly in use on the terrace under the palm trees.

Tériade came often. Sometimes there was Jacques Prévert, the whimsical, mischievous poet, always his true and uncontaminated self, coloring everything with his unpredictable, subversive, disturbing wit, his caustic disrespect for every form of establishment, his soul-fulfilling quest for liberation and his changeless youth. Only once did I see him become aggressive and attack, with cruel humor, a rather mannish woman—who obviously suffered from lack of confidence—until she dissolved into tears. He loved women, but he couldn't bear mannish ones. He was warm and congenial, endlessly entertaining and funny, his cigarette wedged in the corner of his mouth and a glass of red wine permanently in his hand.

Jacques Lassaigne was a prominent art critic and historian, an enormous, heavy man with a gentle manner. He was a fathomless source of enthusiasm and his devotion to Marc was absolute. He had carried out negotiations with the heirs of Ambroise Vollard so expertly that Marc was able to purchase the three great engraved works at an incredibly low cost. But Marc did not always appreciate the absence of ulterior motives by some of his most loyal friends. Oddly enough, some far less scrupulous people often managed to possess him.

Jacques's former wife, Assia, a gifted writer and a rich personality of Russian origin, was stricken with tuberculosis. She came to live in Vence at my suggestion, in an effort to prolong her fragile existence that had been so crammed with adventure. She had astonishing joie de vivre that carried her on miraculously against all predictions. She even had a perfectly healthy child by her lover, but she was never allowed to take him in her arms. He was kept by a foster mother in the country, near Paris, and I once took her to see him. She remained seated in the car and the child was presented to her through the window. She smiled a radiant smile, no tears, no self-pity. With her doctor in Vence she joked endlessly, even about her own inevitable death. Marc was afraid to let her enter our house (he had an obsessive fear of contagion), so I used to visit her in her *pension* where we had many enriching conversations.

When Marc went to Paris in 1946 and 1947 he stayed with Assia, already separated from Jacques. She was a seductive and beautiful woman with ash-blond hair and pale greenish eyes. She had conquered tuberculosis momentarily and was declared non-contagious. It was not until he came home that Marc told me he had been staying with a young woman. He thought I might have feared he would fall into temptation. He told me that Assia had made advances, but he had remained aloof. He said that she was a present-day Marie Bashkirtseff (a Russian poetess who lived at the beginning of the century; a romantic, impassioned creature who died at twenty-four of tuberculosis). That sort of woman scared him; there was no danger of him falling into her trap, he explained. Besides, there was the question of possible contagion.

In his account of innocent flirtations with the young girls in Vitebsk, one had the impression that promiscuity and contagion were one and the same in his mind. He spoke of the "traps" set him by the so-called "violent" Aniouta, with whom he had been flirting for four years. At last he gave her a kiss—a terrible kiss, he said, and a few days later she fell ill. Her face was covered with red pimples and he asked her if it was because of the kiss.

Marc was an essentially chaste man and prudent where relations with the other sex were concerned. He was totally faithful—temptations were never great, for the tremendous temperament went into his paintings.

His mother remained a central figure in his life. Bella was his ideal fiancée, his first love and his bride, yet she became something of a mother figure as well. With Ida the relationship was tinged with passion and there was a strong identity between them, but she was also something of a mother figure. Women have always played an important part in his life. Again and again in his paintings, he is so completely involved in them that the artist-lover's face melts into the face of the loved one.

He had, as most artists do, a strong feminine counterpart to his masculinity. A woman, in his mind, is synonymous with purity. He once said to me, after reading a story of rape in the newspaper, that if I happened to be the unfortunate victim, he would feel considerably cooled off for some time with regard to our physical relationship. "Bella was a virgin," he said. "I asked her when I came back to Vitebsk, after four years' absence, whether she was still pure, and she answered yes. I believed her implicitly."

But what he preached and what he practiced were somewhat different. He told me that a cousin of his, a young woman from Vitebsk, came through Paris during his first stay there on her way to get married, and they spent the night together making love. I remarked with a chuckle, "I hope her fiancé didn't have strict ideas about virginity like you."

Assia went back to Paris with resolute courage to meet her death. She was aware of everything that was happening to her, but only sought humor and affection from others, never pity. She used to carry on long conversations through the fence at the end of the *pension* garden with two little American boys. They were the sons of Arkady and Rose Leokum, who later became our friends.

I had asked Arkady to write me his recollections of the close friendship that had developed between us all. The relationship was particularly satisfying to Marc, who was totally relaxed in their company. Arkady confessed that when Rose and I got to know each other one day in the village, he was not particularly excited at the prospect of getting to know the painter, Marc Chagall, unaware of his importance in the art world. Their relationship was all the more straightforward and spontaneous from the start.

Marc discovered, much to his pleasure, that Arkady spoke perfect Yiddish. Moreover, his mother, Katia, who came to stay in Vence, and with whom Marc had a warm relationship, spoke Russian. When the two families were together, four languages were spoken and there was a joyful communion between us all. When we went to the Leokum's house for a meal, Marc often expressed his good humor by asking for paper and crayons and making sketches on the dining room table for our friends.

Marc liked showing his paintings to people whose vision was unspoiled, who had a fresh approach owing to their unfamiliarity with his work. Once he asked Arkady to give his honest opinion about a painting that Marc said he couldn't understand at all, and Arkady's innocent explanation was a revelation to him.

Arkady used to talk about Marc's "astonishing offer." Marc was so pleased by the happy relationship between the two families that he wanted to preserve it, and he proposed to give them an acre of his property and help them build a home there. We would bring up our boys together, and arrange for them to have Hebrew lessons. Marc's dream of bringing up David as a Jewish boy would thus become a reality. He liked the idea of my having Jewish friends, intimate friends who were almost part of the family. He had been brought up in a big family, and he longed for another.

But Arkady was running out of the money he had made from the proceeds of a best-seller he had written called *The Temple,* a novel about building a Jewish Temple in the town of Westport, Connecticut. He was planning to go back to work in an advertising agency in New York, so our charming friends left us in 1950. I never saw Rose again, for she died a few years later.

Marc asked Arkady if he would become his agent in New York to try and obtain commissions for murals. Although Arkady felt honored, he declined, saying that as a writer he could not live off someone else's creative work. He agreed, however, to contact a certain number of people and subsequently approached the directors of the luxurious Temple Emanu-El on Fifth Avenue, who were simply not interested. Only a few years later, the finest public buildings in New York were vying with one another to commission mural paintings and stained glass by Chagall, such as the Metropolitan Opera in Lincoln Center and the United Nations.

Paul Eluard came to Vence with Dominique, a warm, spontaneous young woman he had met in Mexico at a peace conference and whom he had married almost immediately afterward. During the years following the death of his wife, Nusch, Eluard, at first crushed with grief, transformed his love for Nusch into a universal love for repressed mankind. He wrote militant poetry and defended the cause of democracy in many countries. He was a gentle, dreamy person, but he was burning inside with an unquenchable fire and was sometimes given to voluble outbursts. He was already affected by the trouble that carried him off in 1952, and his hands trembled so violently that he had difficulty holding a glass of wine.

The art dealer, Aimé Maeght, and his wife, Marguerite, were frequent visitors. Marguerite was warm and direct. I have never forgotten the cooking tips she gave me with her colorful *accent du Midi:* the meridional specialty bouillabaise, made with rockfish from the Mediterranean and cooked not more than ten minutes on a hot stove, and the famous aioli, a mayonnaise made with garlic that is crushed to a paste with pestle and mortar. Marguerite had the gaiety and simplicity of an uninhibited *bon vivant.* Aimé was less of an extrovert; he never quite let himself go. But his small blue eyes observed everything and his thin lips wore a faint smile that was half amusement, half diplomatic amiability. He was gifted with a rare natural flair for discerning true quality in art along with a brilliant business mind, two gifts that might seem antagonistic.

In the end, Maeght won the battle against Carré for exclusive rights in representing Chagall. From then on he won all the battles, and became the most celebrated and powerful dealer in France.

There was already talk of Maeght's plans for an important foundation in St. Paul de Vence, near the house where he had recently settled. His original idea was to set up a place where the best artists from all countries could come together to work, exhibit, and exchange ideas. The Spanish architect, José Luis Sert, had already been appointed to design it and Joan Miró, who was a frequent visitor to St. Paul, contributed to the general excitement around this ambitious project. Miró was always beaming with secret pleasure, eternally curious about everything, always bustling with activity. He and Marc had a warm relationship, indeed it was practically impossible not to have a warm relationship with Miró.

Ida had worked very hard to promote her father's fame since the war, and wished to earn a living by acting as his freelance dealer. She retained a limited interest in Marc's business dealings, an arrangement Maeght reluctantly agreed to. He was an "all or nothing" man and Marc was torn between the two of them (after I left, Marc's wife Vava opted for Maeght to handle all of the work and Ida was sacrificed). In 1949, thanks to Ida's successful business dealings, she was able to buy an ancient house on the Quai de l'Horloge near the Pont Neuf, in Paris; one side of the house looked out onto the Place Dauphine, just opposite the back of my parents' house.

She furnished it in the distinguished manner she had inherited from her mother, with her father's paintings and the objects d'art and furniture he had divided between himself and Ida. She managed everything with great efficiency and Marc was proud of her. In speaking of his daughter, he observed, "People who walk on the tips of their toes and raise their little fingers are very practical people." Sometimes it happened that Marc and I agreed on some plan of action that Ida disapproved of, and Ida would talk him into agreeing with her. He would then quickly disavow me, assuring her that he had never been of my opinion. He was childishly disloyal. In later years he was disloyal to Ida in turn, and Vava became the family's sole oracle.

As a rule, Marc was on far more friendly terms with Matisse than he was with Picasso. He was proud of the fact that Ida had posed for a series of drawings by Matisse, but he was jealous of her admiration for him. Still, Marc also admired Matisse and was slightly in awe of him—an unusual state of affairs indeed, for Marc rarely admired living artists. Matisse had great respect for Marc as well, although he, too, judged the painters of his time with severity. He once said, "Chagall has a mystical sense and an incomparable dramatic power." He spoke to Marc of his graphic work and admired it very much, and during one of our visits they looked through the Boccaccio book that Tériade had just published, with illustrations by Marc. Since Matisse had become bedridden he had rather lost touch with the world of painters and lived instead in a world of books.

We visited him in his spacious apartment high up in Cimiez, overlooking the Bay of Nice, with its wide balconies shaded by colored awnings and flowering shrubs. Lydia Delectorskaya, his Russian-born secretary and companion, imparted a discreet radiance. Her admirable face and voice reflected all the harmonious qualities of her character. Thanks to her, Matisse was able to live an immensely productive but tranquil life, in spite of his serious disability, and lived to a much greater age than was expected. When he died, Lydia disappeared into the obscurity she longed for.

Whenever we visited Matisse, he was usually either lying in bed drawing on the ceiling with a stick of charcoal on the end of a bamboo pole, or cutting out large pieces of brilliantly colored paper, which he instructed Lydia to paste onto a board. The latter were the basis for designs which Tériade had commissioned for an important book, *Jazz*. He was always congenial and talkative, though a trifle intimidating with his steady, discriminating eye. Marc was always on his best behavior with Matisse, like a young pupil visiting the master.

The balcony was full of the restless bustling of white doves, contrasting with the cool tranquillity inside. Some gray-and-white kittens were rolling over each other in the sun, and Matisse gave us one of them. This cat roamed contentedly in Vence, and the children and I adored the cat until one day it disappeared. Marc was rather jealous of this *"chat de* Matisse," especially when I fondled it too tenderly.

When we came to live in Vence, Matisse's former house, Le Rêve, was empty, following his move to Cimiez in 1948. His friend and neighbor in Vence, Jean Darquet, was bereft. Matisse was the only person to whom Jean ever showed his paintings, and to this day he has chosen to remain obscure. Matisse considered him a talented artist. In fact Jean also has a vast knowledge of art history and a brilliant mind. He has a deep familiarity with almost every great art museum in the world, having memorized every worthy book and catalog on the subject. He was a pupil of André Lhote, one of Marc's great friends and an exceptional teacher, whose own paintings are always solidly constructed.

I know no other example of an artist of Darquet's quality refusing to show his work, even to his wife, his mother or his closest friends. Marc often pleaded to see his work, but to no avail. He always replied that he had not yet made sufficient progress and was not ready to show it. Marc scoffed a little at this excessive timidity—or was it pride? As they lived in the Avenue Henri Matisse, a short way from Les Collines, we saw a lot of each other and the Darquets became (and are to this day) my intimate friends. Darquet's mother, Edmé Casalis, was a woman of great character to whom we had given the nickname of "La Comtesse" because of her impressive airs. She was the closest friend of Catherine Pozzi and came to live in Vence to be near her; I enjoyed a close friendship with her as well.

One day a very old friend from Russia came to visit Marc—Allia Berson, a tiny, elderly lady. Her father was a well-known art collector in St. Petersburg in the days when Marc had been a struggling art student, and it was she who had paid for his lessons at the school of Léon Bakst. "I am ashamed to say you paid three months for nothing," said Marc. "I was so vexed by Bakst's humiliating criticism that

I didn't go back until I had got everything straight in my mind again
—I simply returned to my own ideas and he finally came around to
them."

"Then it was worth it," said Allia good-humoredly.

Marc was pleased to see his old friend; he so rarely saw anyone
from the Russian days. He was still homesick for Russia, and never
gave up hope of returning. But he knew that before he could go back
there, things would have to change a great deal. His art would have
to be accepted; his paintings would have to be brought out of their
hiding places and shown to the public.

So he sent Ida to Russia as a messenger and "trailblazer." She had
left Russia when she was six, and while Vitebsk no longer looked like
her father's pictures (if it ever did), she plunged into a bath of Rus-
sian-ness and discovered her roots. She took masses of presents and
messages for her aunts (Marc's sisters, of whom three or four were
still alive). In return they gave her souvenirs for her father and even
a camera for David, inscribed "Daragoy (Dear) David."

Many years later, in 1973, Marc went back to Russia with Vava,
at the invitation of Madame Furtseva, the minister of culture, who
organized a special exhibition in Moscow at the Tretiakov Gallery of
all the pictures the museum possessed. It was a great day for Marc,
for a surprise was waiting for him: the three famous murals he had
painted for the Jewish State Theater in Moscow were spread out on
the floor, and he was asked to sign them. For years he knew nothing
of their whereabouts, for the Jewish Theater had of course ceased to
exist. Apparently someone had taken them down when the theater
was closed and deposited them at the Tretiakov. Marc had tears in
his eyes when he saw them. Fifty years had passed!

He saw his remaining sisters during this trip, but he didn't go to
Vitebsk. The war had changed everything; even the graves had disappeared. It was the period when Soviet Russia had begun to show
particular hostility toward Jews anxious to leave the country, and
Marc's visit was hotly criticized in Israel.

From Broomfield, Godfrey wrote regularly with news of Jean:

> She refuses to take either of us seriously. It puts new life into me
> to be considered with such refreshing spontaniety.
> Once, when we were walking along arm in arm, talking of this and

that, she suddenly stopped and looked up into my face. "Of course, *you* are my daddy," she said.

I feel in the presence of something new and unique, something untouched and rather wonderful. If it broke in one's hand, it would be irreplaceable. When I see her sleeping I think: "What a delicate, beautiful piece of work; it could be crushed like a butterfly, but it might be capable of blowing up the world."

Her longing for you and David goes on all the time, like a toothache.

I also missed her more and more. I went to England in April for her tenth birthday, bringing her a present from Marc—a splendid pen and a watercolor portrait of herself he had painted in Orgeval. Godfrey proudly hung it in the dining room, where it stayed for twenty-five years, until both my parents had gone. I also brought the special Chagall issue of the art catalog *Derrière le Miroir,* published in 1950 in conjunction with the exhibition at the Galerie Maeght. Godfrey and I had many discussions.

He: "Why a double face, why houses upside down?"
Me: "Why not?"
He: "All right, if it has some meaning."
Me: "Maybe *you* can find some meaning, if you must have one."
He: "I believe it's just a stunt."
Me: "Just let yourself enjoy them, relax."
He: "Okay, I *do* enjoy them as blazes of color, but the mass of apparently irrelevant material interferes with my enjoyment."

Meanwhile, Marc was impatient for my return. He wrote:

When you're gone everything is sad, except David who makes me laugh. He is adorable. He says that when the tomatoes are red, Maman will come back. I would like to write you a whole book, but I write French like a Russian pig.

The summer holidays brought Jean home for good, much to my delight and hers. The English school experience and my parents' affectionate care had been positive in many ways, and she had personally opted to stay until the end of the school year. The old feelings of rejection were stifled momentarily and the idyll with David continued, stronger than ever.

Chapter

VI

Advice to Young Painters
Biblical Paintings
Ceramics and Sculpture
Israel

In those days young painters occasionally came to the door with an armful of paintings to ask Marc for advice. They were mostly foreigners; the French painters never imagined they could come unannounced. Marc enjoyed these impromptu visits and received the young artists kindly. His faculty for seeing with the vision of others and understanding their problems was remarkable.

A young Italian painter, grave and earnest as a priest, once appeared with paintings that were full of dark violence. He was absorbed in obscure theories and used elaborate terms to explain them. Marc said, "You are far too preoccupied with theories when all that matters is quality, and one is born with that. There may be quality in your work, but it is obscured by schools of thought. If your cloth is not of good quality, your suit will be worthless, however well it is tailored. Any part of a good picture is good, like a fine piece of cloth. All that matters is the plastic value, the form comes of itself.

119

Klee is an artist of quality because of the purity of his plasticity; Mondrian, too."

The young man said that what he admired in Chagall was not his plasticity, but his poetry. Marc replied that without plasticity, poetry didn't exist.

"Don't you think," said the young man, "that in this atomic age, our plasticity should be full of atomic energy?"

"Mon cher," Marc smiled, "if you possess atomic energy, well and good, but if you don't, it's no good searching for it! Say what you have to say without troubling about the manner in which you say it. Whatever qualities you possess will then be evident."

To a Scandinavian painter he said, "Don't confront nature with a knife, but with a prayer. Don't bother yourself with texture. Perhaps the 'cuisine' of Braque and Matisse doesn't suit you. You're not French. Search for your weltanschauung, your personal conception of the world."

Another painter showed him a very violent painting and Marc asked him, "What gave you such a shock?" The man explained that his wife was very hostile to his work.

"Never mind," said Marc. "You must be patient and steadfast. Be calm, don't search so far away. Do a chair or a bowl of fruit. All this fantasy is foreign to you. In any case, it's banal fantasy."

To a Dutchman whose paintings were heavy, obscure and confused, he said, "You must wash your paintings just as you wash your body."

To two Americans he said, "You must reevaluate your currency. You need a dollar that has one hundred percent value. Your values, your talent, your chemical qualities, *these* are your capital."

One of them asked whether it was advisable to study in an art school, and he replied, "If you have a small talent, you will lose much, but if you have a big talent, you will lose nothing. I advise you to forget about poetry, feelings, love—you won't lose those. Concentrate on your plastic quality while you are young. The older you grow, the less spontaneous you will be. A child paints with passionate intensity, that's the quality you must preserve. Above all, don't think too much about your direction. Daumier never had time to think about his direction, he had to earn his living. But he found his direction quite naturally, because he found his true value."

To one very young painter he urged, "Don't exhibit, because if you are successful, you will be tempted to repeat your success. Your painting is too fragile, don't use it as a means of livelihood, you might destroy it completely. Earn your living any other way. Keep your painting innocent."

One time he held court with a group of painters who had arrived: "Don't wait for ideas, they come with production. If you prepare yourself too much, you might never be ready. Creation is itself a preparation. I have been producing like a madman ever since I was sixteen. Don't be afraid to do inferior things, the first fruits are always small and sour. You must work a lot, it clears the brain."

"In art, two and two don't make four, they're more likely to make five," he remarked with a chuckle to a severe, symmetrical abstract painter.

He never failed to give these young artists the significant criticism they needed that would put them on the right road in pursuit of their personal quests. He was surprisingly tolerant of their shortcomings. His judgment of some of his colleagues' work, however, was much less tolerant, especially if they were successful artists. At an exhibition of the Austrian-born painter Oskar Kokoshka's work, Marc exclaimed, "It's a bouillabaisse delirium! He just throws *anything* onto the canvas," and he made a gesture as if to flick something from his nose.

But whenever an artist came to visit him he was full of courtesy and deference. When we were on Riverside Drive he received two visits which gave him—and incidentally me—much pleasure: those of Henry Moore and Graham Sutherland. Needless to say, the conversation was centered around Chagall, for that was the object of their visit. Apart from Matisse, Marc never paid a single visit to another artist's studio while I was with him, and this was a disappointment to me. But Marc seemed to feel uncomfortable in the presence of other artists and avoided discussing their work with them.

At that time I started drawing again, timidly, and Marc was quite encouraging. I compared his kindness to John's cruel disparagement. Marc had more respect for a humble, self-taught artist, a naïf painter or an artisan than for a successful artist who lacked authenticity.

I asked him once what he thought of the mystical English artist

William Blake, who, to my mind, was above all authentic, even to the point of artlessness. "Blake," he said, "was a visionary mystic who wanted to express his mysticism in his paintings, but his vision was too great and his means were too small. Van Gogh, for instance, is both effective and authentic; there isn't a single brushstroke that's not in keeping with his deepest feelings. In all humility he put his burning religious fervor into his paintings. His pair of boots speaks for all of suffering humanity, and the simplest tree or bouquet is charged with religious feeling. He was a prophet preaching in the desert; he cried out, 'Freedom for everyone! Freedom for the artist! Crucify me if you wish!'"

It was fun visiting museums and picture galleries with Marc. He always made a beeline for whatever interested him most and wasted no time on the rest. He knew very well that a human being's capacity to absorb works of art intelligently is relatively limited, and he never examined more than a dozen paintings at a time. I was grateful for this, and I have a living memory of the pictures we looked at together. Whenever he looked at pictures the other spectators were ruled out; there was no room for them. He would take one step forward, two steps back, put his head on one side, make his pronouncement and then signal to me to move on. Sometimes I lingered behind disobediently.

Coming out of the Jeu de Paume museum in Paris he summed up three painters as follows: *"Renoir, c'est une orange; Monet, c'est une pomme; Van Gogh, c'est une prière."* Renoir is an orange; Monet is an apple; Van Gogh is a prayer.

Marc felt more of an affinity with Rembrandt than with any other painter in history and his greatest ambition was to be worthy of him. One of the last lines of his autobiography is: "I am certain Rembrandt loves me." This was written in an effort to console himself for the treachery of his artist friends in Vitebsk, who had turned against him after he had named them professors at his art academy, and for the antagonism toward his art shown by the new leaders of Russia.

Jacques Lassaigne, who apart from being an art historian, was librarian at the Senate in the Palais Bourbon in Paris, took us to see the famous Delacroix ceilings. Marc was particularly fascinated by

Delacroix because of his daring experiments in technique and his free heroic style. Later it was Monet, especially, who bewitched him, and the influence of Monet's spiritual sensuality became visible in his work.

We made frequent trips to Paris, where Marc worked on lithographs in Fernand Mourlot's studio in the Rue de Chabrol, near the Gard du Nord. These were happy and prolific hours for Marc; he felt at home with Mourlot and his technicians in the enormous old studio where he was the center of attention. It was here that he made the lithographic posters for Maeght's exhibitions each year, and a series of splendid lithographs for *Derrière le Miroir*, published on each of these occasions. Tériade also commissioned color lithographs for this art magazine, *Verve*, which are among the best of Marc's work in this medium, especially the three based on the "Paris sketches," made in December, 1952. In the following years he produced many lithographs of a disappointingly inferior quality. They became confused and woolly, heavy with repetitious strokes and devoid of structure.

Ida had arranged the ground floor of her house, overlooking the Quai de l'Horloge, as an apartment for us, and organized lunches and dinners for us there.

Marc was torn between a desire to simplify and tone down his relationship with Ida, and his urge to use the powerful identity between them by making her his confidante and ally. He was constantly impressed by the efficient way that she managed his business, but he feared the emotional scenes. Her brilliant, busy social life was the opposite of the one he desired, and although he was excited by her whirlwind of activities, he was also exhausted by it. As long as he was working, he felt no great need for company, however sociable he might be.

In Vence, Marc would start to work immediately after breakfast and stop only for an hour's walk before lunch. Occasionally, the children or I accompanied him. Walking with Marc was a spasmodic affair, because whenever he got carried away by the conversation he would stop and make wide expressive gestures. In winter, before leaving the house, he would look to see if we were well covered up. "Don't catch cold," he would say, "doctors cost a lot of money."

Marc never engaged in any form of sport, except an occasional swim in the sea. To wield a brush from morning till night and to walk an hour every day seemed to have been sufficient to develop his impressive muscular system. Our occasional outings made him relaxed and good-humored and would result in a sketch pad filled with new ideas, but usually he worked nonstop until supper. I introduced the custom of picnicking, which my family had always enjoyed; it brought back memories of the rare and happy times in my school days when my parents would come home for the holidays.

Once we went down to Antibes with the Leokum family to have a picnic on the beach. As we began to enjoy the good things we had brought, we saw that a little way off, Picasso was doing the same with his friends and family. Marc looked over with an uncomfortable feeling that he had been robbed of his privacy, but he waved feebly and Picasso raised both arms in greeting. Picasso was holding court, receiving the homage of his loyal admirers. People were taking photos as Picasso performed. Marc was obviously envious that no one had noticed his presence, and it was the last time we had a picnic in Antibes.

Marc read the papers in a fragmentary fashion, but he consumed the pages on art. Occasionally he seemed to glance nostalgically through the sports pages. I remember him telling me that during the peaceful years before the war, he sometimes went to football matches.

As for books, I rarely saw him read one right through. He begrudged almost any activity that prevented him from working. Still, he seemed to "absorb" books, while ordinary people were obliged to read them. He had an uncanny intuition about things he didn't consciously know, and sometimes said astonishingly revealing things about books he had hardly glanced at. He had a gift of divination and an uncommon lucidity about works of art in general, as if they were perceived by his second nature. Hence his extraordinary power as an illustrator of books. He seemed to be able to live through the creative experience of the author, letting the work mold him, as it had molded its author.

But if he seldom read, Marc loved to be read to as he worked. Far from distracting him, it seemed to set his painter's intuition free by giving the intellect something else to dwell upon. Sometimes I read articles on art in papers and magazines. Lives of artists interested him far more than novels. He was intensely curious about the lives of

Goya and Gauguin, about their frustrations and misfortunes. Van Gogh's letters to his brother moved him particularly. "I *must* know all that," he said. "but I have no time to read." After a while I had no time either, and our reading was constantly interrupted by the telephone or visitors.

Listening to music was also a welcome accompaniment, giving him wings for his work. He had a deep need for music. Long-playing records didn't exist at that time, and our little gramophone had to be wound up continually. Finally he switched to the radio and listened to his heart's content. Moussorgsky stirred the melancholy fibers of his Russian soul; Monteverdi awakened his imagination; Ravel made him marvel at the magical inventions of the human brain; Bach touched a religious chord in him; but perhaps Mozart, more than any other, fulfilled his deepest needs. Sometimes he sang while he worked—a song from *Eugene Onegin* in a plaintive, minor key, full of romantic melancholy, or the captivating wedding dance from *The Dybbuk.* I liked to hear him sing; his voice was warm and melodious and it was a sure sign that the work was going well. He told me that as a boy he had sung in the synagogue choir. His voice was so beautiful that he thought he would become a singer, but his uncle Neuch "who played the fiddle like a cobbler" gave him violin lessons. He thought he'd become a violinist instead. Then he learned to dance and everyone said he was graceful, so he thought he'd become a dancer. Finally, he began writing poems in Russian which astonished everyone, and decided to become a poet . . .

When we were in Paris we sometimes went to Henri Langlois' cinemathèque (film archives) in the Avenue de Messine where we saw films that stirred us with moving memories: old films by Pudovkin, Dovenko and Eisenstein; Marc was not curious about modern feature films.

Marc's intuition with regard to people was not as sure as his insight into works of art. He could only have feelings for people when nothing about them interfered with his peace of mind.

He was blessed with a number of devoted friends, but he was not much interested in their problems—they had to be adoring and utterly disinterested in his wealth and position. While this was true of most of his acquaintances, the richer he grew, the more he distrusted people—even some of his most devoted friends.

But he had a way of bringing out the best in people. His gracious manner was a "fluid drive" that carried him through existence. He loathed the boorish manners of people like the painter Chaim Soutine, who refused to make social concessions—but the polished life didn't really satisfy him either, although it was a revenge for past humiliations and a mark of success. In *Ma Vie* he wrote, "I am a workman's son and when I get bored in a drawing room I feel like soiling the waxed floors." He longed for a simple life, but fame and riches made it increasingly inaccessible.

There were some gifts he gave willingly: One was his brilliant smile that tilted his eyes to an astonishing angle and lit them up with humor and tenderness and sometimes a tinge of mischief. In company he always gave of his best. Another was his generous inscribing of Chagall books for friends and acquaintances. He never refused to embellish the title page with a drawing or a watercolor. Sometimes he incorporated the printed letters into the design, thus preventing the easy sale of the work by his friends, should they fall on adversity. Some of the sketches are full of beauty. This gift had the added advantage of costing him nothing, though it was valuable. Everything that had to be bought with money seemed to him an extravagance, whereas it amused him thus to create a gift "out of nothing." He gave drawings and sketches to all his best friends and often donated works in aid of worthy causes, but if a friend wished to buy a picture, he had to pay the full price. It was a question of principle —prices must be kept high. Marc pretended not to know anything about business matters, and in the old days he always passed customers on to Bella, but it was plain that he maintained control behind the scenes. A would-be purchaser once told the story of how he saw, reflected in a mirror, a sign from Marc to Bella, indicating the price she was to ask for a picture. Now that he sent everyone to Maeght or Ida, matters were simplified.

There was one form of generosity he never practiced: He resented lending money to a friend; it went against his belief that if you lend money to a friend, he will surely become your enemy. If Ida or I ever prevailed on him to do so, his feelings for the borrower became chilly.

A complex man, Marc was full of contradictions—generous and guarded, naive and shrewd, explosive and secret, humorous and sad, vulnerable and strong.

Marc was obsessed by his desire to do large-scale religious paintings. He started repainting the big *Abraham and the Three Angels,* begun
in 1940. Next he began *Moses Receiving the Tablets of the Law* and *King
David,* both of generous proportions and based on the gouaches he
made as a preliminary to his Bible etchings. Of all the prophets,
David was nearest to his heart because he was an artist—a complex
personality with all the faults of ordinary mortals, as well as the
loftiest of virtues.

Marc ardently longed to make these paintings for a specially constructed building where their religious character would be respected.
This idea had been growing ever since he had seen Giotto in Padua
and Fra Angelico in Florence.

He began to concentrate his dreams around a little stucco chapel
in Vence, the Chapelle des Pénitents Blancs. It was painted ochre and
had a roof of glazed green tiles. It was no longer used for services but
it still belonged to the parish. The door was always locked and the
walls were growing damp. He examined the available wall space,
assessed the light sources and inspected the state of the masonry, and
when people of importance in the art world came to Vence, he took
them to see it. The diocese was duly notified of his desire to decorate
the chapel, but for months there was no progress in Marc's negotiations with the curé of Vence, however polite the latter seemed. He
had obviously received orders from the bishop of Nice to use delaying tactics.

Since Léger, a communist, had decorated the facade of the church
of Assy, and Matisse, an agnostic, had created his own chapel, there
were very few acceptable arguments against the decoration of a
moldering, unused chapel by Vence's famous citizen.

Seeing no progress in that direction, Marc became interested in
another more or less abandoned chapel in Vence, the Chapelle du
Calvaire. He even made a plan for its reconstruction and decoration,
in which each biblical painting had its symbolical place. This plan
served as a basis for the later Message Biblique, founded in 1973 in
the Cimiez section of Nice. Neither of these chapels was given to him
and Marc became embittered against the diocese.

Meanwhile, Père Couturier, a cultured and intelligent Dominican
monk, himself a painter, asked Marc to create a work for his modern
church on the Plateau d'Assy, in Haute Savoie. This is a mountain

resort of great beauty which caters to respiratory patients. Couturier particularly wanted Chagall, a Jew, to decorate the baptistry. He was captivated by one of the St. Jean gouaches, *La Madonne au Buisson,* a white virgin in a blazing bush with a great fish floating over her head. The fish, he said, was the symbol of Christ.

We went to visit Couturier's church of Notre Dame de Toute Grace. The huge Léger mosaic that decorates the whole facade gives it a theatrical air; a row of massive, rough-hewn pillars support a disproportionately fragile roof. A luscious yellow-tiled altarpiece by Matisse, a shimmering painting by Bonnard and some dark, hypnotic windows by Rouault decorate the interior. Germaine Richier's bronze crucifixion expresses the horror of decomposing flesh. A strange bronze virgin by Lipchitz bears the inscription, "Jacob Lipchitz, a Jew faithful to the religion of his ancestors, made this virgin for the good understanding of mankind upon the earth, as long as the Spirit reigns." Above the altar, Jean Lurçat's powerful tapestry gives the church a festive appearance.

Marc was impressed, and felt tempted to participate in this ensemble, but he hesitated, fearing he might feel guilty toward his fellow Jews if he agreed to decorate a baptistry.

For months he weighed the conflicting opinions of Jews and Christians, and got no nearer to his own truth. He called a meeting of Jewish notables, together with the chief rabbi of France to discuss the matter, and on the whole they seemed unopposed. Abraham Sutzkever, an old and faithful friend of Marc's who lived in Israel and with whom he corresponded regularly, came to visit him in Vence and they talked the matter over. Sutzkever seemed to have no objections either. Marc discussed the various problems with Arkady. He said he feared a priest might conduct people around the church one day and interpret his paintings in a Christian manner.

Marc even wrote to Chaim Weizmann, the president of Israel, who answered that he should act according to his own conscience and intuition, that he could give him no better advice. Arkady remembers that Marc had expected Weizmann to react to his plea for guidance by commissioning him to do mural paintings for public buildings in Israel, which he would have much preferred to decorating churches. Marc was understandably disappointed by Weizmann's lack of imagination.

Marc Chagall at his Riverside Drive apartment, New York, 1945.
Photo by Charles Leirens.

David's first photos with his mother and half-sister. Jean McNeil, High Falls, New York, 1946.

Chagall with son David in High Falls, 1947.

Chagall painting Liberation, High Falls, *1948.*
Photo by Charles Leirens.

Chagall and David in High Falls, 1948.
Photo by Charles Leirens.

High Falls, 1948.
Photo by Charles Leirens.

Chagall and Virginia in High Falls, 1948.
Photo by Charles Leirens.

Chagall and David in High Falls, 1948.
Photo by Charles Leirens.

High Falls, 1948.
Photo by Charles Leirens.

Jean and David. High Falls, 1948.

Chagall with his daughter, Ida, in the tiny village of Orgeval, near Paris. This is where he and Virginia first settled on his anxiously-awaited return to France after the war, in 1948.

Father Couturier, the Dominican monk who first approached Chagall for a work to decorate the Baptistry of his church in Haute Savoie, with Jean Cassou, the writer and director of the Museum of Modern Art (Paris) in Orgeval, 1948.

Chagall and Virginia in Venice, 1948.

James Johnson Sweeney who, as director of the Museum of Modern Art in New York organized the big retrospective exhibition of Chagall's works, visited him in Orgeval, 1949.

The journalist Max Lerner and Chagall in Orgeval, 1949.

Ida, Marguerite Lang, Chagall and Tériade, one of the two most famous avant garde art editors in Paris at that time. This photo was taken in St. Jean Cap Ferrat in the South of France, 1949.

Chagall picnicking with the children, 1949.

Arnold Rudlinger, who became director of the Kunsthalle in Bern, with the art critic Charles Estienne, Ida and Marc at Les Collines, the house Chagall and Virginia moved to in Saint Jean Cap Ferrat, 1950.

Marc with the poet, Claire Goll, in Vence, 1950.

The art critic Jacques Lassaigne, a frequent visitor in Vence, with Virginia, Marc and the children, 1950.

The poet Paul Eluard and his wife, Dominique, with Chagall in Vence, 1950.

Jean and David in front of Les Collines, 1951.

Jean, Marc, Virginia and David in Vence, 1951.
Photo by Mako.

Virginia and Chagall in Vence, 1951.
Photo by Mako.

Virginia's brother, Stephen Haggard, the late British actor, 1935.

Chagall and Virginia in Israel, 1951.

Chagall in Jerusalem, 1951.

Virginia with her father, Godfrey Haggard, and Chagall in Vence, 1951.

Chagall painting Ida's portrait. Vence, 1951.

Ida, Franz Meyer, Ida's husband, and Chagall in Vence, 1952,
the year of their marriage.

Charles Estienne, Jean, Arnold Rudlinger, Chagall, Ida, Franz Meyer, Bush Meyer Graefe and Virginia in Vence, 1952.

Chagall's good friend, the poet Jacques Prévert, dancing at the reception of Ida's marriage to Franz Meyer at Les Collines, 1952.

Charles Leirens, the Belgian photographer, at Ida's Wedding.

Chagall toasts Ida and Franz. The wedding lunch took place in Chagall's studio, where the big Circus *painting can be seen in the background.*

Chagall, Ida and Prévert at the wedding luncheon.

Chagall and Prévert dance at the wedding reception.

Chagall at the Madoura pottery works in Vallauris, 1952.

Chagall and David in Paris, 1954.
Photo by Roger Hauert.

David, Chagall and Ida with her children, Piet and the twins, Meret and Bella in
Paris, 1954.
Photo by Roger Hauert.

David sits beneath a photo of his father, surrounded by postcards of his paintings. 1954.

David with his first guitar, 1956.

Jean and David, Brussels, 1983.

I drove Couturier to Nice after a visit to Les Collines, and we discussed Marc's ambition to paint biblical murals for a religious building. I said I imagined a sort of temple where all the religions would be brought together in an all-embracing mystical philosophy. Couturier disagreed with this notion with icy politeness. As an after-note I must say that I was pleased when this very same idea was carried out in Marc's great Message Biblique Museum in Nice in 1973.

But Couturier had his way as well. In 1957 Marc finally carried out and donated to the baptistry in Assy a monumental ceramic mural representing the crossing of the Red Sea; two delicate stained glass windows and two splendid bas-reliefs in marble. Above the door he added this inscription: "Au Nom de la Liberté de Toutes les Religions" (In the Name of Freedom for all Religions).

In the spring of 1951 the bishop of Nice, thinking he ought to dispel any possible resentment, decided to call on Chagall in person when he came to Vence for a confirmation service. I received the telephone message about the bishop's visit, which I completely forgot to pass on to Marc. When the day came, we went off to the beach for a picnic with the children, and when we got back the gardener and his wife greeted us with a mixture of hilarity and awe. They said the bishop and his suite had exchanged incredulous glances—*"Ah, ces artistes!"* Marc didn't scold me; in fact, he rather enjoyed the joke.

One of my tasks was to take care of the correspondence, which I did to the best of my ability. Marc wrote in Russian and Yiddish, but his written French was so poor that my own efforts were preferable. Ida presented me with a copy of Larousse's *Le Parfait Secretaire,* but I never managed to live up to the title. I worked in a little room adjoining the studio. It looked out onto vines and tangled foliage behind the house, where frogs croaked in summer from the cisterns. Every now and then I went to see what Marc was doing. I watched him for a while, gave him a kiss and went back to my den.

It was the first time in years that I had had a room of my own, and I made it my domain, where no one could intrude upon my privacy. I started writing down ideas, reflections and observations. I saw this as a starting point for a new, more autonomous life, and I began to question other people's hitherto accepted criteria. I bought myself a large notebook with an imitation leather binding and Marc drew me an angel on the cover—"to give me wings"—and advised me to write in ink because "only ink gives rise to permanent things," but it was precisely the permanence of ink that made me feel inadequate. As for the angel, I was so intent on being worthy of it that I tore out page after page, until only the cover remained.

I found Rosa, a merry Italian housekeeper whose husband worked all week 'n the mountains, digging highway tunnels. Rosa took a liking to us all, especially to David, who kept her constantly amused. When she climbed up to Les Collines in the morning, I could see her head bobbing in and out of the mimosa and the laurel. She had the youthfulness of a schoolgirl, even though her round, good-natured face was covered with a fine network of wrinkles.

Marc wanted a vegetable garden and I found a big, handsome man named Alexandre, who undertook the task of growing vegetables. He had the meridional's laziness, and the cunning to get away with it. He ordered a large collection of tools, many of which disappeared unaccountably, but he had such charm and kindness that it seemed ungracious to criticize. Marc tended to be suspicious, even when there were no grounds, so I was careful not to give Alexandre away. Besides being a talented gardener, he was also an excellent driver and handyman, and I felt we could well afford to contribute a few tools to his well-being. The vegetables grew so abundantly (there are no Japanese beetles in France) that he and I were soon able to give away large quantities to our neighbors. Marc made a tour of inspection every now and then, and whenever he saw rotting tomatoes he complained that they had cost him a fortune.

I had the basement made into an apartment for Alexandre, his wife and their three-year-old boy, and whenever we went away they cared for Jean and David with devoted affection. Thus our frequent absences were not too keenly felt.

During this period I made photographs of all the new paintings and mounted them in an album with titles, dates and dimensions. This cataloguing had never been done before, and although my photographic efforts were poor, they were sufficient for identification. Little did I imagine that one day I would become a professional photographer!

I had dozens of small sketches, drawings and watercolors mounted by a couple of young artists and put away safely in big portfolios.

These works of small dimensions, often of great beauty, had been hitherto piled up in helter-skelter fashion.

In the big downstairs studio, which was used for mounting, framing and storage, I taught the children modeling in clay and painting in oils, and with the help of Alexandre we made a marionette theater. When my sister Joan came to stay in a *pension* in Vence with her husband and four children, our art classes expanded. Marc always enjoyed having members of the family around him; they were all there to make his life pleasant and he was charming to everyone. Sometimes he came downstairs to inspect the children's work and give them advice; it reminded him of the orphan children he had taught in the Malachovska children's settlement during the revolution. "They were ill-clad and famished," he recalled, "and they seized hold of the paint as if it were meat." The single-mindedness of the children and their passionate fervor fascinated him. Without doubt they influenced his work.

David's paintings were explosions. "I'll draw a picture of thunder. The thunder is Papa and the moon is Mama, who feeds the little stars. Then I'll make a picture of Belle [the neighbor's cow who was butchered]. She's going up to heaven in a nest." The cows butchered by Marc's grandfather also went to heaven. Marc wrote, "And you, little cow, naked and crucified, you dream in the sky." Marc's images, whether written or painted, were very close to a child's vivid world.

Jean turned the playroom into a stage. Its frosted glass doors, pasted with children's drawings, served as curtains. When lighted from behind, they glowed like stained glass. A backdrop for *Le Corbeau et la Renard* (The Crow and the Fox) had a cutout transparent moon with a candle flickering behind it, and a tree on which the crow (David) was perched, with a large piece of cheese in his mouth. By the time the words *"ouvre large son bec, laisse tomber sa proie"* (opened wide his beak and let fall his prey) were pronounced, most of the cheese was gone.

We had an old magic lantern that projected any picture that was placed under it, and the children fed it with picture shows of their own invention. Marc enjoyed these immensely.

Vence was full of old people and who had come to end their lives in this sunny place; two such people, both well over eighty, were good friends of mine. Edward Gordon Craig, the son of the great English actress Ellen Terry, himself a famous actor, producer and especially designer and theorist of dramatic art, had come to settle in a modest *pension,* but he was bored and lonely. He and Marc were not drawn to each other, for Craig had become somewhat misanthropic and his remarks about people were often sarcastic. But he was delightful to children and meek, anonymous people like myself. With his once stately figure, now stooped and slow, his silver hair, his handsome nose protruding from under his flat broad-brimmed hat, he had become a familiar sight to the townspeople of Vence. He shuffled along the streets in his black corduroy trousers, trodden down at the heel; his eyes were piercing and truculent. He never spoke of the past, he was only interested in the present. He complained of the way that old and famous people were always being thrust back into their past.

My other friend, Aglet, aged eighty-five, agreed with him. She was Baroness Von Hutton, author of the "Pam" novels that were much loved by schoolgirls. She was entertaining and eccentric and owed her longevity and excellent health to her doctor's prescription: a glass of milk in the morning with two cloves of raw garlic grated into it, and in the evening half a bottle of champagne. Sometimes I joined her for a glass of champagne on the cream-colored veranda of her old-fashioned hotel, under festoons of potted ferns. When her husband, the famous actor Henry Ainley, took to drinking heavily, she divorced him and married a German baron. Her actor-son, Richard Ainley, was also one of my most steadfast friends; his generosity and tolerance were a rampart during the difficult years in England and America. He was John McNeil's friend, the only one who never completely gave him up during the difficult years we were together. Richard had served in the U.S. forces during the war and was wounded in the head on the German front. He recovered enough to continue acting, although his arm was paralyzed and he had to wear a brace on his leg. Now he came to Vence to visit his temperamental mother, his old friend Craig and me. Two other friends joined the octogenerians occasionally: Count Michel Karolyi, first president of the Republic of Hungary, a great champion of freedom, and his wife Catherine, known as the Red Countess. Catherine's fight for women's rights following World War I brought her out of the privileged class into the open struggle, leading her to care for lunatics and delinquent children and to play an important part in Michel's brilliant and hazardous career. Their life was full of astonishing feats, mad defiance of danger and confidence in justice. They settled in Vence and created the Karolyi Foundation, which gave young artists and writers an opportunity to live and work, for a time, in peace and security.

After our shopping, Jean Darquet's wife, Ziazi, and I would sometimes meet for a cafe créme on the Grand Place. We were close friends and confidantes, and we gave each other moral support. Sometimes she was short of money, but I couldn't lend her any. Marc gave me neither a banking account, nor housekeeping money. I had to ask for money whenever I needed it and explain what I wanted it for. I got all the food on credit and he paid at the end of the month, a practice which undoubtably cost him double, for the tradesmen were not always above a little "arranging." Curiously, he trusted them more than me! Perhaps he thought I would be tempted to give money away to people in need. Taking checks for Marc to sign was always an ordeal; he invariably grumbled and scolded.

It began to weigh on me to have to ask for every penny I spent. I had no autonomy. When I was earning miserable wages, at least they were mine to spend as I wished, but this was something Marc could not understand. He reminded me repeatedly that he had saved me from poverty and given me inestimable material benefits, and of course I was grateful for these, but there were other things on which I set a higher price—freedom and independence. However, it was impossible to explain this to him. If I had been more mature, I could have insisted on this independence, and he would have had to give in.

He wanted me to wear fine clothes and he told his friends, with a note of pride, how undemanding I was because I preferred simple ones. But if I asked for a raise for Alexandre and Jeannette he refused, saying that he couldn't be sure he would be selling any pictures next year. When I reminded him that he probably had enough in the bank for at least twenty years, he replied that riches were no guarantee against ruination, that he was brought up in a poor family, and his father had taught him the real value of money. With characteristic paradox he would declare, "One can't afford to be poor these days."

In fact, he had been making considerable profits lately, and he instructed Ida to make investments. While he recognized that works of art were excellent investments, he wanted only his own. Stocks were uncertain, so Ida bought two bars of gold and an immense cut diamond. She asked me if I wished to wear the diamond on a ring, and I laughed: "Can you see me wearing a diamond?" It was put in the safe, together with the bars of gold and several of Marc's important pictures. The latter were wrapped in blankets, in an effort to console them for having to live in a cold, dark vault. We carried them reverently into their mausoleum in the Credit Lyonnais on the Boulevard des Italiens in Paris, where Picasso also kept his pictures.

Marc feared I would never become a worthy guardian of his possessions because I had no respect for money, but he still hoped I might change with the years. One day he announced that he had made out his will and left all his possessions in three equal parts to Ida, David and me. I was moved by this gesture, but I had a vague, inexplicable feeling that I would never touch that money. Here I was back in the privileged class again, and I felt concerned. Marc had the same lack of concern for the underprivileged as my parents; he wouldn't accept the view that fortunate people owed something to those who were needy.

Soon after we moved to Les Collines, Marc made friends with Serge Ramel, a potter who worked on the Place du Peyra (where the enormous tree, with its circular bench, had been painted by Soutine). Ramel was the great-nephew of Ingres. He was not only a man of intelligence but a sound and sensitive craftsman as well. He taught Marc the rudiments of ceramics, following his whims and fantasies with such respect that every new piece was an exciting discovery for them both. Clearly they were on the same wavelength: Ramel sensed instinctively the effects Marc wanted to obtain, although Marc had not yet acquired sufficient familiarity with the capricious medium.

Under Serge Ramel's guidance Marc produced a number of exquisite pieces. His first attempts were some oval dishes. Next he made a series of ceramic plaques that had a richer texture, made of reddish clay mixed with "*chamotte*" (a coarse, granulated substance) and colored partly with a transparent glaze, partly with thick, brilliant opaque touches. These pieces, such as *David and Bathsheba, Woman with Bouquet* (inspired by a gouache for which I posed) and an extraordinary crucifixion all had the glowing mysterious quality of icons. Later he directed Ramel in the construction of sculptured ceramic vases, which he finished off himself with detail and color. Little by little, these became freer and more elaborate. One of them was a crouching nude. When Serge carried it away to the kiln, Marc ran after him with a brush.

"Vous permettez?" he asked.

"Je vous en prie!" said Serge, and Marc put two pink spots on the breasts.

Serge was delighted with his pupil, in spite of his fidgeting and fussing. Marc said, "If you had a lot of pupils like me, you'd become pregnant!"

Another time, Marc went on elaborating an already beautiful plaque with needless detail. Serge called out: "Chagall, Chagall, *arrêtez!"* and Marc stopped obediently.

Whenever we came into the workroom, Serge would throw up his arms in jovial greeting. *"Ah, bonjour!"* He would offer us each a little finger to shake, because his hands were plastered with clay. We spent many good times eating and drinking together. Once we drove to the town of Seillants to see a famous altarpiece. Serge went to the curé's house to ask for admission to the church; the curé was a small man with a black beard, surprisingly resembling one of the rabbis in a Chagall painting. He seemed very preoccupied and in a great hurry; he had just brought back the butcher's bicycle to repair. Evidently the butcher's wife was ill and he had many more duties to fulfill. Serge asked him if we could see the altarpiece.

"Impossible," the curé cried, "there's a procession in the next village today and they're all waiting for me."

Serge insisted politely, "I have come from Vence with a famous painter who has very little time."

"I'm sorry, *cher* monsieur, it's really impossible, I'm late already."

Serge refused to give up. "Chagall would like so much to see the altarpiece."

"Chagall?" said the curé. "Chagall here? Oh, in that case, God will just have to wait."

It is not generally known that Marc worked with this talented artisan. His modesty was such that their collaboration has been more or less wiped from the records.

It was thanks to Serge Ramel that Marc had the courage to go and work with Ramié at the Madoura pottery works in Vallauris, Picasso's private hunting ground. There is an amusing story told by Jean Paul Crespelle in his book on Chagall.* Picasso came one morning to Vallauris and found Marc hard at work. His presence upset Marc so that he went off for a "breath of fresh air." When Marc came back, the plate he was about to work on was decorated with a beautiful "Chagall." He couldn't have done better himself!

Doing sculptured vases gave Marc an urge to do real sculpture. On his walks he often stopped to watch his neighbor, an Italian marble cutter whose yard was opposite the entrance to Les Collines. Marc was fascinated by the blocks of glistening marble that stood in his yard, the slabs of blue granite and the rough yellow sandstone. He began to imagine beasts and trees and lovers. He drew forms in pencil on the blocks, then instructed the marble cutter on how to chisel them out. He did this remarkably well, getting to feel more each day what Marc was driving at. Thus, they completed a series of bas-reliefs. The figures were pleasing and graceful, but somehow they still remained imprisoned in the stone. Then Marc began a series of more elaborate stele forms, and the figures came to life. He did little of the chiseling himself, only adding details, once the main shapes had been rough-hewn from the blocks. The two bas-reliefs in marble, which he did some years later for the baptistry of the Church of Assy, are among the most successful of his sculptures.

I have never read any mention of this humble marble cutter who introduced Marc to sculpture. He has been forgotten, like Serge Ramel.

Sometimes Marc would visit the Matisse chapel on his morning walks. He admired its pure simplicity and its delicate coloring. The handsome windows, especially, pleased him and he began to wonder what he might do himself in that medium. Little did he imagine at

*Chagall, l'Amour, le Rêve et la Vie. Jean Paul Crespelle. Presses de la Cité, Paris, 1969.

that time what masterly works he would one day create in stained glass—the windows for Metz, Reims, Jerusalem and the Message Biblique, among others.

Marc's palette was a thing of beauty, its tone surprisingly delicate. It looked more like a Turner color scheme than a Chagall one. He sometimes used color fresh and pure from the tube, and blended it with others on the canvas. He used paint tubes down to the last smear, cutting them open with scissors so as not to lose anything. When the pots of gouache were completely dry, there was still a crust at the bottom that a little water could soften. He usually gave the pots to the children when a new lot arrived from Lefèvre Foinet, exciting him with their inviting smell, the color oozing out from under their lids. But weeks later, wandering around the children's room in search of their paintings, he would come across the old pots and carry them off again, much to their amusement.

One day Marc flew into a rage with an awning merchant whom he accused of charging too much for a handmade awning for his big studio window. I thought the price was very reasonable and interceded on the man's behalf. Marc, furious, flung his palette at the man. He ducked just in time and the palette alighted neatly, like a flying saucer; it was not even cracked. Even when he was in a rage, Marc instinctively protected his precious materials.

In the summer of 1950 we spent a couple of weeks in Gordes with Ida and Géa, in the beautiful seventeenth-century stone schoolhouse which had been lying abandoned for so many years. Ida had restored the tall shutters, the fireplace and the school bell in its gable. The walls had been preserved, sound and dry, by the scorching sun. Marc was apprehensive about going back there again, for it was in Gordes that he and Bella had spent their last happy year together before leaving for America.

Now Marc fell under the charm of the quiet village again. The sun beat down furiously on the smoldering walls and the crickets chirped deliriously. The children ran wild with their friends in the streets of this superb, half-ruined village; it had been a prosperous shoemaking center until industry made it obsolete. After a few days, Marc's sadness evaporated in the wholesome air. The studio was still the same, with its cool tiled floor and its long tables, and he spread out his sheets of paper, eager to set down impressions of rugged well-being and permanence.

As usual, Ida's crowd of faithful friends arrived, and there were rowdy and joyful meals in country taverns. Ida was not made for living tête-à-tête, and her company was much sought after.

One visitor in Gordes was Willem Sandberg, the dynamic, avant-garde designer, director of the Stedelijk Museum in Amsterdam, who had organized a Chagall retrospective in 1947, after the one in Paris. He carried his sixty-odd years with astonishing youthfulness, and wore his silver hair in a nonchalant mop. Charles Estienne also came, he was preparing a book on Marc for the French publisher Somogy. Together we rambled over the dry, stony countryside, climbing up to castles and rocky villages that sailed on blue seas of lavender.

In October, 1950, we drove to Bergamo for an international exhibition of drawings in the beautiful Palazzo della Regione. Ida joined us there with Géa and an American couple and we all went to Verona, Venice and Florence. Again we were carried away by the feeling of lightness and well-being that we had felt before in Italy, the sense of limitless potential and the spirit of adventure. But Marc was also moved by the extraordinary peace of Angelico, lost in thoughts about the virtues of a monk's life. "He had walls to paint," said Marc with envy, "and no worries." The Medici Chapel, the Ufizzi and the Pitti Palace were so full of staggering impressions that he was silent most of the time, digesting the Titians, Ucellos and Mantegnas, impressed rather than moved by the Michelangelos, and more than ever lost in wonder at the Tintorettos.

Traveling with Marc was exceedingly pleasant; these were some of our best times together. We gave each other more attention, and Marc was always gay and more loving. At home he was always at work, and I was always on the move. The phone calls and visitors had doubled in the last year.

For a nervous man, he was surprisingly relaxed and confident when I drove him; he abandoned himself to the motorcar, that wondrous monster, scribbling or gazing dreamily at the landscape, and his eyes saw things that were in his own mind, visions that the changing landscape revealed. His sketch pad filled up with rough ideas for compositions; sometimes there were remarks in Russian, observations, color notes.

When we stopped somewhere to have a meal, he went off to the nearest butcher shop to find out what was the best and most advantageous restaurant. The method was infallible, and I personally never had cause for regret, but as we continued our journey he would see several other restaurants that looked better still. He seemed always to be pursued by an unconscious feeling of dissatisfaction. When he sat before his meal in his chosen restaurant, he couldn't help looking over to the other tables to see what his neighbors were eating, often regretting his choice.

Marc's curiosity was endless. He enjoyed stopping to look in all the shop windows, but he would usually turn away, shrug his shoulders and say, "I have no money." One of his rules was never to enter a shop if the shopkeeper was standing at the door. It was a sure sign the man had no customers.

In some lonely place in Tuscany, the fan belt on our car broke and enormous clouds of steam rose from the radiator. I wondered what on earth to do, but Marc was not at all anxious. The steam was pouring out in impressive billows and he was enjoying the sight. By chance, a peasant was working in a nearby field and he came up to us with a radiant smile. He made us understand that he would fix the belt for us. He brought it back half an hour later, perfectly mended, and refused to be paid for it. I can still see his small dark eyes, amused by our relief and gratitude, and the deep verticle furrows on his cheeks.

There was one superstitious habit Marc had which he bade me observe along with him. Before departing on a journey we always had to sit down for one minute. As we took off, he would heave a sigh of satisfaction and expectation, mixed with a slight apprehension that would only disappear once we were well on our way.

Marc maintained that an artist had a right to be an egotist, because his work was too exacting to permit his considering other peoples' feelings. Of course a certain dose of egotism is necessary to guard against the wasting of one's time by other egotists, but that precisely is what he often failed to do. Other egotists took advantage of the flaws in his armor, but those who cared for him and tried to protect him received little gratitude. No one should stand in the way of an artist, but neither should one lie prostrate in his path to be walked over.

Jung wrote, "An artist is the instrument of his work and subordinate to it. . . . The artist is not a person endowed with free will who seeks his own ends, but one who allows art to realize its ends *through* him. . . . A person must pay dearly for the divine gift of creative fire." Jung doesn't say that others must pay dearly as well, but this seems often to be the case.

An artist's companion (if the artist is a man) has to be herself totally, she must be strong and autonomous; only then can she coexist in harmony with an artist. But all too often she is effaced and frustrated, as I was. Ideally, she should serve his art without being subservient to it; she should have her own life as well. The *"veuve abusive"* is one who played a disappointing role in an artist's life and failed to be anything on her own. The *"muse abusive"* is one who possesses the artist through the protection she gives him, and plays a dominant role. Both fail to develop their lives in a truly autonomous fashion.

An artist's companion in the role of a disinterested protector is more necessary than ever, because the artist is constantly in danger of being harmed by a ruthless system of speculation. But his own voracious ambition can harm him as well, and no one can protect him from that.

Marc pursued riches, and thought that he was acquiring freedom. But freedom is elusive—if one tried to grasp it too tightly it seeps away unnoticed, like grain from a worn sack.

I was too immature to avoid being crushed by the weight of the formidable establishment that Marc's life was becoming. I had no freedom to experiment; no way to search for a personal identity. Marc was settling down at last, beginning to accumulate a vast fortune (only Ida knew how much) and acquire an immense reputation, but I didn't feel at all like settling down. Gone were our bohemian days. Chagall had become a grand person, very much in the public eye. Ida seemed also to have turned against the more happy-go-lucky attitude of Géa. She became more conscious of her public role, and sought to promote her standing. Soon I would also have to live up to certain standards expected of Marc's companion, and I felt I would not be able to do so. Invisible barriers were beginning to grow up around me; I was being gently and imperceptibly forced into a mold. Even Jean was having her role mapped out for her, and soon it would be David's turn. I felt we had a right to be unpredictable. I wanted to be with people who were not conditioned in some way by success, people for whom money was nothing more than a necessary commodity, who dared to question accepted rules of behavior. Marc, for all his seemingly free lifestyle, was not liberated.

During the summer of 1950 I made friends with a group of young people who answered to this description. They lived in a big house in Roquefort-les-Pins. A handsome couple with emancipated ideas lived in a trailer on the wooded grounds. They had a young poet friend who was convalescing from severe tuberculosis. A strong empathy grew up between us. The poet owed his spectacular cure, after years of medical bungling, to the natural therapeutic methods practiced by the owner of the house, and he felt deeply indebted for this, but he disliked the owner's sectarian ideas. The latter had married a naive rich girl who believed implicitly in his moral superiority. They were strict vegetarians, and even their dog was allowed no meat. When their baby was born, they considered him a superior specimen, a sort of baby Jesus, because he was being brought up in strict observance of all their principles. The owner's little girl by a first marriage came to feel that, however hard she tried, she would never be quite up to scratch. She was treated with charitable indifference, and the rest of us tried to give her the affection she lacked. Jean found in her an echo of her own jealousy of David and they became good friends.

I was impressed by the young poet's remarkable cure, and began to learn some of the nature-cure methods. Marc began to have symptoms of prostate trouble and I urged him to try a cure, but he was skeptical. I, in turn, was full of mistrust for orthodox medicine, having seen the havoc wrought by it, especially in the case of my young friend. I tried to reform Marc's diet, hoping it would have a favorable effect, but Marc was recalcitrant. I believe vegetarianism appealed to something puritanical in my nature, instilled perhaps by my Protestant upbringing. This may explain my occasional attraction to this form of asceticism, which was in contradiction to my naturally fun-loving nature. Happily, the latter has supplanted the former, and

I sympathize with my family for having had to put up with my fads.

Marc went to Roquefort-les-Pins several times and seemed to take a liking to my three young friends. When he went to Paris to work on his lithographs, I would stay there with the children; at last I could give them my undivided attention. The rocks and pines suggested by the name of the village were real and as yet unspoiled, and there were narrow paths winding through needle-strewn hummocks. An icy brook of pure mountain water tossed itself into a dark secluded pool, and on hot days we stripped and dived in, oblivious of bathing suits. Needless to say Marc knew nothing of the latter—he would have been shocked!

In November of 1950 we sent one hundred and forty-eight paintings to Zurich for a retrospective exhibition at the Kunsthaus, the biggest show yet of Chagall's work, but the house was empty and cheerless without the paintings. Marc was not able to go to Zurich, for shortly afterward he entered a clinic in Nice for a prostate operation in two stages. Ida flew to Nice to be with him, then flew to Zurich for the opening. The clinic was an old-fashioned place, but Marc had a pleasant room. The doctor thankfully had a good sense of humor and knew how to handle his overly sensitive patient. The humiliating and painful examinations were dispatched with speed and reassuring good humor, followed by absorbing conversations on the arts. The whole process took two months in those days, and Marc, rather than return home between the two operations, preferred to stay at the clinic. I slept in his room for the whole period.

Marc showed a dogged patience throughout the ordeal, bearing everything with grim determination. He never smiled and rarely talked, as if he were keeping all his strength bottled up, ready to let loose as soon as he got back to work. He had a piteous expression all through these two months, even though the physical discomfort was far from intolerable. He was completely wrapped up in himself and uncommunicative, and the warm contact between us suffered. I read to him a lot—a life of Mozart, some classics: *Le Rouge et le Noir* and *Eugénie Grandet,* as well as books on Velasquez and Tintoretto. After this operation his health became remarkably good, and as soon as he was back at work his good humor returned.

Shortly after Marc's operation, the children, too, underwent minor surgery—for tonsils and adenoids. I was carrying Jean from the car,

wrapped in a sheet with bloodstains on it, and Marc happened to
come down the steps of his studio. When he saw the pale little girl
in my arms, he wept with emotion. He was profoundly upset by the
sight of physical suffering.

Jean was now eleven and attended a boy's secondary school simply
because there was no other *lycée* in Vence. She seemed unconcerned
about being the only girl in the school. Marc was proud of her good
grades, and began to plan her future as guardian and curator of his
works. In short, he saw her as yet another mother to eventually care
for him devotedly. In the meantime, though, she had to remain
obedient and predictable, which in fact she did.

In March, 1951, we went with Ida to Bern where Franz Meyer, the
director of the Kunsthalle there, exhibited one hundred and thirty-
five of the works shown the year before in Zurich. At the Zurich
exhibition, Ida had become friendly with Meyer and his friend and
colleague Arnold Rudlinger, who wrote the preface to the catalogue.
Meyer was later appointed director of the Kunsthalle in Basel (where
he is to this day) and Rudlinger succeeded him in Bern. Ida and Géa
had separated, and we guessed that something new was in the air.

It was the first time that I had seen some of the important early
pictures from Germany and Switzerland, and it was a joy to be in
Marc's presence when he greeted his beloved children after so many
years. He stroked each picture lovingly, feeling the texture to see if
the paint was holding well, then he appraised it critically, his head
on one side. Then he said softly (so that only I could hear) *"Ça c'est
un bon tableau, un tableau magnifique!"* and he laughed with pleasure.

Here was the daring *Hommage à Apollinaire,* one of his greatest meta-
phorical paintings. In the center of a disk or clock dial is a double
figure of Adam and Eve—two bodies sprouting from one pair of legs.
It has the magic of Robert Delaunay's color wheels with mysterious,
metaphysical ramifications.

When Marc first went to Paris he was struck by the freshness and
candor of Delaunay, who became his close friend (the only close
painter friend he had, beside André Llhote). But Delaunay's Orphism
was not for him, nor was any other "ism." He fled from them all—
expressionism, Cubism, Futurism, surrealism— but he was not insen-
sitive to some of their qualities, those of Cubism especially.

Another great painting was the *Self-Portrait with Seven Fingers* (again the magical number), a powerfully fantastic painting, high in color and solidly constructed out of five elements: the painter, his palette, Paris, Vitebsk and, on the easel, the painting *To Russia, Asses and Others,* which is today in the Musée national d'Art moderne in Paris. *Golgotha* was also there, a crucifixion scene in brilliant colors, showing Christ as a baby and his parents under the cross. It has staggering intensity and vigor, and the richness of an icon or a stained-glass window. Marc wrote in *Ma Vie:* "Perhaps my art is completely mad, like flaming mercury." It is interesting to compare this "mad" painting with the *White Crucifixion,* painted in 1939. The latter resorts to story-telling to get its message across, whereas *Golgotha* has the visionary quality of a legend.

Marc returned to Paris, where his lithographic work with Mourlot was going full swing. Ida was glad to have her father all to herself. They were seeing more and more of each other these days. She enjoyed organizing lunches and dinners with the elite of artistic circles in Paris, and "Papochka" did everything she wanted.

Marc wrote me:

> Idochka is about to leave for Israel for the opening of my exhibition and everything turns around her like the planets around the sun. One hundred seventy-nine works are to be shown in Tel Aviv, Jerusalem, Haifa and Ein Harod—a great event! I have been invited for a month's visit in June, my first official visit to the State of Israel!"

He took it for granted that I would accompany him, but I shrank from the idea of an official visit. I dislike ceremony, and I feared that in Israeli eyes I would appear inadequate as the companion of their greatest Jewish painter. But Marc insisted. Perhaps I seemed rather too drawn by my new friends in Roquefort-les-Pins, and he preferred not to leave me behind. But he also wanted me to be with him to share this exceptional experience. I was touched by his unreserved desire to introduce me, his goy companion, into official Israeli circles.

I left the children in Roquefort during our month of absence. From Marseilles we took an Israeli boat that carried only a few passengers; we were given a luxurious suite and ate at the captain's table. Six days later we arrived in Tel Aviv and were met by Mokady (I don't recall his first name), the minister of culture, with whom we immediately struck a good rapport. He spoke French with ease and, being a painter himself, made a perfect companion for Marc during the month's visit.

I must have felt rather disconnected, for the whole trip seemed unreal to me, fascinating but strange, as if it were happening to someone else. My mind was elsewhere. Yet the kindness that greeted us was warm and real, and there was an informal atmosphere everywhere we went. Jews are blessed with immediate switching-on facilities, ordinary problems of communication are eliminated. Everyone spoke to me in English, and communication was simple and direct. The Israelis have a refreshing eagerness, an exhilarating desire to get rid of old conventions. They welcomed me as if I were one of them; they gave me a Bible in Hebrew for David, a photo album for Jean with a picture of the Wailing Wall and several other gifts. And yet I couldn't help feeling I was there on false pretenses. What could I give them in return? Marc was slightly reserved with all these exuberant people, who welcomed him not only with enthusiastic admiration, but with unbounded affection. The Israelis sought to lure this illustrious son of the Jewish people; he was their figurehead and they needed his support and prestige. Moshe Sharret, the foreign minister, offered him a splendid home in Haifa and living expenses, if he would come to Israel for a month or two every year. Marc said nothing but nodded gratefully, melting all those sensitive hearts with his wonderful smile. No wonder they felt let down when, a year or so later, he had to disappoint them.

Marc knew that fidelity to Israel had to be unconditional. They were an all-or-nothing people; they had fought for their lives and survived. But Marc was cautious, he wanted to stay in everyone's good graces and France came uppermost—that's where his art would be considered universal. He didn't want to be branded a Jewish artist, and for the Israelis this was treachery.

We saw the famous *Dybbuk,* played in Hebrew by the actors of the Russian Habimah theater, who had settled in Israel. Golda Meir was sitting next to Marc, and they conversed in Yiddish. I was immensely impressed by the beauty of this play, of which I understood so little; perhaps that added to its mystery and spurred my imagination. But I also saw it with Marc's eyes—it was one of his strongest theatrical experiences, and he often sang snatches of the haunting music. Once, in High Falls, after a good dinner with the Opatoshus and plenty of wine, he danced the bride's dance from the wedding scene of the *Dybbuk,* twirling a table napkin over his head.

As it turned out, the leading actors were friends of his and he was moved to see them again. But his old friend Michoels, who had been for years the leading actor of the Habimah theater in Moscow, was not among them; he had probably been murdered by the K.G.B. in Minsk in 1947. Marc had last seen him in New York in 1946, a few months before his death with another close friend of Moscow days, the poet Itzik Feffer. Marc had given them two pictures to present to the Tretiakov Gallery, two gouaches entitled *Burning Village* and *Mother and Child,* both painted in 1943. They were refused by the Tretiakov, and after the death of Michoels, his widow sold them to the great Greek-Russian art collector, George Kostakis, who took them with him to Athens. Kostakis was granted permission to leave Russia on condition that he leave half of his collection behind. One year after the death of Michoels, Feffer was accused of conspiring against the Soviet state with a group of Jewish intellectuals, and executed.

Of Michoels, Marc writes in *Ma Vie:*

> Often he came and stood near me, his eyes and forehead prominent, his hair disheveled, short nose, thick lips. He followed my thought, preceded it, and with his arms and legs at right angles, hit on the essential. Unforgettable! He looked at my paintings, borrowed my sketches. He wanted to become intimate with them, try and understand them. He said: "That has made me change my character. From now on I know how to use my body, my movements, my speech in a different way. Everybody looks at me and no one understands what has happened."

Sadly, Marc and his friends recalled the death of Michoels, Feffer and others, the death of Bella, too. Countless deaths, for not a single Israeli had been spared the death of some loved one during the tragic war years.

Marc found many old friends who had greeted him and Bella on their first trip to Palestine in 1931, when he was working on the Bible etchings for Vollard. Abraham Sutzkever, the Yiddish poet, editor of *Die Goldene Keyt (The Golden Chain),* a literary quarterly to which Marc contributed poems and drawings many times over the years, was one of his oldest friends. They had first met in Vilna where Marc and Bella had gone in 1935, before Sutzkever emigrated to Israel. He was one of the rare friends with whom Marc was perfectly in tune. A much younger man than Marc, he was adoring and faithful through thick and thin. To Marc, Sutzkever was a link with his Yiddish past. They wrote each other innumerable letters. Marc's letters are quoted in Sidney Alexander's extensive and masterly book on Chagall:*

> More than once I thought to myself: If only I could run off to my small but deeply loved land to live out my years near you and breathe the air of real people. . . . The older one gets, the more one is drawn to the source. I am envious of you—you are in the land."

Needless to say Marc had no desire whatever to go and live in Israel.

Sutzkever came to visit Marc in Vence in 1950, and they would go off together for hours. I had little contact with Sutzkever—perhaps he felt I was an intruder; no doubt he missed Bella. After all, I was a goy, I spoke no Yiddish, and I knew nothing firsthand of the past he shared with Marc. He squared Marc's conscience with regard to Bella by being slightly aloof with me.

He reassured Marc about his work for the church; everything Marc did met with his approval. He knew and understood little about painting, but that didn't matter, he understood Marc's poetical mind.

Sutzkever fought to preserve Yiddish in a country where it was doomed to disappear, and came up against a great deal of opposition in the process. He supported Marc unconditionally through the various disagreements he had with the Israelis in the following years, first because of the important work he was doing for the church, and later due to Marc's anger at the unacceptable manner in which his superb stained-glass windows were placed in the graceless and awkward building of the Hadassah Hospital in Jerusalem. Sutzkever's friendship was like an oasis to Marc, and on this particular trip he was happy to meet up with his old friend.

Mokady and his wife showed us around from one end of the country to the other. We visited several kibbutzim; Nazareth (where Marc sketched in the primitive streets, peopled almost entirely by Arabs); the incomparable Galilee, beautiful but stifling and oppres-

---

Marc Chagall. Putnam's, New York, 1978 and Cassell, London, 1978.

sive; St. Jean d'Acre, the crusader town; and the impressive excava-
tions at Caesarea. The heat was tremendous, and we were urged to
eat salt herring, olives and salty cheese for our breakfast, to make us
drink and replace the moisture we lost in perspiration. Marc was in
great form and took the heat and subsequent fatigue in his stride. In
Jerusalem we climbed up the Tower of David, the only point from
which the dazzling old town is visible, and Marc made rapid drawings, stirred with emotion. Jordanian Arabs controlled half of Jerusalem at that time, and beyond the green strip of no-man's-land we saw
the gigantic old walls, where Arab soldiers stood ready to shoot at
the slightest alarm.

We attended the funeral of an Israeli writer, a simple and moving
gathering without any ritual whatever, and I was impressed by the
fact that true feeling had taken the place of the usual empty formality
of religious funerals.

We visited the army headquarters of Moshe Dayan and dined with
Golda Meir, Moshe Sharret and David Ben-Gurion. The latter was
jovial and straightforward. He told Marc that he had not been to see
his exhibition in the Museum of Jerusalem, which had been opened
by President Chaim Weizmann. He didn't understand a thing about
painting, he said, and Marc must forgive him. He spent the years of
his youth hewing stone to make roads for Israel; he was a true sabra.
But in literature, he said, he was not so ignorant. His favorite author
was Plato.

The last visit of the trip was reserved for Chaim Weizmann, brilliant disciple of Herzl, who obtained from Lord Balfour the famous
declaration, in exchange for services rendered to Britain as a scientist
during World War I. Speaking in French, he recalled the letter Marc
had written him a year earlier, asking his advice on the question of
whether he should do works of art for churches. Weizmann repeated
his answer: Personally he had no objection whatsoever, it was a
matter between Marc and his conscience. But Marc insisted: "My
conscience has no objection either, but I don't want to be misunderstood by the Jews. What I would love best of all is to do mural
paintings for Israel." Weizmann nodded approvingly but nothing
came of this hint, which Marc repeated constantly over the years.
Marc donated a large picture *Jew with Dreaming Cow* to the Knesset, and
it was hanging there when we went in, but he never received an

official acknowledgment of the gift. It was several years later, in 1961, that he made the stained-glass windows for the synagogue of the Hadassah Hospital in Jerusalem, and donated the tapestries and mosaics to the Knesset. The Hadassah windows are the only works Chagall has ever made for a Jewish religious building. The law against the representation of the human figure obliged him to resort to symbolic and abstract forms, which give the windows great strength and beauty, although unfortunately the building is unworthy of them. But many of his works are a reminder of a world the sabras are anxious to forget—the ghetto life of the Russian Pale of Settlement which for Marc was full of highly significant memories —and perhaps this partly explains why the Israelis were not in a hurry to commission works. But whatever the reason, they had little justification in criticizing him for decorating churches, as some did.

The opening of Marc's exhibition at the Tel Aviv Museum was a great event for the Israelis. The museum already possessed a few Chagalls and Marc promised the curator to donate something toward the "Chagall room." Outstretched hands and smiles greeted him on all sides, and he responded with exuberance. His face was bronzed like a sabra's and his half-moon smile was all the more dazzling. Openings were among the best moments of his life; unlike some artists, for whom the quicker they are over the better. Marc really believed the compliments. He knew the value of his work, and the more people expressed their admiration, the happier he became. His legendary doubts were more on a metaphysical level.

In Jerusalem we stayed at the King David Hotel. During the war, it had been a center for Allied officers and war correspondents, and my brother Stephen had stayed there when he was sent on missions by the Department of Political Warfare in Cairo. From the King David, he set out on his last journey in 1943, at the age of thirty-two.

Stephen and I had been estranged for years owing to my marriage to John (whom he hated), but he had written me a long affectionate letter of reconciliation shortly before he died. Thoughts of Stephen clouded my mind, making me even more absent throughout our travels.

On our way back from Israel, we first stopped in Italy to visit Pompeii. Marc was filled with excitement and wonder; he made rapid sketches from the mural paintings and stuffed them into his pockets.

He always had to register powerful impressions immediately. During the whole trip, Marc and I had had very little warm contact. He seemed ever so slightly distant, and I didn't know if it was unconscious or intentional. Perhaps he felt that I was beginning to disconnect, since I was choosing my own friends; but he said nothing.

On our return to Vence, I wrote to my parents:

> We are heartily glad to be back after three successive storms, crowned by a really good mistral as we came into Marseilles, and this after the terrific heat and the endlessly tiring official receptions. Vence is comforting, what sweetness in the air! The brown hills of Jerusalem are majestic, austere and awesome; they have produced deep impressions that will take a long time to digest.

Marc was impatient to get back to work, but a job was waiting for him that was not the work he was longing to do. He had to begin the arduous task of signing nine thousand prints of the La Fontaine etchings and coloring four thousand of them by hand. Ida set out long trestle tables in the vast studio in Gordes, and Marc set to work courageously until his wrist ached and his head was heavy. Ida, Jean and I would take away the etchings when they were dry and spread out new ones. The monotonous hand-coloring of a hundred different subjects was particularly trying, and I couldn't help feeling that it was a mistake. It was Tériade's idea, not Vollard's. The luxuriant etchings certainly didn't need coloring. (*Rehaussé* is the term, but how can perfection be "heightened?")

I made trips to Vence with the finished parcels and fetched new ones. It was good to escape alone on these long drives in the blazing sun, wearing a light summer dress, my hair streaming in the wind. Every excuse to go off on my own was welcomed. My father noted that as a child I liked to play by myself, and took it as a sign of selfishness and noncooperation. That I should detest team games struck him as unnatural; it was only much later in life that he began to understand me. As a small child, I frequently gave the slip to my governess and wandered off alone. I recall when we lived in Havana how I explored neighboring streets and entered houses where large families were gathered together in a noisy cheerful room. As a girl, I often rode away on my bicycle in search of other worlds where I would feel free of criticism and convention, jealousy and possessiveness. They were not lonely places, but anonymous places, where contacts were freer: villages, market places, cafés. When my more gregarious sister chose to go to a fashionable finishing school in Paris, I asked to be sent to a country *pension* where I was the only pupil. The inhabitants of this dilapidated château were like people out of a Balzac novel, and it was an extremely instructive period for me. In my little room, I wrote down my impressions.

I reflected on all this as I drove to Vence, stopping in Roquefort on the way to see my friends.

Marc was beginning to pass judgment on my inadequacies. Gone was the wonderful feeling of being loved and accepted, of being trusted, that had made our first years so blissful. It was inevitable that I should wander off in search of people who would accept me as I was. The desire to improve is all the stronger if one's imperfections are tolerated.

Ida was taking charge of things more and more. She was shrewder, more experienced, more intelligent than I; it was normal that she should do so. And since she had given up painting and no longer had any means of creative expression, her life was now centered on her father's. Marc's attachment to me was obviously a threat to her possession of him, and she began to undermine it quite unconsciously during the next year. She made herself as indispensable as she could, ruling over his work and his conscience. As they carried on all their conversations in Russian, I was excluded. Her criticism of his paintings increased; he began to depend on her more and more.

After Gordes, Marc and I and the children went to a quiet seaside place called Le Drammont. While the children searched for shells and spent hours in the water, Marc sketched on the beach or worked in the little house. Once I posed for him there in the nude. It was, surprisingly enough, the first time he had asked me to do this, and it was a pleasure. The result is *Nude in Le Drammont,* which he finished only in 1954, when I had departed, and which he presented to his wife, Vava.

Le Drammont was a turning point in our life together, the last really peaceful intimate time we had. Three of the gouaches he did there: *The Blue Boat, Sun in Le Drammont* and *Nude in Le Drammont* seem to contain a shadow of things to come. In *Nude in Le Drammont,* the lover's head and arm encircle the sleeping woman as the sun goes

down, and in *Sun in Le Drammont,* a huge multicolored sun is also going
down, while a martyred Christ lies limp and piteous in the foreground, watched over by a mother and child. *The Blue Boat* shows the
lover and his veiled bride leaving the shore in a boat under a setting
sun-moon, while a young woman remains behind. There was something inexplicably melancholic about these paintings.

One day we were walking in the hills above the village, when Marc
saw a handsome young man ahead of us. "I wonder what our David
will be like at his age. I'm scared to think of it."

"Why are you scared?"

"Growing up is so difficult. What will he do in life? What if he
should turn out to be a failure? A *peintre raté,* for instance, like
Picasso's son? He'd much better be a lawyer or an architect."

I said, "Of course, Paul's main disadvantage is having a name like
Picasso. David will have more of a chance since his name is McNeil."

I didn't intend to be unkind, but Marc was pained. He was understandably distressed that his son still bore the name of McNeil,
David's legal father.

My divorce alone could bring some consolation to Marc, and fortunately a month later it became possible at last. John wrote to me
announcing the death of his mother and saying that it had altered his
whole outlook on life; he was no longer opposed to our divorce.

I went over to England to get things going and Marc wrote to me:

It's an unpleasant Russian kasha, but it has to be gone through. Don't
worry; it will soon be over. The house is cheerless since you've gone.
Come back quick! We'll all go down to the beach for a picnic.

Chapter

VII

Denouement

During the summer Charles Leirens, the Belgian photographer who had visited us in High Falls, wrote from America asking if Marc would agree to let him make a 16mm film in color at Les Collines in the fall, and Marc consented. Charles wanted to make a little fantasy "à la Chagall" in which the house, the garden, the animals and the children would all play a part.

Since our last meeting in High Falls, Leirens had been very near death with coronary thrombosis, but he had made an excellent recovery. He was thinking of coming back to Europe for good because he was heartily disgusted with American politics.

I sometimes went to visit my friends in Roquefort when my absorbing life left me time, and sometimes they came to Les Collines. Marc had begun to criticize my friendship with these people. He couldn't accept the fact that I had interests outside of himself and his work. "I believe you're in love with that young poet," he said teasingly.

"Maybe I am!" I said in the same tone. Marc raised his eyebrows, wondering if I were serious. Then he gave me a playful kiss.

One day as I was leaving for Roquefort with the children, I called up to the studio to say good-bye and Marc leaned over the parapet. "I forbid you to go!" he ordered.

"I'll go all the same," I replied playfully, and he looked at me with a stern smile, half reproachful, half admiring.

I *was* attracted to the young poet, but this was a romantic reverie I kept entirely to myself; the poet may have sensed it but he made no response. He had great respect and friendship for Marc. I always liked free, adventurous relationships charged with unexpected vibrations, half amorous, half comradely. Platonic relationships seek no resolution; their peculiar magic is in their suspended state. I reassured Marc that this was nothing serious.

Nevertheless, I longed for some of the passionate tenderness that filled Marc's paintings, and it was something I couldn't explain to him. By nature, Marc was shy and undemonstrative in love. More and more, his tenderness seemed to be expressed in creation. He talked a lot about love in general, he painted love, but he didn't practice it.

When I wasn't there, he missed me, he was worried. But when I was there, he took my presence for granted. His gracious smiles and his warm, winning manner were for the visitors. My High Falls lover had forgotten how to play; he only worked, worked, worked. I was still young and immature. I sought many experiences, contacts with all kinds of people; I wanted to be useful to others besides Marc. I drove carless people around, shared our vegetables with neighbors and visited sick and lonely friends. He teasingly called me "Lady Bountiful" and objected that I had no time to waste on such things.

I began to spend more time than ever writing in my little den that adjoined Marc's studio, and when I went to bed, Marc was often asleep. He complained about my staying up late, but I began to need those quiet times alone when everyone else was asleep. The rest of the day was crammed with activities. He professed to be in favor of my writing, but in fact he resented my choosing my own time for it.

Marc sensed that I was drifting away, but instead of trying to understand me, he complained to Ida. She, in turn, was becoming more and more of a confidante and a mother figure. Since I began to have activities of my own, she saw an opportunity to keep him more to herself. Marc loved nothing better than to have her constantly preoccupied by things that concerned him. I had hoped that when we settled in Vence, he would become a little more autonomous, but he soon became incapable of making the least decision without consulting her, and this even seemed to apply to his life with me.

The phone calls between them were longer and more frequent, all spoken in Russian, of course, and Ida came to Vence more often, too.

My relationship with Marc had always been simple and gay, almost a brother-sister relationship. We had always told each other everything spontaneously, and we literally never quarreled. Often, Marc's vague and generalized irritability was vented on me, as I was the most convenient depository. Sometimes it was wearing, but I was used to it and took no offense. Now he became more secretive; he was no longer impulsive and spontaneous with me, no longer gay. Even though he felt he was losing his hold on me, he did nothing to win me back. His fatalism was taking possession of him again, as it had done in Sag Harbor. As for me, I was closing up, too. I didn't speak of my Roquefort friends any more, especially since he disapproved of them. It never entered my head that he might suspect me of being unfaithful. Only now, looking back, I wonder whether he was perhaps suspicious, but he said nothing.

Ida came to stay for a couple of weeks. As usual, she arrived with her arms loaded with presents—tasty edibles, a Hermès bag for me, and for the children an antique clockwork merry-go-round that she had picked up at the Marché aux Puces. As usual, too, she was charming and vivacious, smartly dressed and handsome.

Ida had been longing for Marc to make a portrait of her, and this was a good opportunity. She posed for several days, but the portrait remained in an unfinished state; Marc was not satisfied with it. Perhaps he was disturbed by her overpowering personality, perhaps he was too anxious to please her and afraid to take liberties. He had never again found the strength of the early portraits, the superb rabbis, his parents and Bella. One of the last portraits of Bella, painted in 1934, *Bella in Green,* betrays his unconscious desire to please the model, which had become uppermost. Perhaps this "desire to please" sums up all the last period of his life and might explain a weakening of his tremendous conviction, except in the more exacting works like the Bible paintings and the stained glass, for example.

Ida announced that Franz Meyer, who had become an intimate friend of Ida's since the big exhibition in Zurich in 1950, was coming to stay. We had not seen him since the exhibition in Bern in March.

Marc was totally surprised and delighted when they made the additional announcement that they were going to get married. Marc liked Franz; he was exactly the sort of husband he wanted for Ida. He had only the most serious intentions, he was solid and dependable, his father was a rich art collector, and, last but not least, he already had an excellent reputation as an authority on modern art and as the energetic director of the Bern Kunsthalle. Franz, with his ready smile and quiet, confidential manner, was a combination of candid sincerity and shy discretion. I liked him, too; his shyness was appealing to me. He was one hundred percent honest and incapable of fakery or flattery.

I was happy about this marriage, for I thought that Ida's life would at last develop in a more personal direction. I hoped she would be less involved with Marc, but she had obviously chosen exactly the kind of man who would never be a rival for her father. As it turned out, her marriage did nothing to diminish her activities on her father's behalf. On the contrary, Franz joined her in this work. He served Chagall faithfully for a number of years and wrote two important books, both of which were translated into English: *Graphic Works* * in 1957; and in 1963, in collaboration with Ida, a complete catalogue of Marc's principal works, *Marc Chagall, Life and Work,* * a massive volume comprising a biography and bibliography, an artistic appreciation of each important work and hundreds of reproductions.

My three friends left Roquefort when the owner of the house began to dabble in occultism with a group of fanatical women who worshiped him, and after that, I rarely saw them. I missed their company, and I was glad when Charles Leirens arrived in late autumn to make his film.

He was a man of about Marc's age, eternally curious about everything and outspoken in his opinions. When music was mentioned, he became impassioned. He had a flair for quality and an intolerance for mediocrity. He was never without his Leica. In the street, he examined faces, buildings and shop windows, always on the lookout for a good photo. He listened to conversations and turned around to scrutinize people without the slightest constraint. He had a teasing, *pince sans rire,* or dead pan, sort of humor and got on well with our friend, the poet Jacques Prévert, who was also inclined to be caustic.

*Both published by Harry N. Abrams, New York.

He had a relaxed and playful relationship with the children, which they enjoyed.

Marc liked him, too, and we had many amusing conversations. Marc told him about his unhappy apprenticeship to a photographer in Vitebsk and his hopeless ineptitude for retouching.

"The photographer was fat and prosperous looking and lived in a hideous house. He said that if I worked for a year for nothing, I would get rich too. I thought to myself: The last thing I want is to be fat and have an ugly house, so I left. But my first experience in photography is when my mother decided to have herself photographed by a distinguished photographer—his signboard had gold medals on each side, very impressive—so in order to take advantage of the occasion and economize on the price, the whole family decided to be photographed together on one small card, complete with uncles and aunts. My mother was dressed in dark red velvet with gold buttons, and my sister and I, aged five and six, stood on each side with our mouths wide open, the better to breathe. When we came back to fetch the photo, my parents bargained a little as was their custom, and the photographer got angry and tore up the only print. But I picked up the pieces behind his back and stuck them together when I got home."

Charles enjoyed Marc's company, and the filming work went well. Marc gave full play to his remarkable gift for performing. There were scenes where he sketched our bantam family, the goats and chickens on the neighboring farm, and the ancient olive trees with their splitting trunks. The scenes filmed at the Madoura pottery works show him enchantingly frisky, spinning a vase on the potter's wheel, while he flicks drops of glaze from a brush. The superb ceramic panels he was doing at that time are also shown. They were made of tiles assembled twelve or sixteen at a time and painted in a bold liquid style, like a gouache.

No one had ever made a film on Marc before, which is surprising, considering what an excellent and photogenic actor he was.

Henri Langlois, director of the French Cinemathèque, had begun a film on the art of Chagall in the spring of 1951, and Frédéric Rossif, the french documentary filmmaker, had come to film all the pictures in the bright sunlight. But after that initial visit, Langlois quarreled with Rossif and we heard no more about the project. The film was never completed, even though Langlois, now dead, had asked various people to help him, including the famous documentary filmmaker, Joris Ivens. Langlois even went to Moscow where the widow of the great filmmaker, Dovjenko, took him to see what remained of the typically Chagallian places; but when he spied an old-fashioned horse and cart exactly like the ones Chagall had painted, she forbade him to film it, saying that such carts are not supposed to exist any more in modern Russia.

Charles Leirens' film work amused Marc. Some of the reels were ready to be viewed, and Marc was fascinated by the result, though he complained that it took him away from his work. Technically speaking, the film was far from perfect, for Charles was still a *débutant* filmmaker.

Although it is the only surviving film about Marc up to that period of his life, it was not the first time Marc had acted in a film. In *Ma Vie* he wrote that he played the part of an artist in a feature film during his first years in Paris. He had to row a young lady in a boat, but he was incapable of rowing and was shamefully embarrassed. The best scene by far in the film was when all the ladies with their cavaliers had to sit around a big table and eat a good square meal. Marc had not eaten so well for a long time, for during those first Paris years, he lived very frugally. "I cut a herring in half," he wrote, "the head for one day and the tail for the next."

Charles was intrigued to learn that it was in our house that Paul Valéry had spent many happy hours with Catherine Pozzi, the lady of his heart. Claude Bourdet had taken away the delicate watercolor portraits of his mother made by Valéry that had filled the living room when we first arrived. Charles' own friendship with Valéry began when the poet came to lecture at La Maison d'Art in Brussels and Charles asked him to pose for a portrait. The result was so much to Valéry's liking that he wrote this dedication to Charles in one of his volumes of poems:

> Si je me trouvais placé devant cette effigie,
> Inconnu de moi-même, ignorant de mes traits,
> A tant de plis affreux d'angoisse et d'agonie
> Je lirais mes tourments et me reconnaîtrais.

If I were confronted with this effigy,
Unknown to myself, oblivious of my face,
At the sight of such anguish, such lines of agony,
I would read my own torment and recognize myself.

The more I took to Charles, the more Marc became reserved toward him. As Charles had to spare his heart, I carried the camera around for him and was appointed "assistant." Marc looked on without enthusiasm while Charles began to teach me some of the rudiments of filming and photography.

During Christmas, Charles returned to Belgium, and I wrote to him:

> I was really sorry to see you go. I shall try and find some words to explain what a friendship like yours means to me. Since you came to Les Collines, everything has been colored by your humor and your joie de vivre. They even got the better of Marc's occasional irritation. You must not worry about having taken up so much of his time; he finds the result excellent and feels it was worthwhile.

Near the end of that year of 1951 my parents arrived in time for Christmas and Marc and Godfrey finally made each other's acquaintance. Now that my divorce proceedings were at last going ahead, Godfrey felt it was proper for them to meet and talk of the future. He obviously expected there would be talk of marriage, but Marc avoided the subject. Godfrey was now sixty-seven, three years older than Marc. Ida also came for a few days and my parents found her charming.

Godfrey was immediately taken by Marc, as Georgiana had been before him, and it was a happy time for us all. I went for long cross-country walks with them, as we had often done in the past, my father having always resolutely refused to own a car. Other delightful memories came back, of walking holidays in Wales, of shrimping holidays in Brittany. How I had taken all their kindness for granted! Coming down from the steep *"baou"* (one of the venerable crags that rose above our house), Godfrey started running like a carefree youngster and sprained his ankle. And as he sat with his foot in plaster, he watched the constant procession of visitors: Tériade with a new project for *Verve* . . . Maeght with plans for Marc's next exhibition in March, and his special Chagall edition of *Derrière le*

Miroir . . . the director of the Galeries des Ponchettes in Nice, who was organizing a big retrospective for February, and had chosen for the poster the beautiful blue gouache entitled *St. Jean* which Marc had given me . . . Rosengart from Lucerne with plans for an exhibition of gouaches . . . and Henri Langlois who came to discuss his film on Chagall.

Marc, inevitably, was unable to penetrate behind the controlled facade, the polite manners and the careful French of my diplomatic father. Decidedly, English people seemed to him unfathomable, but he didn't attempt to find out what was going on in my father's mind; it didn't seem to him worth the trouble. He later told me, "Your father is a fine piece of bookbinding, but I don't know if the book's worth reading." As for Godfrey, he was charmed and endlessly astonished by Marc. He envied his extraordinary spontaneity, even his moody behavior—when he was bad tempered, he was simply bad tempered; and when he was tired, he made no bones about it. Of course, my father was not an important person in the art world, and Marc had no need to put on his seductive performance, but when he was in a pleasant mood, he was twice as charming as anyone else, and when the important people filed past, he was the most gracious of hosts.

They spoke very little together—Marc was always busy working or deep in his own thoughts—and Godfrey was unable to broach the subject of our future "regularization," which seemed far from Marc's mind and mine. My father returned home disappointed, wondering whether Marc and I were really cut out for each other.

A year after I left Marc, Godfrey saw him in Paris in the café *Les Deux Magots* on the Boulevard St. Germain. They were both having a café crème and reading a newspaper. Godfrey approached Marc in a friendly manner and extended his hand, but Marc immediately turned away and cut him dead. Godfrey was hurt and puzzled, but I was not surprised at Marc's reaction. In his rancor he had put the whole family in the same boat.

Charles returned to Vence to film Ida's wedding in January, and the guests began to arrive: Franz's father and sister; Arnold Rudlinger, his best man; the Bourdets; Jacques Lassaigne; Charles Estienne and Bush Meyer Graefe, widow of the Bauhaus architect Meyer. They were joined by the Maeghts and their two sons Adrien and Bernard,

Tériade, Jacques and Pierre Prévert, the poet André Verdet, Ribemont Dessaignes and others. Marc's big studio was cleared, and trestle tables were arranged in a horseshoe. Jean decorated the menus and Ziazi Darquet arranged the flowers. The wedding took place at the town hall of Vence, and Marc wore an expression of great solemnity during the ceremony. But the wedding breakfast, which took place in Marc's studio under *The Blue Circus,* was a hilarious event. Jacques Prévert was in brilliant form; he and Marc tried to dunk Ida's nose in a glass of champagne. Jacques danced a mad waltz with Ida's mannish housekeeper, who had made the journey down from Paris in a tweed suit and brogues. Ida crowned Franz with the last tier of their wedding cake, and the fun continued in the drawing room under *The Cattle Dealer* and *The Bridal Pair at the Eiffel Tower* with more guests and more champagne. Charles dodged in and out taking photos, and the children ran around like excited puppies.

The next day Ida and Franz left for Corsica. Estienne brought out his Tarot cards. Marc had gone back to his work, and the cards were set out for him without his knowledge. We were all dismayed by the ominous prophecies they contained. Marc, he said, was about to go through an extremely painful period. For Charles, he foresaw a complete upheaval, followed by happiness. No cards were drawn for me.

Charles left the next morning to tour Italy, and he wrote to me from Florence:

> The hours I spent in Vence have been a series of revelations. You are all a part of my life now, and I consider myself very lucky to have had the inspiration to write to you one morning, after a long sleepness night in New York. My stay in Vence was a sort of oasis where I was able to let go at last, after the frenzied life of strife and struggle. I feel a bit lost right now, and you are responsible for that. You treated me so well, you even spoiled me in such a natural manner that to thank you would be out of the question.

On the day of Marc's vernissage at the Galerie des Ponchettes, I was obliged to leave for London because my divorce proceedings had been scheduled for the next day. Richard Ainley, my faithful friend, testified on my behalf, and I was granted a decree nisi and complete custody of Jean.

Marc wrote to me: "There's no doubt about it, I love you even more!"

Happily, the relationship between John McNeil and his daughter was in no way affected by the divorce, and to this day, Jean has remained on affectionate terms with her father. John did keep to his plan to return to his painting and produces work that has a strange bewitching quality.

Marc and Ida were waiting for me on the doorstep when I got back. Ida had brought me a handsome leather suitcase to celebrate the occasion, and asked us in an offhand manner when we were thinking of getting married. I had no doubt that she was acquainted with Marc's intentions in this matter at least as well as I was, for he told her everything. Marc had not mentioned the subject to me for some time. He replied in a careless fashion: "We're in no hurry. What's marriage? A piece of paper!" I agreed, but this was a far cry from the Marc who had always glorified, almost sanctified marriage.

Marc and I had often discussed marriage as the only means of giving David his father's name, but now that the false father was out of the way, Marc seemed to be tranquilized for the moment. Also, he remembered our conversation in Le Drammont about the handicaps of carrying a famous name. He was biding his time, as if he wanted me first to prove myself worthy. He was observing the changing conditions of our life together. I didn't feel at all that he "loved me even more," and that sense of slight distance remained between us. I wasn't sure that I wanted to get married.

One day, Marc asked me to move out of my little den because he wanted to work completely alone. This was surprising, since he detested solitude. I was distressed because it was the only place that was really my own. I had decorated the walls with some of the small pictures Marc had given me, and my collection of photographs. When we moved into Les Collines, I had a spiral staircase put in to give this room a separate access to the downstairs studio, so as not to disturb Marc each time I went in and out.

But he wanted me to write in our bedroom. Perhaps he unconsciously wished to relegate my work to the woman's domain, where personal work is usually regarded as an agreeable pastime, rather than a necessity. Besides, this would make it impossible for me to write at night after he had gone to bed.

Then he asked me to find someone else to do the secretarial work. This work took a lot of my time and was not particularly gratifying, but that was not the reason why he wanted me to find someone else. I knew only too well that my unprofessional efforts were unworthy, but that wasn't the reason either. He wanted to punish me, no doubt, by keeping me away from the studio.

Then he complained that I gave too much time to the children, and asked me to give them their supper separately, because they disturbed him. I retaliated, rather unkindly, by bringing him his supper on a tray in the studio instead. He said nothing, but complained to Ida when she arrived two days later. She was there almost all the time now, acting as an observer and sometimes intervening. She chided me and asked for an explanation. I replied that suppertime was one of the few moments when we could be with the children, but I promised, nevertheless, to feed them separately. Marc saw very little of the children these days, and their joyful cries in the garden drove him crazy. I kept them on the other side of the house, as far away from the studio as possible.

Marc criticized me for being interested only in what he called the "secondary" things of his life. He considered his public life to be of prime importance, not his private life, and Ida willingly and brilliantly ruled over the first. She took care of the business dealings, organized exhibitions and negotiated with editors, journalists and art critics. I was not qualified to do any of these things, so I concentrated on entertaining a constant flow of visitors, running the house, driving Marc around, photographing the new paintings, having them framed by Alexandre or mounted by our young artist friends, answering the telephone, typing the correspondence. Sometimes Marc needed help in the studio, squaring out a canvas, moving pictures around; this is what I enjoyed most. A marvelous disorder reigned in the studio, but I never tidied up the innumerable objects that were strewn about on the tables. The most I did was to caress them with a feather duster. Marc liked his disorder. For him, it was an ordered world, made of relics (family photographs) and *trouvailles* (stones picked up on the beach, feathers, color samples, and so forth).

Marc was working hard to finish some new paintings for the next Maeght exhibition. A series of ceramics also had to be finished, and I drove him several times a week to the Madoura pottery works in Vallauris. But instead of staying beside him and watching him work as I used to do, I now took advantage of the free time to write in a café. We were slowly growing farther and farther apart.

Charles Leirens came back from Italy to film the pictures at the Gallery des Ponchettes, and Alexandre drove the two of us down to Nice several times to give us a hand with the pictures. These drives brought us close together, holding hands in the backseat, unnoticed by Alexandre. We were beginning to fall in love.

Charles had a natural elegance; he liked well-made, original clothes and had distinctive tastes—brown suede, corduroy and rough tweed. One of his eyes was green, the other brown; and these were his favorite colors. He disliked blue, whereas blue was Marc's favorite color and matched his eyes. Marc often wore a bright blue jacket, and I had a dress the same color. I began to wear it less often.

Charles' work was now finished, and he planned to await the results of films and photos in Paris, pending Marc's exhibition. On the eve of his departure, I went to his room to help him pack. Over his suitcase, we exchanged a kiss and a look of bewildered emotion. To decide never to see each other again had become as impossible as to go on seeing each other. I told Charles I would never leave Marc because I still loved him; besides, there was David.

Charles left by car in the morning, and I drove Marc to Nice to take a train to Paris. I was to follow later by car with the sculptures and the new ceramics, which still had to be fired.

Marc wrote from Paris a few days later:

> It seems as if an eternity has passed by! The time wastes away, and I want so much to work, but I have to be here. Do you think of me? Phone me from time to time; I need to talk to you.

His letter had a wistful note, and he ended it by saying that I would have to guess how much he loved me, because he could express it only in a painting or a Russian poem.

I wondered if he really loved me or whether he loved the person he still hoped I might become, the refined elegant wife, worthy of Bella, the protector of his property and a match for Ida. My wild streak was emerging again, and I was feeling disobedient. The word "Haggard" (apart from its more common meaning) is defined as "wild or intractable, untamed; said of a hawk caught after acquiring adult plumage."

I believe there is something untamable under the polished gloss of some members of my family. This was certainly true of Rider, my great-uncle, who escaped from the discipline of a civil servant's life to write strange and mysterious tales; and his brother, my eccentric grandfather, who resigned from a promising career in the Indian Civil Service because he was opposed to British policy in India; and in my own brother, who never hesitated to turn down a promising acting job if it was not strictly in accordance with his ideas.

In the midst of good breeding and apparent loyalty to traditions, suddenly the wild streak emerges. It amounts to an irresistible urge to disobey. I often feel it boiling in my veins.

The one thing I was certain of was that I didn't want to be always compared to someone else. I wanted to be accepted as I was.

As soon as he got to Paris, Charles phoned me: "I know there isn't the slightest hope, but I *must* see you just once more, alone. Tell me honestly, is this madness?"

Of course, it was madness, but I let him come. He took a plane to Nice, and I drove him to a small mountain village called La Turbie where we spent a day and a night together, and the madness continued.

Then he wrenched himself away to keep a painful appointment back in Paris—he had to show Marc and Ida the wedding photos, as promised. He didn't dare to let them down; he was afraid to arouse their suspicions.

I wrote to him:

You have let something loose from inside me, something that was screwed up with nuts and bolts and wanted desperately to come out. I believe all this could make us all better, rather than unjust and cruel. I like to think there is some sort of mysterious equilibrium in people's lives that rights itself if it's allowed to. Maybe we should ask: How can we all be more true to ourselves? I have certainly not been true to myself, and this prevents me from making Marc really happy. I feel I can only make him what *he* considers "happy" if I am the person he wants me to be, but I can't be that person now. Ziazi was weeping with emotion this morning. She has been expecting this to happen, and she's filled with anxiety for us all.

Charles answered: "The most tragic things in life are not the sorrows but the half-perceived, forbidden paradises."

The Darquets kept me sane by playing the records Charles had recommended—Monteverdi, De Lassus and Josquin des Près—and we went to see one of his favorite works, *Pelleas and Melisande,* which, by a happy coincidence, was playing in Nice.

The time came for me to leave for Paris, with the ceramics and sculptures carefully packed. Ziazi accompanied me. We met Charles in Auxerre and Ziazi left us there for one last night together. Then I made my way to Ida's house. Marc and Ida were noticeably guarded, but Marc eagerly unpacked the new ceramics, examined each piece lovingly, critically, and stored them away in safety. In the evening we went to the Hotel Voltaire, on the Quai Voltaire, and Marc was ostensibly distant.

Charles had written me a letter, which he gave me as we parted. I was impatient to read it, and I locked myself into the bathroom, but Marc's suspicions had already been aroused, and he was waiting for proof of my treachery. To explain my absence from Vence during our night at La Turbie, I had told him that I was staying with my friends, Elisabeth Sprigge and Velona Harris in Mentone, but I didn't bother to tell them so, because I never thought he would phone them to verify.

Evidently he did. He snatched away the magazine in which I had hidden Charles' letter and found it.

I had often heard the lash of his violent temper, but this was the first time he had ever let it loose against me. He beat me to the floor with iron fists, pounding me on the back repeatedly; and when I began to recover, he pounded me again and shouted, "How could you do this to me? It's the vilest treachery. That man is a monster! He dared to come into Ida's house as if nothing had happened. He's a liar and a hypocrite! And you're no better." He struck me again, but I held back my cries. I was afraid the hotel management would come to my rescue. Certainly they, and the guests in the adjoining rooms, were listening at the door. Marc's voice was thunderous. He stopped beating me; the release had done him good. And now he wanted the truth. He wrung it out of me, every drop, and leaving me like a mangled piece of clothing, he slammed out of the room and went to tell Ida.

I had not expected this sudden and violent showdown. I had been planning to break the news to Marc when I had collected my senses; I was still stunned by my exalting experience with Charles. I wanted time to reflect, time to find a way of telling him. But I had been caught like a thief.

Choking with emotion, I phoned Charles. Immediately, he had the same reaction as Pelleas when Golaud's men closed the palace gates: "Tout est perdu! Tout est gagné!" Everything is lost; everything is won.

He came quickly to meet me and we walked along the banks of the Seine to the Champ de Mars. There was snow on the ground and fever in our hearts.

Marc returned in the evening, and there were more violent scenes, with tears of rage and grief from Marc. "How can you be so cruel to me, me so faithful and trusting? Have you forgotten that I saved you, gave you so much, brought up your daughter? Have you forgotten all that?"

"No, I haven't forgotten, and I'm very grateful."

"Grateful! You call that grateful? You're killing me!"

He walked up and down the room in a frenzy, wringing his hands, weeping, shouting. And so it continued for hours.

The next day he said I must go to Ida's with him, because she wanted to see me. I went.

Ida looked at me sternly. She said that Charles' visit to her house after our escapade shocked her profoundly, and proved Charles' duplicity.

Marc maintained that Charles had prepared his coup right from the beginning and wormed his way into the very heart of our family. It was useless to deny it, to insist that it had all happened within a few days.

By now, all Marc's friends had been informed by Ida, and the news went around artistic circles like a brushfire.

The next day was the vernissage at the Galerie Maeght. I told Marc and Ida that I couldn't possibly face it. I would simply be making a show of myself, now that everyone knew what had happened. They said angrily that I must go. But the next day at the hotel I refused again. Marc was in a tearing rage and said that if I didn't go, he wouldn't go either. He flung himself against me with all his weight and threw me to the floor. So I went to the vernissage—and it was an ordeal. Friends greeted me as if nothing had happened, and I didn't know what to say to them.

The new work excited much admiration; it was the first time Marc had exhibited either ceramics or sculptures. The etchings for La Fontaine's *Fables* had been published at last by Tériade—after twenty years—with two new etchings for the jacket.

Marc was his gracious, charming self and Ida was full of sparkle.

Marc spent the next day with Ida. Charles had left for Brussels, and I was left face to face with myself. I wrote to Charles:

> I have to keep reminding myself that you love me, that you don't consider me a monster. You say the same for yourself, yet we simply followed the road that lay straight ahead of us. We couldn't *not* fall in love. Is there really such a thing as justice, and if so, would it have been justice to refuse this experience?

But it seemed utterly unpardonable to break up my life with Marc —the life that had brought me immense happiness and literally saved me at a time when I was so deep in sorrow that I wasn't even able to feel. Marc was right; I was ungrateful. Had I so completely changed in seven years, or had he? Or had we both changed in different directions—he into a more ponderous man, conscious of his fame and fast-growing riches and I back into a more liberated person similar to the immature girl of twenty who revolted because she wanted to change her life?

I tried, with as much detachment as I could, to define the person Marc and Ida expected me to be, and I clearly saw that I was not that person. Since I had fallen in love with Charles, I was more conscious than ever of that.

The greatest blessing for an artist is freedom, and I tried to give it to Marc, but sometimes it seemed to me that he really wanted to be chained, and to chain me with him. If Ida had not been there, he would have found someone else to dominate him. Of course, he revolted occasionally—he was full of contradictions—but he was giving in more and more to her. Charles wrote:

> All night long I persistently imagined only the *worst*, obsessively repeating to myself that *we* are the ones who ought to accept suffering and sacrifice because we already possess the happier lot—we have had that glimpse into paradise. This morning, I'm filled with grief at the thought of the three of us.

The next two nights were agonizing. How could I make Marc suffer like this? His distress aroused my deepest compassion, because it was stronger than his bitterness. When he spoke of David, I broke down.

"I love David. I can't live without David," he said tearfully.

"I know. You'll *never* live without David. You'll see him as much as I will."

"That's not the same thing!" Marc was suddenly dark with anger. "It's not the same without you. If he lives with another man, I don't want to see him again."

Marc was threatening to become fatalistic and punish himself as a revenge.

For several tortured days, I racked my brain and my conscience. Was I making out a case in my defense, fixing things up with my conscience?

I wanted this new love more than anything, and to turn back was in complete contradiction to my nature. I was not in the habit of retracing my steps, and I never regretted any experience, however painful. My frequent urges to begin again came from a deep feeling of inadequacy. I lived in expectation of a brighter future, when I would at last feel adequate. But each time I brought suffering to others. Perhaps I would stop hurting people when finally I learned to accept myself . . . Meanwhile, I had to rely on other people's acceptance, and now it was Charles who gave me confidence in myself. If he came into my life with such impulsion, it was because something vital was lacking—that acceptance which I needed so desperately.

"But you don't love me," I protested to Marc. "You say you love me, but I don't feel it. When I go away you miss me, but when I'm there, you criticize me all the time. I've not turned out the way you hoped I would, and you're disappointed. You don't approve of my friends. Ida disapproves of me too. Your life is with Ida, more and more."

"Ida looks after everything," he replied. "Without her, I'd be lost. You must realize that. But you've got other interests too!" Yes, I couldn't deny that.

One day he said suddenly, "You don't like Jews," and I looked up astonished. "That's not true!"

I realized for the first time that since the departure of the Leokums, my closest friends were non-Jewish. I had never been aware of the fact, but for Marc it was significant. Charles was also non-Jewish, and that aggravated the situation, however much I denied his accusation. Marc shared a Yiddish world with friends like Abraham Sutzkever and a Russian one with Ida and their Russian friends, and I had no access to either of these. He had no access to my English world and was not interested in it. But the Yiddish world was closed off by more than a language barrier, and he protected it jealously.

Oppen wrote me that he and Adele were coming to Paris. He had brought two gold rings from Israel, one for David and one for his own grandson. "While I was playing with the rings, I got Marc's sad, sad letter. What has happened, Virginia? Have you forgotten your old friends Oppen and Adele? You know we love you."

Our meeting was strained. Adele was distant, incredulous, wounded, as if I had repudiated our friendship, but Oppen was his old sweet self. He kissed me sadly, and we parted.

I knew that if I went back to Marc, it would have to be in total humility and contrition. Even so, I didn't believe that Marc would ever completely forgive me; he had strict ideas about fidelity, and his resentments were tenacious. I would be regarded with disapproval and Ida would take an even stronger position. I wrote to Charles that I felt intensely that nothing could separate us now.

Marc was silent and there was a painful tension between us whenever we were together in the evenings in the hotel bedroom. I was torn between the fear of giving him false hope, and a reluctance to crush the last bit of hope he held out against accepting to the inevitable. Sometimes he drew me to him and kissed me, but I felt nothing. I was a block of ice. I was not the same woman any more. It was too late. How hard I was; how cold and hard!

There was no longer any ground upon which we could meet, in spite of my immense affection for him. Marc said Charles and I were guilty of treachery, and I must never see him again. That only served to numb me and cut me off until there was nothing more to say.

Ida apparently felt that things were coming to a head, and she asked me to have lunch with her in a little restaurant in the Place Dauphine. I was apprehensive and tense, but we had a cool, unemotional discussion. She asked me if my love affair with Charles was just a passing thing, and I assured her of the contrary. Then she asked me, in a matter-of-fact way, if I intended leaving her father, and I confessed that I saw no other alternative. These questions being settled, she went on in a businesslike fashion to outline the various steps that should be taken in order to spare her father's pain as much as possible. She intended asking a friend of hers to live with him for a few months, following my departure. This was a young woman of Ida's age and mine, of German-Jewish extraction, with a cultivated background. It was she who had declined Marc's invitation to live with him as a platonic companion in New York, seven years earlier, before I came on the scene. Ida had not spoken to Marc about this plan. While we sat in the restaurant, the friend phoned from the South of France, as arranged, and said she would think it over. With this friend, Ida knew that she would have complete control of the situation. She said she was going to buy an apartment for Marc in Paris with the money from the sale of the villa in Passy where the Chagalls had lived before the war, and suggested that if Charles and I lived in Paris (as we intended to do) Marc could see David often. I was profoundly relieved by this. She had it all planned, she was quite composed, like a mother who is glad to have her son back again.

After this luncheon, Charles came back to Paris, and we immediately decided to look for an apartment. Everything went with lightning speed. The only apartment advertised in *Le Monde* the first day we looked was for sale (rental apartments in Paris simply didn't exist). We loved it at once, and Charles had just sufficient savings to make the first payment. Of course, Marc and Ida knew nothing of this. We planned to get married, because we thought it would be more settling for the children, and more final for Marc.

I went to see my sister Joan, who was living in Viroflay, and she was warm and sympathetic. I asked her if she disapproved, and she said no; but of course she thought I was a bit mad. We laughed together, remembering our youthful escapades in Paris.

Next I undertook the delicate task of breaking the news to my parents. Godfrey wrote a generous letter, reassuring me:

> Do come over as soon as possible with the children and stay as long as you can. We are happy to be able to offer you a port in a storm. We want you to know that we understand the reasons for the step you are taking and that we sympathize. Only we hope you won't rush too hurriedly into matrimonial chains, but hang on to your new found liberty. Your swans of today do rather tend to turn into your geese of tomorrow. Considering everything, marriage seems unnecessary, and we don't want to go through all this again.

Charles and I laughed, and I was pleased to note that I was now able to take Godfrey's reactions with humor. He was being extraordinarily kind and understanding.

Things were beginning to precipitate between Marc and me, and it was clear that some action had to be taken. Ida agreed that it would be better to have done with the separation as soon as possible. But first I had to go back to Vence and fetch the children and my belongings. Marc decided to accompany me.

Our long drive to Vence was tense, but not stormy. The breach was widening more and more between us. As usual, he scribbled. He was lost in his thoughts and visions, and I felt profoundly sad, remembering all the delightful journeys we had made together.

I had planned to go and stay with my parents for a few months, to ease the children's transition from one life to another, and to make the initial separation less cruel and absolute for Marc. Marc imagined that in England I would have time to reflect and get over my passion for Charles. He promised not to make any scenes in front of the children; they were simply to be told that we were going to stay with their grandparents for a few months.

Marc had forbidden me to correspond with Charles, so I picked up his letters almost daily at the post office. Marc begged me to stay in Vence for a week or two longer. He had to get used to the idea of my leaving, he said, and some of our friends wanted to see me. But he especially felt that being in Vence again with the children in apparently normal circumstances might make me forget Charles and, at least, I wasn't seeing him.

Marc received many demonstrations of sympathy, from his friends, which gave him some consolation; he almost had a sort of pleasure in his sadness. He seemed already to be settling down in this martyrdom he had sometimes unconsciously called for. Decidedly, Marc had a *goût du malheur*—perhaps happiness made him feel insecure.

During the eternity of those two weeks Marc tried to persuade me that Charles was too old for me (he was one year older than Marc); that Charles was in a precarious state of health and had no right to ask a young woman to share his life; also, to crown all, that he was a photographer and far from prosperous. No arguments could have had less effect on me. I was drawn to older men, also to people who are lonely or unloved or vulnerable, perhaps because they made me forget my own feelings of inadequacy. John was all of these things, and Marc himself had been suffering from loneliness when I first came to his house. Perhaps, also, I was still unconsciously searching for a father-lover, and Marc had become more like a brother to me.

The point about which I was most apprehensive was the painful separation of Marc and David. I kept assuring Marc that I would do everything in my power to preserve the permanence of their relationship, but that did little to appease him. Often he threatened never to see David again. That would be preferable, he said, to the torture of having his own son brought up by someone else. I feared he might be capable of something like this, knowing his fatalistic reaction to misfortune.

I knew that Charles would be scrupulous in this matter, that he would unfailingly foster David's love for his father, but it was useless to try and convince Marc. Needless to say, I was full of anxiety regarding the effects on David of this unhappy separation. He was going to have to suffer like Jean had done at exactly the same age, five and a half years old. For Jean, too, it would be yet another painful uprooting. Marc was mercifully unemotional with David—just pleasant, though a little grave, as if he were already trying to accept a new distance between them.

Marc no longer objected to having supper with the children, but he was silent most of the time. Although Marc was a childlike person himself in many ways, a child's world was somewhat foreign to him, and his conversations with children were limited. He was deep in his thoughts most of the time, as he had been for several months, ever since I began to lead a freer life. He plunged deeper and deeper into his work. It became his sole preoccupation, his obsession, his whole life.

Tériade, who was back in St. Jean, asked me to come and see him, and we had a long talk. He told me that I had a sacred duty toward Marc the artist, and that nothing in the world counted more than that. I said that maybe I was not really cut out for the job, that someone else might be able to do it better. I tried to explain why I felt that I was not doing the artist any harm, even if I was making the man suffer. I said that Marc had tremendous strength in him, that he was safe in his stronghold of creation. He had health and fame and riches, whereas Charles had none of these; he was a vulnerable man. Marc was also supported by many devoted and admiring friends who, together with Ida, were constantly attentive. I believe Tériade had a certain esteem for me, but we disagreed on principle, and the talk ended in a stalemate.

Lydia Delectorskaya, Matisse's secretary and companion, phoned me to say that Matisse wanted to see me and that, had he been able to, he would have come to Vence himself. She always spoke of him and addressed him as "Monsieur Matisse." She had been Matisse's model, and her superb oval face was the inspiration for several fine paintings and drawings. I was upset at the thought of this meeting. I had a reverant admiration for Matisse and Lydia, but I knew they would tell me that I owed a sacrifice to the work of a great artist. Lydia was a living image of this sacrifice, and she had found fulfillment in her exacting role. I wrote to Matisse saying that I felt incapable of explaining the depth of my feelings for Charles. I assured him that my decision had been taken in perfect lucidity and after mature reflection. I said that I had the impression that I was not doing anything dishonest, though I knew how much I was hurting Marc. I said I hoped he would understand how difficult it is to defend one's motives when there are so many things it is impossible to explain. I thanked him for his great kindness and assured them both of my warmest friendship.

Neither of them answered this letter, but after my departure, Ziazi wrote saying that Lydia (who was one of her intimate friends) completely understood me and that she had said so to Marc and to both Ida Bourdet and Ida Chagall. She said that Matisse understood why I had not gone to see him, and I was relieved to hear it, but I never saw either of them again.

The Darquets and "La Comtesse" were my greatest support during this painful period. They were among the rare friends who considered the dramatic events from the point of view of each of us, and they were torn between conflicting loyalties. Ziazi showed much compassion for Marc and tried to help him by lending a sympathetic ear to his distress.

I corresponded with Claire Goll, the poetess widow of Yvan Goll, who was our good friend, but she had bitter feelings against Marc, which distressed me. I asked her, "Why such hatred?" and she wrote back:

> I hate no one, I have fraternal feelings toward everyone and more especially toward an artist I venerate. But I'm always looking for the Chagall of twenty years ago, the wonderful friend with whom Yvan and I spent so many fabulous weeks in the country and in Paris. What I can't forget is his hardness toward Yvan when he was dying, because they had quarreled about something. But you mustn't take sadness for bitterness and judgment for hatred.

However, in *La Poursuite du Vent,* the book of memoirs she wrote some years before her death, I found a good deal of bitterness against Marc and others.

Marc heard that he had received the Legion d'Honneur and he was very pleased. Just before leaving for Paris, two new books on Chagall came off the press—the new one from Skira with a text by Jacques Lassaigne, and an attractive little album published by Hazan, both of which Marc presented to me with inscriptions. He talked quietly about the apartment Ida was going to buy in Paris; he would have two residences, he said, like Matisse.

For several days I drove him back and forth between Vence and St.

Jean, where I left him to be with Tériade for the whole day. Tériade wanted Marc to paint two murals for his living room (at last a commission for murals!). He also had a plan for an important album of color lithographs, and he asked me if I had a suggestion for a theme. I remembered that when we first came to Vence and lived in a big house called Le Studio, Marc had made a series of fresh, spontaneous gouaches and wash drawings from nature. I suggested a return to this direct inspiration as a change of themes. Tériade thought it was an excellent idea, but it was not put into effect; instead, Marc did a series of fine color lithos on a variety of themes for several numbers of *Verve* and finally a series of color lithos from the Bible illustrations. All this work, plus the large biblical paintings on which Marc was already working, were going to save him. But, meanwhile, there would be intensely painful moments. Marc had exchanged his severe and pious indignation for a quiet, pitiable expression, and I felt even more cruel. I could take his brutality better than his beaten-dog look. A great silence had fallen between us.

Marc began to make a series of drawings and watercolors in various books which he offered me, adding touching inscriptions. I felt unworthy of these but I accepted them gratefully and with sadness. As long as this apparently normal life continued with the children, Marc couldn't believe that I wouldn't change my mind. Little did he imagine that I had become another person. I had found a new source of unconditional acceptance, and it was not something I could reject. Here, nothing seemed real any more; it was as if we were all acting in a film.

I couldn't sleep any more; the strain was too great. Marc managed to sleep—as long as I was there next to him, he felt reassured.

In secret, Marc took one of my notebooks to our friend, the artist Geneviève Gallibert, in Vence, and asked her to translate certain passages written in English. Years later, Geneviève told me that Marc had been surprised to find warm and loving remarks concerning him. He said to Geneviève: "We ought to have been happy together. Maybe I never realized how happy I was."

One day Marc received the visit of a beautiful unknown woman. She mounted the steps directly to the studio and knocked on the door. She wanted to tell him how much she loved and admired him. He was very touched; he thanked her, and after a short conversation, conducted her to the door. He told me the story and added, "So you see, I wasn't even tempted. I'm too faithful to you."

Marc went on working with grim determination on his large biblical paintings—*King David* and *Moses Receiving the Tablets of the Law.* There was a somber gravity in these paintings.

Then the stony fatalism I had often seen before took possession of him, giving him an extra strength. Marc was in his stronghold of creation, filling me with admiration. Now I felt that it was time for me to leave. Ten days had passed, and I thought that Marc was at last resigned to the idea. I took leave of my friends, prepared my belongings and reserved seats on a train to Paris—where Charles would be waiting for us.

A few days before I left, the Maeghts went back to their house in St. Paul and Marc spent most of my last days with them. They were kind and relaxed and avoided dramatizing. They seemed to think it was never too late to mend things and made various suggestions, which Marc conveyed to me. One was that we should go off to Italy together immediately, but I shook my head sadly. Maeght had also reiterated his desire to be Marc's exclusive dealer and take over Ida's share of the business dealings, but this was not to happen, at least not yet.

Marc still couldn't imagine that I would give up everything that my life with him represented, this life of plenty that so many people envied. He thought I would have my little fling and then come back repentant.

The Maeghts counseled extreme gentleness and reserve, and Marguerite, full of sincere kindness, made one last attempt to make me change my mind. Their chauffeur came to fetch Marc half an hour before I left. There were quiet good-byes. Everything was mercifully undramatic. Marc made me promise to think the whole thing over very carefully. Jean (who was now twelve years old) realized that something serious was happening when Marc took her aside and asked her to try and persuade me to come back again. Marc kissed the children calmly and left. His quiet courage was admirable.

I had left behind some of our books and clothes and took only a few suitcases so that the break would seem less final for everyone.

Jeannette broke down when she and Alexandre came to bid us good-
bye. We got into the taxi and waved, until Les Collines was out of
sight.

And so I went out of Marc's life as quitely as I had come into it
seven years earlier.

That same evening, the two Idas arrived from Paris and mercifully
occupied Marc's mind, but for several days, he ran from one friend
to another to pour out his grief. Already he was searching for someone to keep him company. Ida's friend had once more declined the
invitation to live with Marc, and she knew she must find someone
quickly. Then Ida Bourdet had a bright idea: She had a friend of
about forty, Valentina Brodsky, of Russian-Jewish origin, the daughter of a rich manufacturer in Kiev who had been ruined by the
revolution. She was an intelligent, cultivated woman. She had a
thriving millinery business in London, but at once she accepted Ida's
invitation to come to Vence and act as Marc's secretary. After two
or three months she became so indispensable that she agreed to stay
only if Marc promised to marry her. Marc confessed to several of our
friends that he had no wish to marry, but he wanted Vava to stay,
so Claude Bourdet immediately published the bans.

As far as the children were concerned, our departure from Vence
was a shock to both of them. David discovered only little by little
that we would not be living in Vence with his Papa any more. I had
hoped that the two of them could go back to visit together, but Jean
was not invited and David had to wait two more years. David felt
secure with Jean and me, also with Charles and my parents, but he
must have suffered deep down. He was a plucky little boy, always
gay and uncomplaining, and I had the impression that he was taking
everything in his stride.

I had decided not to tell Jean the truth until we were well on our
way, so that our departure would be less dramatic. She took the news
calmly, but in recent years she gave me the following account:

> Was I sad to leave Vence? I think I shut off any feeling of sadness.
> I wasn't warned that we were leaving. I had no chance to say good-bye

to the place or the people. The idea of a definite parting is not something you can grasp at that age. I was emotionally numb; I had no
feelings for anyone except you and David. Other people came and
went like a shifting scene.

I feel in a way I was your dark side, the side you tried to deny in
all this adventure, your own weakness, your dependence, your desire
for recognition. You were always strong and on top and caring for
other people.

I left behind all the pictures Marc had given me—seventeen in all
—taking only the books he had inscribed and four small drawings,
also inscribed. I stacked the pictures in my little den and I asked Marc
to put my name behind each one, this way he couldn't say I had
refused his gift, but I left him free to confirm it later if he wished.
I dearly loved those paintings, but I never regretted leaving them
behind. I never felt that I really owned them, I owned them *with*
Marc. Shortly after my departure, he had the pictures photographed
and a legal document drawn up bequeathing them to David on his
twenty-first birthday. I was profoundly touched by this gesture, but
I said nothing about it to David, fearing that it might disturb the
normal course of his life. Also, I was not at all sure that Marc would
stick to his original plan, and in this I was unfortunately right.

The marriage ceremony between Marc and Vava took place in July,
1952, four months after my departure, at the Bourdet's country
house in Rambouillet, and Claude made a waggish speech in which
he referred to the efficiency of the "Agency Ida-Ida." They had
arranged everything, right down to the marriage contract. But six
years later, according to Crespelle in his book on Chagall, when there
was conflict between Ida and her stepmother, Marc and Vava divorced and immediately remarried under an agreement more favorable to Vava.

One of Vava's first moves was to turn over all of Marc's business
dealings to Maeght. Ida's heyday was over; she was shouldered
slowly but surely out of the way. I couldn't help wondering if she
missed me just a little!

At the time of my departure, Ida had met Picasso at a theater in
Paris and told him what had happened. Picasso thought it was a good

joke, and Ida admonished him: Don't laugh, it might happen to you. Some months later, Françoise Gilot left him.

Fortunately, Ida took advantage of her newfound liberty to bring up her three children, thus satisfying a maternal instinct lavished, since the death of Bella, on her father, that difficult and demanding "child." She and Franz had a golden-haired, blue eyed boy named Piet, and a pair of brown-haired girl twins named Bella and Meret. The family lived in Basel for a number of years, until Ida and Franz eventually divorced.

In the meantime, however, Ida shuttled back and forth between her children in Basel, her house on the Quai de l'Horloge, another house she had bought near Toulon, and the old place in Gordes that Marc had given her. Ida liked moving around as much as her father. She had bought Marc a superb apartment on the Quai d'Anjou, overlooking the Seine on the Ile St. Louis, five bridges down from Ida's place on the Quai de l'Horloge.

Vava almost immediately became Marc's perfect guardian and protector, curator of his possessions, lucid and imaginative organizer of his life, all of which delighted him. In all of this activity she was a match for Ida and Marc was reassured and consoled that all was well. My traces were quickly wiped away. There was one wound, however, that wouldn't heal—Marc's longing for his son; it couldn't heal because he was determined to punish himself (and David, incidentally) by refusing to have any contact with him for almost two years.

David was now eight years old. He wrote regularly to his father and sent him paintings, but there was no response. One day Ida Bourdet decided she would try to change Marc's fatalistic attitude; she worked on his feelings and prevailed, and at last a loving relationship was resumed. After that, Marc gave him a regular allowance and asked him to Vence for the holidays. Marc and Vava were kind to him and their relationship was a happy one. David's sense of humor, which was already well developed, was appreciated by Vava, who is similarly gifted, and David remembers gay moments. Ida and Franz also had him as their guest repeatedly, taking him to the mountains for winter sports and showing him much kindness and affection.

David has memories of idyllic walks with Papa on the beach, where Marc made him drawings on large flat stones. They would return to the house loaded with them. He remembers a café in Paris where his father took him, a little bistro on the Isle St. Louis that was full of house painters. Marc said to them, "We're all painters together," and he showed them his paint-covered hands. "Even if I scrape, it doesn't come off, there's paint right down to the bone." In another café, the Beaujolais, on the left bank, the waiters knew Marc very well, and often saved the paper tablecloths he drew on. They smiled as he sat down and began to draw, but when David did the same and messed up Papa's drawings, they looked daggers at him. When David had brought back his school results: "excellent" for drawing and music, "could do better" for Latin and history, and for math "a weak effort," Papa was surprised. "Don't you like mathematics? It's pure poetry." He told David that he had met Einstein twice and had conversed with him about mathematics. David, of course, was awed.

David also recalls: "I accompanied him the very first time he went to Charles Marcq's studio in Reims, to work on stained glass for the cathedral. The distinguished specialist looked on amazed while Papa began to work. In fifteen days he had learned everything about stained glass. The big studio was in darkness; only the huge window was bright, where the irregular panes of glass were held together temporarily by leaden cames. Each pane was taken down successively for Papa to apply grisaille with a brush; then they were all baked and assembled again with permanent cames.

"I was with him, too, when he painted the mural *Commedia dell'Arte,* standing on a scaffold and using enormous brushes. I 'helped' on one big patch of blue."

David took it for granted that everything his father painted was perfect; it seemed so natural to him that he never thought of expressing his admiration. But Marc would certainly have been pleased to hear some praise from David; he needed constant expressions of appreciation, even from a child.

David has never criticized his father; he has always been staunch in his unconditional love and support. Any troubles that arose were the result of misunderstandings with Vava, he says.

When David finished primary school, Marc expressed a wish to send him to a boarding school near Versailles, the Ecole du Montcel.

Charles and I were living in Brussels by that time and I agreed to this arrangement so that David could see his father more often. One of David's fondest memories of that time was when Aimé and Marguerite ("Guiguitte") Maeght went with Marc and Vava to visit David at his school and took him out to a lavish lunch in Versailles. Aimé recited poems by Verlaine as he walked down the splendid avenues, waving his arms in expressive gestures. The Maeghts were particularly generous and kind to David and when he was on holiday in Vence, they took him fishing in Cannes.

David's best friend at school was Gerard Liebskind. He took David home for weekends and his parents got friendly with Marc, who was pleased that David had a Jewish friend. When Gerard had his bar mitzvah, David wanted one too (Gerard had received a wristwatch and a motorcycle), but Vava disapproved of the idea. When the Liebskinds couldn't have him at their home for the weekend, he would go to church services—sometimes Catholic, sometimes Protestant, anything to get out of school. One day the director summoned him and said it was time that he chose one of the faiths. David had to confess that he didn't want any of them.

Around this time Marc and Vava had moved from Les Collines to a house in St. Paul. I asked David what he thought of his father's reputation for acquisitiveness, and at once he came to his defense.

"He's haunted by the Exodus obsession—who knows, there may be another Hitler! Prosperity might come to an end. He said, 'My son must earn money.' But he's very generous, really. He was always buying things for Vava and me. In Vence he bought up the farm next door where two old people live, and he let them stay there for the rest of their lives."

"He wanted to make sure no one would build there right next door," I replied, "as they did later, higher up on the hill."

"Okay, but he could have turned them out and used the land for something else. He liked to walk there. He liked the goats and chickens and the stumpy old olive trees. But then that dreadful building was built further up and people could see right into his garden with their binoculars. The authorities in Vence had no regard for his privacy; they could have prevented that. So he cleared out. It was a pity, that house had such charm!"

David explained that the steps to Marc's studio were getting to be too much for him as well. The house in St. Paul was very modern and practical, surrounded by woods for privacy, and the Maeghts were

nearby to watch over him. He could wander to the Foundation whenever he liked and look at his big mosaic *The Lovers,* which he'd given
to Aimé and Guiguitte as a present, or walk down to the village and
watch the *pétanque* players under the plane trees, or have a drink at
the Colombe d'Or.

David told me of Marc's injunction: "You can do whatever you
like, but it must be the best." He often gave David the example of
Picasso's son as a warning: "Paul is a *peintre raté.*"

I recalled the story Marc had once told me to prove Picasso's
hardness of heart: Picasso disowned his son when he was brought
home drunk by two policemen. "You can do whatever you like with
him; I have no use for him." said Picasso, so they left him on the
doorstep.

As David grew into adolescence, Marc and Vava began to show
more severity toward him; when he went to Vence for holidays there
was sometimes friction. They felt that some of his friends were not
desirable, he had to return home early in the evening, and so forth.

At fifteen, David asked Marc and Vava if he could live with them
permanently and go to school in Nice, but they said there was no
room in the house. At sixteen, he began to smoke and come home
late, and they were indignant. At seventeen, coming home from a
journey to Greece, he stopped in St. Paul to see Marc and Vava. They
were absent, but his friend the gardener was there, and of course he
was let in. When Marc and Vava returned, they were angry and
scolded the gardener for letting him in. David was understandably
hurt.

I remembered my conversation with Marc at Le Drammont—
Marc's fear of David's adolescence and maturity. Did he project his
own boyhood fear of adolescence, his desire to remain an innocent
child, as described in *Ma Vie?* David was anything but frightened of
maturity, he was scorching the ground under him, forging ahead
impatiently. He certainly had a wild streak—the old Haggard strain,
and the Chagall one too, that burns in his father's pictures.

Marc fought that strain in his son, as he fought the idea of David
becoming an artist. Marc wanted him to be a dependable, solid individual on whom he—the wild artist—could lean, as he leaned on the
rest of his entourage.

Charles had early-on discovered David's gift for music and was eager to teach him, but David was not an assiduous pupil; he was content to pick up whatever he wanted to know as he went along. He learned to play the saxophone, the guitar and the trumpet (the latter was presented to him in a red plush case by Aimé Maeght). Then he began to sing and compose songs and made several records, first for Saravah, a progressive French company, then for R.C.A.

In 1967 David married Leslie Ben Said, a handsome, dark-haired girl with a Belgian father and a Moroccan-Jewish mother. They had a son named Dylan and settled in Paris.

David and his family visited his father regularly. Once Marc took Dylan by the hand and led him to his studio, a privilege seldom granted to visitors, but David was not invited and he felt hurt. The meetings were not relaxed and he was never left alone with his father. On the other hand his cheerful and affectionate relationship with Ida continued as before, and he paid her visits with Leslie and Dylan.

One day the poet André Verdet brought Bill Wyman of The Rolling Stones to see Marc in St. Paul, and he told me that Marc had said proudly, "My son is a pop singer too." But Marc had never heard any of David's songs—not even the one he wrote especially for his father, called "Magician." He never asked to hear the songs and David didn't offer to sing for him, knowing that Marc disliked that kind of music.

After a while it became increasingly difficult for David to approach Marc. Letters were unanswered, appointments were practically impossible to obtain. Every time David phoned to arrange a meeting he was turned away on some lame excuse. He didn't see his father for years, but he never gave up hoping. At age sixteen, Dylan phoned to ask if he could see his grandfather, but his request was refused.

Marc was deeply fond of his son. He was a proud and sentimental father, but when David began to develop his own personality, he became a disruptive element in Marc's well-organized life. Marc's peace was paramount and Vava was his protector. He hid behind her, and it was she who had to make the unpleasant, unpopular decisions.

Other members of the family and some devoted friends were kept at arm's length as well, on the pretext of sparing him every possible disturbance. He could have refused this "protection" if he had really valued the love of these people, but perhaps he would have had to sacrifice a little of his own precious peace. He sought protection from life and bought it at the cost of deeper and more spontaneous feelings.

Marc was not a weak man, as some would have it, but a strong one turned inside out, made vulnerable by his desire for protection . . . is that why most of his paintings lost their prophetic, visionary quality in later years? Perhaps this excessive protection was not good for his art.

But the monumental works that he did in collaboration with master craftsmen—the mosaics and the stained glass—brought him out of his lair. Again he was the struggling artist confronted with all manner of technical and human problems. The superb Paris Opera ceiling is an example of the immense difficulties he conquered; it was his "Sistine Chapel." His stained glass has a powerful new dimension —a timeless quality. His Message Biblique ensemble has the cohesion of a noble ideal—the bringing together of all sincere searchers for some deeper truth that goes beyond creeds and customs.

A great artist is the most complex kind of individual. He possesses the whole gamut of human potentialities from the lowest to the highest. As his oeuvre takes shape and becomes something totally new, the fragile human being that he is—the unpredicatable, vulnerable individual—continues to grope for ordinary human happiness. If he achieves fame and fortune his problems are inevitably greater and his family have their share in these as well.

After the death of my parents, Jean reluctantly sold the beautiful watercolor of her that Marc had given her for her tenth birthday. It had been hanging in their house for twenty-five years. Jean had at last embarked on a painter's career and she was very grateful to Marc for the substantial contribution he had unknowingly made toward her development.

She had received her baccalaureate in Paris and studied social science at the London School of Economics. For years she earned her living in London without daring to admit to herself that what she really wanted to do was to paint. Finally she won a scholarship to an art school, and now she devotes herself completely to this passion.

I asked her if her life with Marc, so full of vicissitudes, had given her a grounding in painting experience. She had often watched him at work and had perhaps absorbed some knowledge in this way.

She said, "Living with such a famous painter was probably inhibiting; I thought that unless I had a great talent it was not worth doing it. That was the message you conveyed too, that if one had not enough talent, one had to serve someone with more. But it did, of course, give me an interest in painting because art was going on all around me. I was moved by it and somehow felt involved in the production of it, like a worker in the Chagall factory. The attitude in conversations about art seemed very critical. Painters were judged severely, to make a bad painting was like a sin."

It is especially remarkable that Jean has returned to her first love, having grown up under the influence of such a stringent attitude.

In 1972, when David was twenty-six, he received, in lieu of his promised legacy, a collection of eight small gouaches and paintings. The portfolio presented to him by Marc's lawyer also contained something for me—a watercolor of me sitting under a big bouquet that he had painted in Vence. I was moved by this apparent sign of Marc's forgiveness and I wrote him a grateful letter.

Charles Leirens had died in 1963, after years of suffering. It had been truly rewarding to live with this fine, courageous man, in spite of all our tribulations. It seemed that since the death of Charles, Marc's bitterness had faded.

In 1977, Sidney Alexander, a distinguished American art historian and novelist, who has written books on Renaissance history and an important trilogy on Michelangelo, was commissioned by G. P. Putnam's Sons to write an extensive biography on Chagall. He was refused access to his illustrious subject, though he tried repeatedly to persuade Vava to grant him a meeting. The reason for this refusal was never given.

Alexander nevertheless wrote a vivid portrait of Chagall, together with a rich and profuse account of Chagall's times and a remarkable critical analysis of all the art movements of the period.

No biographer had ever mentioned my existence before, the Chagalls having always refused to offer any information concerning me. So, according to all the biographies—excepting this one—Marc is supposed to have lived completely alone for seven years. For anyone familiar with Marc's character, that would be inconceivable.

Sidney Alexander's encouragement helped me to pursue still further remembrance of things past, and it has taken me seven years to relive my "seven years of plenty" to the full.

Although I never had the least regret over what had happened, a deep remorse pursued me for years. I had recurring dreams of Marc suffering with a wound that wouldn't heal. I wrote to him several times; the first time was to congratulate him on his marriage. I wanted him to know that my memories of him were full of joy and loving gratitude, and I asked his forgiveness. Not surprisingly, he never answered, but Vava wrote me a kind letter, thanking me for my good wishes. Once, when David was about ten, we met Marc by chance at an exhibition of his at the Galerie Maeght. He kissed David and shook my hand and that was the last I saw of him. For years he sent presents and messages to the children at Christmastime and once, when Marc had an appendix operation, Jean went to visit him in the clinic. Mercifully, he was alone and they were delighted to see each other again. But after that, he became inaccessible.

Now my remorse has gone. I realize that Marc's life turned out exactly the way he wanted it to. He received all the honors he could hope for and many others he never dreamed of. He outlived all of the most illustrious artists of his generation and reached the great age of ninety-seven without ever putting down his brush. He acquired a handsome fortune. He had a devoted wife, children and grandchildren and countless hosts of admirers; he is known from one end of the world to the other. He accomplished his Message Biblique, his opus magnus, and his soul is in peace.

When I first returned to see my old friends in Vence, I felt almost like an intruder. But now I am at peace with the venerable sphinxes that watch over the town, the Baou Blanc and the Baou Noir, and the rugged faces I know so well. Things look different, but they still have an aura, an imperceptible radiation of their former nature.

For years, every time I returned, I always hoped I would see Marc again, and I tried following the course of his morning walk, but I never chanced to meet him.

Les Collines fell into ruin after Marc and Vava moved to St. Paul de Vence. Sadly, I walk up the winding, overgrown driveway and survey the crumbling buildings and a feeling of desolation grips me when I look up at Marc's big studio window.

Then suddenly I have a tremendous feeling of joy as I think of all the splendid creations that flew away from that window—and from windows in Vitebsk and Paris and High Falls. I think of them flying away over the ages, endlessly beautiful, bringing joy everywhere.

EPILOGUE

One morning at eight o'clock the radio announced: "The great painter Marc Chagall died yesterday evening, March twenty-eighth, 1985 at his home in St. Paul de Vence at the age of ninety-seven." I rang David out of his sleep; he was shocked and dazed. He had been thinking of his father with particular intensity the night before and drew a picture for him—a long flight of steps leading to the sky. He had stayed up until four in the morning—somehow he hadn't been able to go to bed.

"Chagall" in Russian means "to stride." Marc strode all his long life and was still on his legs when death came gently and wafted him away. Only three days earlier he was seen working on drawings and watercolors.

Ninety-seven years old! Right to the end he was true to his magic number. His Message Biblique Museum was inaugurated on his birthday, July 7, 1973. In 1977, he entered the Louvre with an exhibition of sixty-two recent paintings, an honor shared only by Braque and Picasso before him. On July 7, 1984, his ninety-seventh birthday, Adrien Maeght and Jean Louis Prat, directors of the Foundation since the death of Aimé Maeght, inaugurated a big retrospective exhibition of his work.

Each apotheosis seemed final, but Chagall continued to astonish, like a rocket that produces more, and ever more spectacular stars.

The funeral was in the cemetery of St. Paul where clusters of cypress trees press against the old walls and the graves have grown into the rock. The village is like a ship that has run aground on the spine of a hill, and the cemetery is its prow. The procession wound its way along the narrow ramparts. Over the rocks, everywhere, there were mountains of flowers.

David and Leslie kept discreetly in the background, but when Ida's children saw them, they embraced each other with emotion.

The ceremony was simple and moving. Jack Lang, France's minister of culture, made a short speech. Marc had expressed a wish for the simplest form of burial, without religious rites, but as the coffin was lowered into the ground, an unknown young man stepped forward and pronounced the Kaddish, the Jewish prayer for the dead.

—Brussels, 1985